*Unfinished
Business*

By the same author

To Gerry,
love from Kate
25 . 6 . '90

Unfinished Business

Kathleen Conlon

GRAFTON BOOKS

A Division of the Collins Publishing Group

LONDON GLASGOW
TORONTO SYDNEY AUCKLAND

Grafton Books
A Division of the Collins Publishing Group
8 Grafton Street, London W1X 3LA

Published by Grafton Books 1990

A CIP catalogue record for this book is available
from the British Library

ISBN 0-246-13590-5

Printed in Great Britain by
William Collins Sons & Co. Ltd, Glasgow

Unfinished Business

1

'Sophie Stephenson would be late for her own funeral.'

This was a sentiment that had been expressed, at different times, by innumerable nursery nurses and child-minders and schoolteachers, by various damp-palmed young men waiting at pre-arranged points of rendezvous, by female friends, driven by impatience and boredom to order one too many G and Ts, or spritzers, or kirs royale, when they looked up from their restaurant tables booked for twelve-thirty to find that the clock said one-fifteen, by dinner-party hostesses and casting directors and the second of two husbands. (The first one had suffered from the same sort of affliction so presumably had no justification for complaint.)

Dee, waiting with Valerie at the barrier on Platform Three, scanned the passengers alighting from the 6.27 and almost said it too. 'Sophie Stephenson – ' she said, and then bit her tongue because Valerie was recently widowed and there was still a tacitly-accepted index prohibitorum appertaining to words like funeral.

They waited close to the spot where, years ago, there had stood a machine which, in return for twopence, rewarded Dee and Valerie and Sophie Stephenson – and anyone else who cared to invest – with thin strips of metal stamped with their names. You got twenty-two letters for twopence, so Diana Mary Wyatt and Valerie Ann Philips were no problem, but Sophie Stephenson, whose middle name was Magdalena, had to be content with an initial.

'Sophie Stephenson what?' Valerie said.

'She's obviously not on *this* train, is she? Do you think she's missed the Intercity or missed the connection? When's the next?'

Of course it wasn't Stephenson any more. Except professionally. Legally, it was presumably still Hawley. ('As in Crippen,' Sophie had said.) Hawley had been the second and, as far as they knew, most recent husband.

Valerie went to look at the timetable. The print was tiny and someone had scrawled 'Gaz is a tosser' across the relevant part of it so she had to put on her glasses. When she put on her glasses she strongly resembled her mother, a neurotic woman who had festooned the bathroom with small linen cloths – the purpose of which Dee, in childhood, had never been able to fathom – and refused to allow her daughter to borrow books from the public library because of soup stains and worse.

She was beginning to walk like her mother too: a kind of hurried, tituping, bit-left-in, Margaret Thatcher gait. It irritated Dee. So did the way that she carried her handbag over her arm and the way she folded her handkerchief ever so precisely after blowing her nose into the centre of it. But then so many things, lately, irritated Dee. She put it down to her hormones, her temperament and the circumstances of her life, but not necessarily in that order.

'Not till seven-thirteen,' Valerie said. 'They're less frequent after six.'

She said it in a melancholy way as if realising that this was yet one more necessary but unwelcome item of information that she, recently bereaved wife of a man who, during their marriage, had chauffeured her everywhere she needed to go, must now be expected to assimilate.

'God, I hate railway stations,' Dee said.

Once, in the tin-strip-stamping days, there had been a

waiting-room with leather-covered benches and pictures of the rolling stock of the Lancashire-Yorkshire Railway around the walls, and a coal fire that the guard kept stoked. They had looked for other pictures in the flames of that fire, looking to see their futures. Their futures – it went without saying – were destined to be marvellous.

Now there was a kind of Portakabin that was called the Travellers' Rest where you could purchase a polystyrene container of something that somebody had the effrontery to call coffee and sundry varieties of additive-packed snacks that looked as though they could never, at any stage, have had any connection whatsoever with anything grown above the earth or beneath it.

'I hate railway stations,' Dee said again. She tore open sugar packets and tipped their contents into the ash-tray, one after the other. Her nerves were bad. She'd recently stopped smoking. Mind you, her nerves had always been bad: before, during and after her life as a smoker.

Valerie drank the liquid that was called coffee and said, 'You keep saying that.'

'Well I do. *Freud* says that railway-station *Angst* is only on arrival or departure, but I only have to walk into the place . . .'

Of course, Freudian explanations were unnecessary. She knew quite well why she hated railway stations. 'I'll be back,' he'd said, standing with her at the barrier of Platform Three. After he'd gone she'd put fourpence into the machine and stamped out his name as well as her own. She still had that piece of tin. She'd kept it for twenty-five years.

And every time she came into a railway station she would remember that she was still waiting, because – unless you know *why* someone never came back, unless you can convince yourself once and for all – the waiting never stops.

The waiting for Sophie Stephenson could also be said never to stop. 'Why does she *always* have to be late?' Dee asked, pushing her hands down deep into her pockets where they would be unable to obey the rogue impulse that might draw them towards a kiosk where cigarettes were to be had.

'I don't think she can help it,' Valerie said. 'It probably started off as a deliberate thing – for effect, I suppose – she thought she was Marilyn Monroe – then it just sort of took over.' She stirred her coffee and then, adopting an even more highly irritating expression of anxious concern, said, 'Oughtn't you to be getting back? In case Pixie needs anything?'

Pixie was Dee's totally unexpected grandchild: offspring of her son Tom and his current girlfriend, peripatetic musicians who had availed themselves of the babysitting services of an available grandmother in order to embark upon a European tour. Dee was not pleased, either at being a grandmother (considering herself to be too young for the role, apart from being totally unsuited to it) or being exploited as a childminder. Though, at present, Pixie was being kept an eye on by Valerie's home-help.

'What on earth could she need that Hilda can't supply?' Dee said. 'Hilda's perfectly competent, isn't she?'

Hilda had helped to clean Valerie's house for the last twenty years. Six weeks ago, due to financial embarrassment, this partnership had been formally dissolved, but Hilda still continued to arrive at nine o'clock prompt on Tuesdays and Fridays. As she said, she had got used and besides, now she had her pension, the money wasn't that much of an issue.

'Yes,' Valerie said, 'I'm sure she is. But – Pixie's – such a very little baby.'

She could hardly bring herself to utter the ridiculous name. Dee refused point blank.

'She's bound to be more competent than I am. I'll wait with you for the next,' Dee said magnanimously, as if she wasn't pleased to be placing the greatest amount of distance between herself and Pixie for as long as possible, 'and then I'll go back.'

'If she's not on the next, I think we'd both better go back and try to ring and find out what's happened to her. There doesn't seem to be a phone here that's working.'

'We'll go back and let her ring *us*,' Dee said. 'I'm sure *she's* better able to afford it.'

True, undoubtedly. But they knew all the same that they'd wait a little longer and then they'd try to get through to her. Somehow it always happened that way.

2

Sophie

I only ever did Chekhov once. It was when I was at LAMDA: *Three Sisters* – I was Irena. My first piece of miscasting. I got it because we had a guest director who fancied me and I was pleased more at the thought of putting the other female noses out of joint than actually landing the part. I've never had much time for Chekhov. All that yawning and sighing and looking regretfully backwards or apprehensively forwards. Nobody *does* anything – well, apart from shooting themselves at the end. Granted their options are limited, but they could do *something* instead of just waiting for life to overtake them. 'But that's the whole *point*,' Dee used to say in those days when we were prone to engage in deeply-meaningful discussions. She was a great fan. She was a great fan of anything that didn't appear to have a happy ending.

Anyway, when I was looking for a key to the thing, a 'hook' (they were very keen for you to have a hook upon which to hang your interpretation), I always used to think of Parklands Station at about one o'clock on a still summer afternoon when all the shadows lay precisely at angles of ninety degrees and the geraniums were so red it hurt your eyes to look at them and the sky had that kind of glassy blue shimmer suggestive of a storm on the way. On such afternoons you always imagined that something was due to happen: a desperate soul about to hurl himself into the path of the 2.35 and achieve decapitation; a fight breaking out in the Ladies' waiting-room, Richard Hannay running full-pelt across the cast-iron bridge and down the steps to be carried away by an electric train just in the nick of time, forcing the pursuing posse to a stuttering halt.

In fact, it was just a little suburban station where we boarded the train for school, the train that ran parallel to the sea, clattering past the golf links and the sand dunes and the thin line of pinewoods within the depths of which not one single corpse, headless or otherwise, had ever been discovered, a little station bright with lobelia and geraniums, surrounded by whitewashed stones and picket fences where our fathers (those of us who had them) disembarked from their journey from the City, where our mothers (mostly middle-aged, middle-class ladies with large bottoms) rendezvoused to embark upon a day's shopping punctuated by coffee at the Kardomah and lunch at Marshall and Snelgrove.

Nevertheless, Dee must also have sensed the Chekhovian overtones. She once wrote a story about it: a man and a girl saying goodbye on a quiet little station platform, watching the signals dropping all along the line as the fateful train approached, hearing the chimes of an ice-cream van in the distance, playing some sentimental Victorian ballad. It was one of those stories in which nobody has a name. I find *that* irritating for a start: I like to know if it's a Roger or a David or a Jacqueline, then at least you can start to put a face to them because Dee is the sort of writer who never tells you what her characters look like.

I also found the story somewhat unconvincing: presumably it was meant to be set in the present day (ice-cream van chimes, etcetera), and yet the chap had TB. I didn't think anyone had TB any more except perhaps a few tramps in doss-houses.

It was called 'Nevermore', that story, Dee being as keen on Poe as she was on Chekhov, and (most appropriately)

13

I read it in a magazine that I bought to while away a train journey between Leeds and Birmingham. At that time I was in rep in North Yorkshire and going for an audition at ATV for a part in a soap they were starting. It was between me and a blonde girl and the blonde girl got it. I told myself it was because they'd wanted a blonde.

Anyhow I was languidly flicking through this mag when suddenly it jumped out at me: 'Nevermore' by Diana Wyatt. I was so amazed and excited I almost nudged the chap in the next seat and said, 'Look! I know her. She's my *friend*.' Though I don't suppose she was any more. I hadn't heard from her for five years; nobody had.

I was thinking about this, remembering those days, from the moment the train emerged from the last of the straggling city suburbs and the smell of the river began to change into the smell of the sea and the breeze fluttered the flags on top of the golf-club houses and I glimpsed in the distance the building that still loomed on the horizon, the building: gabled, turreted, tall and isolated against the skyline, that had fascinated us so as schoolgirls. A prison? An asylum? The reality, as always, had proved to be more prosaic: it had been built by a ship-owner in the early nineteenth century, fallen into a period of desuetude followed by use as a boys' preparatory school, then, during the war, requisitioned for troops, and afterwards opened as a convalescent hospital.

I was thinking and remembering and daydreaming to the extent that I almost missed the damn station. Probably because there was nothing faintly Chekhovian about it today (not in my terms, anyway); high summer it might be, but it was raining so heavily that I could scarcely see through the steamed-up windows of the carriage.

When I was young and lovely men used to help me with my luggage. When I was young and lovely there existed a body of persons called station porters. Now I could heave my guts out while searching the platform vainly for a trolley.

I'd expected changes; you do. There was no longer a Ladies' waiting-room, just a kind of three-sided shelter made of vandal-proof glass. More to the point, there was no longer a Ladies' lavatory. Most to the point, there was no sign at all of Valerie Lamb, née Philips, or Diana Mary Wyatt (Ms).

It wasn't as if I was late. I was actually early. '*Do* try to be on time,' Dee had said. I could hear again that cool sarky voice over the phone as I looked along the platform, towards the barrier and over the bridge. They were nowhere to be seen. They were one minute, five minutes, quarter of an hour late. 'Your persistent unpunctuality is symptomatic,' Dee said once. 'Symptomatic of what?' I'd enquired. But she hadn't yet reached that chapter in her Teach Yourself Psychology book.

After twenty minutes I thought I'd better ring someone. The three-sided glass shelter was hardly weatherproof and I couldn't get much wetter by searching out a phone.

There was no reply from Dee's, so I tried Valerie's. Her help answered. Places like Parklands, I thought as I watched my ten pence dwindling, must be the last bastions of employment of that sort of domestic help: women from the other side of town, turbanned, pinafored, with big prominent leg veins who would know their place and allow themselves to be treated with kindly condescension. The cleaners who came to me from the agency were never less than daunting: either they had First Class degrees in Philosophy or else Daddy owned half the Highlands.

Valerie's was called Hilda and was a sort of family heirloom. She was also a bit deaf. There was a baby crying very loudly in the background and that didn't help matters. Eventually it was ascertained that Mrs Lamb and That Miss Wyatt had gone to the station to meet their friend from London.

'I am their friend from London,' I said. 'And there's no sign of either of them here.'

'Well now that's funny, dear,' Hilda said. But even as

she was saying it we both realised what might have happened. I said, 'Have they gone to the terminus?' And Hilda said, 'Don't say they're waiting at Church Street while you're stuck there like Piffy on a rock?'

You forget that there are still people who use those quaint old Northern expressions in their everyday parlance; you think they're all just dreamed up by *Coronation Street* scriptwriters.

'I guess that's exactly what may have happened,' I said. She said, 'Are you the one that was in that film? I saw it, you know. At the Odeon,' just as though I wasn't the same Sophie Stephenson she'd known from about a million years ago when, as a schoolgirl, I'd visited the house of her employers: Valerie's late husband's parents, for tea and buns and Bible study.

I supposed I'd have to get whoever was in charge of the station to put a message through to the terminus and I was walking back across the bridge, my lenses all misted up, rain squelching out of my shoes, towards this end when the pain started and I thought, yes, that's right, you bastard, start now when there isn't a glass of water in sight to help me swallow down the pill. Isn't it ever thus: pain striking in the middle of Act Two of *A Long Day's Journey Into Night*; period starting to flow on the train between Inverness and Euston when you haven't packed any tampons?

He gave me a glass of water, the porter or guard or whatever he was, and let me sit down in his office. I'd have acted the 'If you don't give me shelter I'll pass out' routine, but I didn't need to act. I was sitting there waiting for the pill to take effect and listening to 'Thriller' which was issuing faintly from the headphones of his personal stereo, when I saw Dee's head passing the ticket-window.

She looked like the wrath of God. For that reason, I let her walk past. But also because I daren't ungrit my teeth to call her name until the spasm had passed. I counted. I'd got to fifty-five and, I guessed, she'd trodden the length of

16

the platform and peered into the glass shelter and the doorway of the Gents' lav and down the subway before I dared to breathe out and she, returning, glanced through the window and saw me.

'We said Church Street,' she said without preamble, pushing her face towards the glass. 'Church Street, not Parklands. We've been waiting there for over an hour. What's up? You look terrible. Is it your stomach?'

When I was seventeen I developed a stomach ulcer. Pretty unheard of. It would have made me famous, had I not been famous already.

'Good job it occurred to me,' she said. 'I'd left the car in the B & Q car-park – it was the only place I could find – and they've started wheel-clamping if you're not a customer. It'd been there that *long* . . . We *said* Church Street.'

She picked up one of my cases and I took the other and walked behind her to where she'd left the car. She was still chunnering but because she walked so much quicker than I did I couldn't make out the gist of it. She used not to walk quickly; in crocodiles teachers would look back over their shoulders and shout, 'Come on, you, the girl at the rear, Diana Wyatt, don't dawdle!' She used not to moan either.

'People change,' my mother used to say with the kind of sagacious air that made you think she was passing on eternal wisdom rather than yet another of her shop-worn clichés picked up, no doubt, from customers across the counter. Actually, because she never lost her accent, it came out as 'pipple tchaintche' which, I suppose, made it *sound* more like eternal wisdom. Customers were charmed, or intrigued, or enchanted, by her accent. She told them she was Austrian, but actually she came from Bavaria. My father, part of the army of occupation, had brought her back when discharged, married her, impregnated her and then, apparently, left, whistling. I remembered nothing about him except for a greatcoat and a

17

rough chin and a baritone voice singing 'Röslein, Röslein, Röslein rot, Röslein auf der Heiden'. After he left, she had to live on her wits. She got a job as a hotel receptionist and pretended she was Austrian. Nevertheless there were some bad moments. One man spat in her face. Once, when we lived in the flat above the butcher's shop, someone put excrement wrapped in Stork margarine paper through our letter-box.

All this apart from the fact that being a hotel receptionist was considered to be somewhat infra dig in those days. I used to say that she 'went out to business' but never explained what the business was. When I got older someone told me that my mother was a tart. She wasn't. It was simply that men liked her. Not one of them liked her enough to marry her though.

Dee had changed. She used to be thin and tentative; there's more flesh on her now and she moves decisively. She used to be – either pale and skinny with a nimbus of frizzy hair, or willowy and pre-Raphaelite, depending upon whether or not we felt well-disposed towards her.

Life has changed Dee. If life has changed Valerie, then it certainly doesn't show on the surface. Valerie has always been five foot three with dark curly hair and thickly-fringed brown eyes and a neat nose and two dimples, one in each cheek, equidistant from her mouth. Valerie has always taken a 34B cup, worn beneath her pale grey or sage green lambswool jumpers. Valerie's tights were, and are, ladder-free, her lipstick a go-with-anything shade of rose, the length of her legs, the span of her waist, the distance from her neck to her hem, all perfectly proportionate. Valerie is, was, perfectly, proportionately, average.

We should have hated her. She embodied everything that a healthily-rebellious adolescent should hold in deep contempt: diligence, respect for authority, conformity; she was the type that the headmistress trusted to welcome governors and keep order and present Lady Muckheap with a bouquet on speech day. But Dee and I were not healthily-rebellious adolescents and, far from wanting to *épater* the bourgeoisie, desired nothing more – albeit covertly – than to emulate it and thus be drawn invisibly into its ranks. We wanted to be familiar with forks, to be invited to Young Conservative Balls, to play mixed doubles with the daughter of the local squire, and Valerie – bank manager's daughter, therefore indisputably, unambiguously and thoroughly bourgeoise (if only of the petty variety) – might provide us with the key.

She knew all the right things. She always knew, for example, how to manage that cheeks-barely-brushing gesture that passes for greeting. Dee never attempts it and I, even after years of theatrical gush, am still not quite comfortable with it.

Valerie did it now, turning to me as I installed myself in the back seat of the car and kissing air. Then she said, 'You don't look too good.'

'Thanks, Valerie.'

'Oh I don't mean that how it sounds. I mean, you look a bit under the weather.'

Well, *which* weather? Does she mean today's, with heaven crying bitter tears and the geraniums shedding their scarlet petals and all their foliage flattened to the ground? I could have that in London and certainly feel under it. Or does she mean Chekhov weather: that hot, still, bright and slightly menacing sunlight? Because that's the weather I want to be under, that's what I've come back for. If I can get back to that: the waiting weather when everything was still to come, then maybe I can make sense of some of the things in between.

Barmy, I know, but it's how I feel and, right now, I'm better off being barmy.

19

3

Hilda met them in the hall. She put a finger to her lips and stepped exaggeratedly in the manner of a pantomime villain trying to creep up unheard behind the hero. She said, in a whisper loud enough to wake any baby with a healthily-functioning auditory nerve, 'I've just got her off. She's been crying fit to burst.'

Sophie, wriggling, said, at normal volume, 'Talking of bursting, I need to pee. Still in the same place, is it?'

She had visited Valerie perhaps twice during her married life but was, as was Dee, perfectly familiar with the geography of the house. They'd known it since their youth when it had belonged to the Lambs Senior. It was a big Victorian house that had servants' bells and a butler's pantry and a chauffeur's flat above the garage – though by Mr and Mrs Lamb's day, chauffeurs and butlers and maids were largely extinct and they had to make do with Nancy who housekept and Annie who cleaned and Gretchen who wiped the noses of Richard and his sister and fed them Scott's Porage Oats and marmite soldiers.

If you did not disembark from the train at Parklands as Sophie had done but carried on through to Church Street, your attention would probably be caught by a big sign in cast-iron lettering that was elevated above a factory building. It said 'J. F. Lamb, Bolts and Rivets'. When they first met Richard, Dee, who was a scornful girl, always referred to him as Richard Lamb-Bolts-And-Rivets.

They met him through church. Small town girls met young men through church or the tennis club (unless they were common in which case they rode pillion to leather-clad youths on motor-bikes and congregated outside fish and chip shops and came to school with thin nylon scarves wound round their necks to conceal the love-bites), and as the Lambs, apart from being rich, were churchwardens, their house was thrown open on a regular basis for evening meetings of the Women's Guild and Bible Study groups and gatherings of the young people of the parish. The young people of the parish (at least the females) were always keen to attend because Richard, almost alone among his seventeen-year-old contemporaries, was an extremely good-looking young man and though it was obvious that he was after Valerie Philips, hope, at that age, still sprang eternal.

'Jesus Holy Christ,' Sophie said to her reflection in the bathroom mirror and scrabbled about among her cosmet-ics for the means of disguise, remembering how some young men had skulked outside Valerie's house because she was pretty and other young men had hung about outside whatever flat she, Sophie, happened at that time to be inhabiting because they detected the faint but unmistakeable aura of sexual promise. As far as they knew, nobody had ever waited outside Auntie B's cottage in the hope that Dee would emerge. Dee had been neither conventionally pretty nor overtly sexy. She'd pretended not to care, but she did. Hence the scorn.

'Grotesque,' Sophie said, striving with foundation and blusher and lipstick to create the impression of a living, breathing human being but only succeeding in producing a clown's death mask.

She put it away: all the red and the black and the blue stuff; more could only mean worse, and went search-ing through the bedrooms (matrimonial, judging by the wedding photograph on the dressing-table – oops! ex-matrimonial; the two that were kept like shrines: aeroplane models, encyclopaedias, football pennants, to children-now-flown-the-nest) until she arrived at what was presumably to be hers: a biscuit barrel at the bedside, a vase of gypsophila and pinks, and two books: a Barbara Pym and a biography of Ellen Terry. Thoughtful, you couldn't deny it. Always had been. Drove you mad sometimes though: Garibaldi biscuits and Barbara Pym, when what you actually felt like was gin and Molly Parkin.

In the natural course of events Sophie would have stayed with Dee but now, of course, there was the baby. And the smoking. 'You can't stay here if you still smoke like a chimney,' Dee had said on the phone. 'I'm practically climbing the walls as it is. You'll have to go and pollute Chez Lamb instead. You'll love that: she empties your ash-tray before the first flake of ash has started to drift downwards.'

Well perhaps that was a small enough price to pay. When you were feeling under the weather. Dee's house-keeping was of the sort that is kindly described as erratic: the concept of aired beds and biscuit barrels did not immediately spring to Dee's mind as being synonymous with hospitality, whereas Valerie had practically written the book. 'What did Richard die *of*?' Sophie had asked Dee when Dee had rung to inform her of the event. 'Heart attack,' Dee had said. 'Officially. Personally, I think she *cleaned* him to death.'

Downstairs, in the kitchen, Valerie checked the casserole and sautéed some croutons for the soup and tried to suppress the unease she had never been able to rid herself of whenever she thought of Sophie and lavatories. It was an unease that dated from a visit to London many years before when she had misguidedly attended a party of Sophie's and, through the buzz of conversation, had heard her describing, without reticence, an infestation of pubic lice – legacy of a brief and unwise encounter: 'Mi*nute*, but just *exactly* like crabs.'

Perhaps it had just been Sophie showing off. She'd always been very adolescent in that respect; saying things deliberately to shock: 'I *think* it was four abortions I had, in all. Or was it five?' or 'I never knew what sodomy actually *was* until I met my first husband.'

A show-off certainly, but you could never be sure.

In the sitting-room Dee apprehensively approached the sofa where Hilda had deposited the carry-cot containing the now blessedly-somnolent Pixie. One tuft of hair stood upright on her skull giving her a look reminiscent of a coconut. She was not an attractive baby, unlike Tom, her father, who'd been an infant of the competition-winning kind.

Hilda, seated opposite the television set, rubbed at her varicose veins and said, 'She's certainly got a powerful pair of lungs. I thought the ceiling was coming in at one stage. I daresay she's missing her mum.'

'Poor mite,' said Dee, under her breath.

'Poor mite,' said Hilda.

The television set was tuned to a soap opera – it was the soap opera for which Dee had scripted some episodes and this was one of them – but in deference to Pixie's slumber the sound had been turned down. Dee was thankful for small mercies.

There were a great many mirrors in the Lamb household. At intervals, as she came down the stairs, Sophie's brightly-coloured and heavily-disguised reflection was thrown back at her. From whichever direction it came she could detect no improvement. 'Sick,' she said in her Sybil Thorndike voice, 'sick unto death.' Then she repeated it in an Edith Evans voice. By the time she reached the kitchen she'd done Athene Seyler and Katharine Hepburn and was on to Bette Davis.

'What?' Valerie said, rather distractedly. She'd cooked dinner-party fare on a regular basis for the past twenty years, but the thought of Sophie's critical eye made her nervous. Sophie, undoubtedly, was used to dining with the famous in those sorts of restaurants where food was theatre and chefs had superstar status. Sophie would, undoubtedly, consider potato and leek soup and chicken casserole and treacle pudding to be peasant fare.

Unless, by any chance, peasant fare had taken over from nouvelle cuisine as the *dernier cri* among the cognoscenti?

'Dinner won't be long. Do go and sit yourself down and have a drink.'

But Sophie lingered, nibbling croutons, lifting the lids off saucepans, reading a recipe for Lancashire Hot Pot that was printed on a tea-towel. Eventually, her back turned towards Valerie, she said, 'Sorry, you know . . . so sudden, like that . . . You seem to be coping very well . . .'

Apart from Sophie's floral tribute and Valerie's acknowledgement of it this was the first time that the topic of Richard's death had been mentioned between them.

'It must have been a pretty terrible experience.'

He'd died in bed, at Valerie's side, Dee had reported. According to the pathologist, she'd lain all night beside a corpse.

'Yes.' Valerie handed her a dish of nuts and said, 'Could you take these in with you?' And Sophie stifled all sorts of ghoulish impulses to ask impertinent questions about rigor mortis and complied.

Hilda had on her hat and coat. She could have left as soon as they came back but she was hanging on to see Sophie. She would tell them at home afterwards that those make-up artists must be miracle workers because, honestly, you wouldn't cross the street to see her in the flesh. Oh, very fashionable: thin as a lath and wearing an outfit that'd probably cost a month's wages and made up to kill. Very *striking*, if you liked a bag of bones, that is, with no chest and that kind of bird's nest hair that they all seemed to go in for these days, but personally, in her opinion, her looks weren't a patch on their Deborah's.

'That film,' she said. 'Now what was it called? I can't bring it to mind. You know, you were investigating this cover-up to do with politics and you got killed. That chap was in it, that one I don't like, big chap with what looks like a toupé to me. *You* know . . . Something about a trial, was it? "Mistaken Identity", was that it?'

'I'm sorry, I don't remember,' Sophie said, a handful of peanuts arrested halfway to her mouth because she'd just noticed the name 'Diana Wyatt' among the credits at the end of the soap on the telly. But she remembered perfectly well. *False Witness*, the film had been called, a sort of Watergate rip-off. The male lead had the worst case of halitosis known to man and liked little girls.

' "Witness for the Prosecution", was that it?' said Hilda, clutching at the air for inspiration.

'*False Witness*,' Dee said mischievously.

'*That's* it. You were having an affair with this other chap – that one I always think looks a bit you-know-what, though he's been married I don't know how many times; he's forever in Nigel Dempster – but he was only using you for his own ends.'

'How life doth copy art,' Dee said from where she was standing by the drinks trolley with a glass of tonic water in her hand. She daren't even drink, for God's sake, because if she did she'd be sure to want a fag.

'Well I'll be getting along then, Mrs Lamb,' Hilda said when Valerie came in. She glanced towards the window beyond which the rain fell remorselessly. 'Looks like I'll be drenched before ever I get to the bus-stop,' she said mournfully. Dee, pouring tonic water, steadfastly refused to take the hint. After Hilda had left, Valerie said, 'It wouldn't have taken you a minute, would it? After all, she did hold the fort with Pixie.'

She put down her sherry glass and shot a covert glance in Sophie's direction. Sophie seemed to be rather heavily into the gin. Sophie had once had what they called 'a drink problem' – it had cost her several good parts at a crucial time in her career – but that wasn't what was bothering Valerie. What was bothering Valerie was the idea of having to fork out for another bottle of gin before the end of the month.

'I can't be expected to ferry all your domestics around,' Dee said truculently. 'And as for the baby, she didn't have to *do* anything apart from *be* here. And she was here anyway ... Why didn't she get a taxi? She's probably better off than all of us put together – well, you and me, anyway; Sophie's in a totally different financial league, of course. Hasn't she got a houseful of sons and daughters all earning: Hilda?'

'Oh dear, poor old Hilda when it comes to the poll-tax,' Sophie said, calling upon memories of a part she'd once played as the guest whose function it was to pour oil on the troubled waters of the household in which she was staying. Rattigan, perhaps? She couldn't remember. Only the recollection of getting through the play on automatic pilot because her period had been late and she was worried sick; it was when she was married to her first husband, Constantine, and, because of being on tour, she hadn't seen him for longer than her putative pregnancy might have existed, and Constantine had shown himself to be a violent man.

Dee, after another gloomy inspection of the interior of the carry-cot, declared that perhaps she ought not to stay for dinner but should instead take Pixie back home and put her to bed. She waited eagerly for somebody to contradict her.

'She can sleep as well here as at your house,' Valerie said. 'And she'll probably only wake up in transit anyway. You brought another bottle, didn't you?'

Dee nodded. 'But if she sleeps now, won't that mean she'll be awake half the night?'

'Dee, she's four months old. At that age they sleep most of the time. The way you talk, anyone would think you'd never had a child. Don't you remember? It's not *that* long ago.'

'Frankly,' Dee said, 'no.'

And who could argue, because no one but Dee had any notion about those days that she professed to have forgotten.

'So how does it feel?' Sophie said, laying down her soup spoon and reaching automatically for her cigarette packet then remembering and desisting for such an action could only be construed as provocative. 'So how does it feel?' Sophie said, having assured Valerie that the soup was simply perfect; it was just that she never had much of an appetite after travelling. (Enough of an appetite for drink, Valerie thought, eventually unable to ignore Sophie's rapidly-emptied glass any longer.)

'How does it feel to be a – '

'Don't say it,' said Dee.

' – grandmother,' said Sophie.

'Very pleasant, probably, as long as your grandchild isn't dumped on your doorstep.'

'Hardly your *doorstep*, Dee,' Valerie said.

'So what exactly happened?' Sophie asked. All she knew so far was that Dee's twenty-four-year-old son, Tom, and his girlfriend had brought the baby to Dee's home and left it there, ostensibly for the weekend while they went back to London to see about a new flat. That had been over a week ago.

'You'll have to ask *them* that, won't you?' Dee said, busy with knife and fork. Dee was a hostess's dream: she'd eat anything put before her if it meant that she didn't have to cook. 'The wandering minstrel and his lady-love.'

She always called him that in a rather unpleasantly mocking way, just as she usually referred to herself as a lady novelist in very definite inverted commas; it was a way of putting herself and hers down before anyone else could do it.

'Can't you get in touch with them?'

'They don't have phones in squats,' Dee said. 'Hadn't you heard?'

'So what will you do?'

'What can I do? Leave the poor little blighter in a phone box with a note pinned to her vest? Trouble is,' said Dee, mopping up gravy with her bread, 'he said they had a tour lined up. Belgium, Holland, Germany. An eight-week tour.'

'Dead Reckoning?' Sophie said. They'd been called Dead Reckoning, Tom's band, two years ago when she met him in a pub near the Front Line in Brixton. 'Hi there,' he'd said. The smell of dope had been enough to knock you out.

Dee shook her head. 'It's Catastrophe Theory now. It's New Age Music – whatever that might be.'

Each of them pondered. For Valerie, New Age Music really meant anything post-Beatles; Sophie had finally acknowledged that she could no longer be bothered to keep up after the demise of Punk; and Dee had only ever played Leonard Cohen and the more apocalyptic of Bob Dylan's ditties, so it didn't apply.

'What I can't understand,' Valerie said, 'is how on earth that girl can just go off and leave her baby, such a *little* baby . . .'

She was watching Sophie's unsuccessful stratagem to make the food on her plate seem less than it was. Not her sort of thing, obviously. A picture of Sophie's gastronomic life glided into her mind's eye: starched napery, larks' tongues, quails' eggs, dishes so rarefied, so obscure, that if you had to enquire of their constituents you didn't qualify to eat them.

'Don't you know anything about this girl – what's her name?'

'Sam,' Dee said. Tom and Sam. They even looked alike: both slight and pale and blond. She'd expected Tom to grow tall like his father, but he hadn't.

'Short for Samantha, presumably. I know nothing what-soever. She never speaks.'

She jabbed her spoon at her treacle pudding as though it had done her a bad turn. She had wanted Tom to go to university, to train for a profession; she had wanted to be able to show him off, particularly to Sophie and Valerie – and he had become a wandering minstrel, and a not-very-successful one at that.

'So you'll wait?' Sophie said. Treacle pudding wasn't so bad. It didn't demand that much of an effort: you could just mush it up and sort of suck it down.

'So I'll wait. And hope I'm not in the workhouse by the time they get back because as sure as hell I'm not going to be able to get much done with that racket going on.'

'There are no workhouses,' Valerie said. There wasn't any racket either. She left the room to check on their next-door neighbour. Neither of the other two had a clue. You couldn't expect it of Sophie, but Dee was just being silly. You didn't forget how to look after babies; it was like riding a bicycle.

'She said that almost regretfully,' Sophie said when Valerie had gone.

'Well I suppose at least the workhouse provided a safety-net.'

'Things are *that* bad, are they?'

'Apparently. Apparently bolts and rivets took a rapid down-turn some time during the last five years. They closed a factory. They had creditors queuing, not least the bank. They *say* it was because of the prevailing economic climate but I wouldn't put my money on it. Richard always struck me as the sort who couldn't run a piss-up in a brewery, didn't he you?'

Sophie helped herself to the last of the wine since it had become increasingly obvious that Valerie had no intention of offering it and said, in an irritatingly dreamy sort of voice, 'Richard used to write poetry.'

'Poetry? Richard? How on earth do you know?'

'It's just something I remember from years ago. One of those odd things that stick.'

'Bad poetry?'

'I don't know,' Sophie said. 'I don't suppose that then I could tell the difference.'

Valerie came back in and said, 'She's still fast asleep.' She had that 'I know you've been talking about me' look on her face, so Dee said, 'Naturally we've been talking about you.'

'And what, exactly, were you saying?' asked Valerie, busy with the coffee pot. They'd had the last of the wine; this was the last of the Blue Mountain.

'Exactly that you can't go to the workhouse because there isn't one,' said Dee, spooning sugar into her cup. Blue Mountain was wasted on Dee; her palate recognised no such fine discrimination. Strange, because her books were full of feasts and libations, every mouthful and sip described in succulent detail. No one but a gourmet, you thought, would be able to produce descriptions like that, and then you looked in Dee's kitchen and saw cans of lager and packets of crisps and boil-in-the-bag dinners for one.

Since the het-up, giggling days of their early adolescence they'd been reticent about discussing sex, but the subject of money was, of course, even less suitable for public debate. Valerie had told Dee that, apart from her meagre state entitlements, it seemed that Richard had left her penniless. She had told her because she was still in shock and at her wits' end, for – worse than penniless – there were DEBTS. The very word was sufficient to make Valerie – still, always and for ever, the bank manager's daughter – start to palpitate.

She moved the cheese board towards the edge of the table (otherwise Dee just kept cutting and cutting) and said, in a flippant sort of way – the only way that made it possible to broach the subject at all: 'I have to get a job. In the not-too-distant future. Any suggestions?'

She'd never had a job. She and Richard had married the summer they'd graduated and she'd become pregnant on her honeymoon. She'd never worked, apart from the kind of charitable/voluntary activities traditionally engaged in by the wives of men who are expected, before too long, to take charge of a prosperous family business and who need their wives beside them, full time, in order to make a continuing success of it.

'You could be somebody's housekeeper,' Dee said eventually. 'Or a companion to an elderly person. You sometimes see those sort of jobs advertised in the local rag. I did it once.'

Dee as a housekeeper. The idea was absurd.

'I was a companion to this woman who was writing her memoirs. Actually, I think the idea was that *I* would write the memoirs. She had a kind of chaise-longue that she used to lie on while she dictated into a tape-recorder. She never really got the hang of the tape-recorder so half of it always got wiped.'

'Did she ever get them finished?' Sophie asked. Surely Valerie couldn't not be going to open another bottle of wine?

'I don't know. I only stayed till about Chapter Two. She was certifiable: she had this notion that she was the illegitimate daughter of the Prince of Wales. Apart from that, she was extremely reluctant to pay me.'

Sophie rose from her seat. 'Valerie,' she said, 'I brought some wine with me.' She'd meant to keep it as insurance against three o'clock insomnia; she'd have to replenish it. 'I'll go and get it, shall I?'

From habit, Valerie started to say, 'Certainly not. I wouldn't *dream* – ' and then remembered about beggars and gift-horses and said instead, 'Ought you to be drinking at all? I mean, if you're recovering from this virus ... What virus *is* it, actually?'

'Not *that* virus, Valerie darling,' said Sophie, advancing bottle-wards across the room. 'So there's no need to

31

disinfect the eating-irons. At least I don't think so. Though I don't suppose any of us can be certain, if what they tell us is true.'

Dee remembered how he had once stopped her from sharing his cup. In the station buffet. He'd got her a sugared tea by mistake so she'd made to sip out of his and he'd pulled it away and said, 'No, don't. Here, get yourself another.' She'd watched Tom like a hawk for any signs, had had him X-rayed at every available opportunity.

I can be certain, Valerie thought, as she began to stack the dishes together, since – apart from one isolated college fumble – I've only ever slept with Richard.

She was halfway to the kitchen before it occurred to her that such sanctimonious certainty was no longer appropriate.

4

Valerie

I'm glad that Sophie's staying here. So much so that I've extended her an open-ended invitation. Though she'd rather have stayed with Dee, I know. They'd sit up half the night wrecking their lungs and their livers while they savaged the reputation of every currently fashionable literary and/or theatrical figure.

It's not so much that I'm glad my guest is Sophie; I'm just pleased to have a guest, any guest. No, not pleased, relieved. I didn't feel it at first: the size and emptiness of this house. The children came home and Richard's sister stayed for a while. But after they'd gone I started to feel so terribly vulnerable.

You see, I don't think I'd ever spent a night alone under this roof before. One time I was so nervous that I almost asked Dee to stay. It was only the thought of seeing that scornful expression in her eyes that dissuaded me. Dee has lived alone for years. Well, perhaps Fred sometimes stays the night, but if he does, she never lets on.

I suppose, like her, I'll get used to it eventually. But was Dee ever afraid in the first place? I don't know. There's a lot about her that I don't know. She disappeared as a highly-strung eighteen-year-old and came back ten years later to nurse Auntie B through her last illness with a ten-year-old son in tow, a published book under her belt and a wall ten feet thick around her.

I didn't know she'd come back until the day I was in Marks and Spencers choosing jumpers for the Twins (I always made a point of dressing them differently because all the books said that otherwise they would grow up with identity problems, but they seemed to *prefer* to look alike and dress alike and share the same activities) when a voice said 'Excuse me' and someone leaned across to get to the 10- to 12-year-old rail and I turned and looked and it was Dee.

She wouldn't have acknowledged me if I hadn't said her name. She'd have pretended she didn't recognise me. But people don't change that much. She hadn't, at any rate. Despite the cropping of all that luxuriant hair that always made the producers of school plays want to cast her as the heroine. (Sophie, being the star, took the male roles because they were always longer and more important.) Not that Dee would ever accept their offers, not since the first year. In the first year she'd walked to the centre of the stage to recite a poem that had been set for the inter-house verse-speaking competition: 'They hunt,' she'd said, 'the tigers in the jungle, The velvet tigers . . .' and then, presumably overcome with the nerves of self-consciousness, she'd wet herself.

If that happened to an eleven-year-old girl today she'd probably take an overdose or run away to London and get introduced to heroin and have to ply her trade around King's Cross to finance her habit. Then you had to endure. Childhood memories are relatively short and I don't suppose she was known as 'Wet-Knickers Wyatt' for longer than a few months, but for Dee it must have seemed an eternity. Her only defence was to adopt an extreme eccentricity of manner. She was an orphan who lived with her funny old Auntie B, she was neither conventionally pretty nor – at first – did she shine academically and, furthermore, she couldn't control her bladder in stressful situations: she had no option but to emphasise her peculiarities, to make them exotic rather than pathetic, in order to survive.

In Marks and Spencers, Dee had picked up a jersey and looked at the price and said, 'Daylight robbery. I'll try the market.' I persuaded her round the corner into a café for a pot of tea and I told her that I had twin sons aged seven and she said she had one aged ten. She never mentioned anything about a husband and neither did I.

In fact the subject was never mooted at all until Sophie came back some months later. She was doing Shakespeare in Manchester: *The Merchant*, one of these new-fangled productions where everyone dresses like members of a Soviet collective – Richard and I didn't care for it at all. Anyway, she stayed on the Sunday night and I persuaded Dee to come round and Richard to go to the golf club and Sophie had lots to drink (and looked as though she'd already had plenty) and said, 'So what about Mr X then?' and Dee stood up – although we'd only reached the pudding stage – and said, 'I have to go. Auntie B's pill's due at eight-thirty,' and went.

'So,' Sophie said this evening after Dee had left, 'how much of your brave face is a brave face? Or would you rather I didn't ask?'

She was slurring her words a bit. Dee wasn't drinking and I never do, much, so she'd had the lion's share of the bottle of wine that she'd brought down from her room. I hope she hasn't fallen prey to *that* again. Once Dee and I met her in London for dinner after a performance and we had to practically *pour* her into a taxi and out of it again. Her husband of that time – 'Harvey Hawley' Sophie used to call him although I don't *think* his Christian name was actually Harvey – met us at the door of their flat and called her a drunken cow and said had she forgotten that she had a fucking audition at ten o'clock tomorrow fucking morning?

'What's the matter, darling? Afraid you won't get your pocket-money?' Sophie had said, draping herself all over him. Apparently he didn't get much work and she provided the daily bread.

'Of course you can ask,' I said to Sophie tonight. Other people had put it more cosily: 'Do you want to talk?' they'd said, magnanimously preparing to spare half an hour or so of their precious time. I knew that if I ever did start to talk I'd need days, so I never started. Consequently everyone thought I was coping marvellously.

Actually, my strongest emotion – stronger by far than grief or fear or anger – was embarrassment. I didn't know how many people *knew*. Had there been a conspiracy and, if so, how far did it extend? To his golfing cronies? The ladies of the Ladies' Circle with whom I helped to arrange fund-raising coffee mornings? His sister? My children? While receiving condolences, or listening to reiterated reassurances that, at least, Richard couldn't have suffered, I would feel the flush rising from my neck to my forehead. I could only hope that it would be attributed to my age.

'I'm not sure it's sunk in yet.'

At least I could be pretty certain that Sophie wasn't part of the real or imagined conspiracy. News of Richard's doings would hardly have percolated down to London. And there was no danger of Dee having informed her for the simple reason that Dee would never have known. She lives in a world of her own, does Dee. It's odd: you imagine that writers, of all people, would be tremendously observant but, with Dee, you sometimes get the feeling that you could drop down dead at her feet and she'd never notice.

Sophie seemed to take my stock response at its face value. She was falling asleep anyway. At ten o'clock she asked for a glass of water and took two tablets. On top of all that wine! She always was an idiot. When she was seventeen she had a stomach ulcer. She was supposed to adhere to a diet of steamed fish and soft boiled eggs; instead she'd sit in pubs with young men (and older ones sometimes too) drinking barley wine and smoking Gitanes.

She picked up her cigarettes and the ash-tray and went yawning to bed. That means that the bedroom will reek tomorrow. I can't open a window in this weather. Anyway I'd hate to be responsible for her catching her death. She looks bad enough as it is. It must have been a particularly virulent bug that she picked up. At any rate it meant that she had to cancel a Canadian tour, she said. Which was a pity because I think she was looking forward to it a lot. Things seem to have been very quiet on the work front of late. Whenever you ask her what she's currently engaged in, she says she's reading scripts or she's done a telly or a radio play that won't be shown or heard until next spring. Of course, by next spring, everyone's forgotten all about it. I can't honestly remember the last time I saw or heard her – apart from that awful advert for the chocolate bar for which she did the voice-over. If it was on when Richard was in the room he always used to say, 'Here comes Sophie doing obscene things to an innocent bar of chocolate.' Of course it wasn't Sophie, it was some very young model.

After she'd gone to bed I got the stool and climbed on to it and reached to the top of one of the kitchen cupboards and felt inside the ornamental egg-holder thing that we brought back from a holiday somewhere or other and fished out the bureau key and took it and unlocked the drawer in which I'd hidden the letters.

Those who are involved in illicit goings-on ought to arrange not to die suddenly. I used to think of that every time I went to the solicitors (which was often of late) and saw that sticker in the window: 'Making a will won't kill you'. Richard had, of course, made a will. He'd left everything to me. Everything turned out to be nothing, however; even the insurance policies had been surrendered once the mortgage was paid; things had, apparently, been that desperate. He'd never said a word.

Topics about which Richard had never said a word: how many were there? How many more? 'Would you like me to clear out the office for you, Mrs Lamb, all the bits and bobs?' Denise had said. Denise was Richard's secretary. I'd said yes thank you very much, because the new owners wanted to move into the building and I was up to my eyes in interviews with accountants and bank managers and solicitors.

There was all the rubbish that you'd have expected to accumulate during two decades in one place: out of date calendars and *Readers Digest* prize draws and invitations to invest in time-shares and exercise machines, ionisers and personalised golf balls. There were memos from 1979 and photographs of the children and a fifteenth wedding anniversary card that he'd bought and obviously forgotten to post. There were stamps of defunct denominations and membership cards for societies of which he'd long ago ceased to be a member. And, in a compartment of the scratched old briefcase that had been a birthday present from me, there were half a dozen letters.

I could never be sure about Denise. Whether she'd read them. Whether she was a party to . . . She'd handed them over and looked me right in the eye. Perhaps she hadn't. She was very religious, one of these evangelical sort of Christians who spend all their free time tramping the streets and knocking on people's doors and asking them whether they've been saved. Richard had always said that it was worth putting up with the odd bout of crusading zeal that got directed at him because she was such a good secretary. Good secretaries were efficient and punctilious – and discreet.

Sophie moved around a lot upstairs. I heard the lavatory flush twice and bathwater gurgling through the pipes. (I hope she's not one of these bath fanatics. The gas bill for the last quarter was *horrendous*.) I waited until everything had been quiet for half an hour or so and then I spread the letters on the coffee table in the order of their despatch and then, for the umpteenth time, I read them.

None of them were dated. They just said 'Tuesday' or 'Friday' or whatever. If it hadn't been for the postmarks I wouldn't have known whether they'd been written recently or years ago. If it hadn't been for the postmarks I'd not have known where they originated from because, as well as being undated, they bore no address. What I did know, having read them, was that they were merely the most recent six in what had been a series of letters stretching back at least over the last sixteen years.

The envelopes were all postmarked 'Bundaberg: Queensland'. In Letter One the correspondent stated: 'We're staying put after all. We've decided to wait until the children are off our hands. Ben's with a radio station in Brisbane and Oliver starts Uni next term, but we feel it would be wrong to uproot Melissa and Josh at this stage of their education. I think I told you last time that Melissa was showing a definite flair for languages; well, this year, she came top in French, Spanish *and* German (didn't you have a German great-grandmother or something?), so we're hoping that, pretty soon, she might be able to spend a vacation in Europe. John's put a "Melissa's European Odyssey" money-box on the mantelpiece and we all put our spare small change into it . . .'

What had happened to the earlier letters, the ones that told of Melissa's linguistic abilities and Ben's footballing prowess and John's operation for a hiatus hernia? Where were they? Had he kept a batch of half a dozen for so long then destroyed them? I'd been through the house with a toothcomb but couldn't find any others. Or anything else incriminating for that matter.

The third letter said, 'I enclose a photograph. It's a bit blurred because Beauty wouldn't stand still. Melissa came third in her class at the gymkhana. Once we thought that she might be going to be one of those horsy little girls but I think she's grown out of it . . .'

The envelope contained no photograph. Where had it gone? Was it stuck behind the drawer of a filing cabinet? Would the secretary to the new managing director of the firm that had moved into J. F. Lamb, Bolts and Rivets, find it one day and wonder about the identity of the girl on the bay gelding?

The sixth letter, which was postmarked in the January of this year, said: 'Well, we've finally got it together. This summer: the Grand Tour. Just me and Melissa. That's all the piggy-bank will run to. Anyway Josh has his summer camp and John doesn't want to leave everything to the new man just yet, so . . . We'll be in the UK in August. For a fortnight. The first week in London. I know nothing happens in London in August, but that suits us fine. We intend to museum and art gallery ourselves to death, with the odd mind-improving play thrown in. Are there any? Anyway . . .'

There was then a space and when the handwriting resumed it was in a different-coloured ink, as though some time had elapsed.

> . . . I don't know whether this is a suggestion that ought to be made. Still, I'll make it. And you can chew it over. You've often said that it grieves you to think that you'll never see her and I've always replied that it's undoubtedly for the best that you won't. I've told Melissa as much as she needs to know, and although John is the most understanding of souls I don't go much for all that cosy let's-get-together-and-be-friends-and-wasn't-it-all-a-long-time-ago business.
>
> Anyway, the upshot of it is that we shall be staying at Bennett's Hotel from 1st to 8th of August. The rest is up to you. The only proviso being that I'd prefer her to remain unaware . . .
>
> Oh, and as an afterthought, *I'd* quite like to see you again, you old rogue.

Richard died in March. There were no unposted letters on his person or in his desk, either at home or at work, so there was no way of knowing whether he'd intended to be in London some time between August 1st and 8th, or whether he'd decided that, after sixteen years, such a meeting would serve no purpose.

'Ba,' she signed herself. 'As ever, Ba.' Barbara, presumably. I racked my brains but couldn't think of any Barbara who might have been on the scene sixteen years ago. I imagined her as tall and dark and rather bossy, one of those women who aren't a bit embarrassed about taking their clothes off in communal changing-rooms. I imagined her as the sort that can change a tyre on the hard shoulder of the motorway, the sort that has one of those voices that carry across hotel foyers and airport lounges, and who never lets cowardice or concern for anyone's feelings prevent her from speaking her mind.

Which is odd, because if Richard ever did express a preference, it was for that kind of vulnerable child-woman who weeps if she breaks a fingernail.

I put the letters back in the bureau and hid the key in the Chinese vase on the landing this time. It wasn't that I thought Sophie would be likely to take to hunting for keys and trying them in convenient locks; simply the habit of concealment was growing on me. Sophie had never seemed that interested in other people's business. It was for that reason, probably, that she often found herself to be a positive repository of confidences. I tried to imagine myself confiding in her, trying to form the words: 'It seems that Richard hasn't two children but three, the youngest being a sixteen-year-old daughter whose mother has been writing to him on a fairly regular basis ever since she was born. What I want, Sophie, is not comfort or condolence, but simply to know how I ought to react. If he were alive I could confront him, scratch his eyes out and then hers and then sue for divorce. But he isn't and I can't even ask, "How many other people knew about this? How many mutual friends have been sniggering behind their hands all these years?"

I went upstairs to bed, reached the first landing and then remembered that I'd neither locked up nor turned off the

41

downstairs lights. They were always his jobs: turning the lights off, locking the doors, providing the income. Mine were running the house and looking presentable and making myself available for conjugal relations without too much demur.

I'd had extra locks fitted after he died and they were stiff. As I struggled, trying to get the tumblers to fall into place, I rehearsed the imaginary conversation that I might have with Sophie. I'd say, 'Don't tell Dee.' And she'd say, 'Why not? Surely Dee's the very person to understand and sympathise, having been in the same boat – even if the boot was on the other foot, pardon my metaphors. Why don't you want her to know?'

Because they are the last people to understand: those who've been in the same boat with the boot on the other foot. I've learned that.

5

'You walk to Leicester Road and get a number 17,' Valerie said. 'You get off at the war memorial, cross over to where the Gaumont cinema used to be – it's Safeways now – and change to a number 4. You want the corner of Ferryside Lane and Beach Road . . .'

'I'll ring a cab,' Sophie said and did so while Valerie stood by making shocked faces at the idea of such profligacy.

In the days when the cottage belonged to Auntie B, Ferryside Lane had not been the smartest of addresses. In those days, before the proliferation of the ubiquitous estates, those great social levellers, the town could be divided into three distinct areas: there was its prosperous end where the property covered a spectrum ranging from rich beyond the dreams of avarice through well-maintained detached (cherry-blossom trees, York-stone paving, rose beds – the homes of bank managers and senior civil servants – Valerie lived there) to modest but respectable semis; its centre: road upon road of boarding houses and Victorian mansions converted into flats (in a series of which Sophie and her mother had made their home); and its north side, bordering the marshes. Here, at intervals along paths that meandered through the dunes, were dotted fishermen's cottages: single storey, whitewashed, lacking indoor sanitation.

Now the area had come up in the world. The cottages, almost without exception, were distinctly des-res: extended, refurbished, plumbed, wired, double-glazed, lovingly restored, superficially, in period detail – although Sophie, passing them by in her taxi, wondered whether poverty could actually be structured in terms of 'periods'. Here was the cottage where the kitchen floor used to be bare earth and ragged children with snotty noses grubbed around in the neglected garden; here the one where the albino lived – you skirted it cautiously; at night the gas-light threw his shadow against the wall as he sat at the window, peering into the darkness with his little red rat-eyes. Now there were Georgian-style front doors and leaded lights and carriage lamps, patios and garages and landscaped gardens, rustic fencing and ceramic plaques announcing that you had reached 'Marsh Farm Cottage' or 'The Dunes'.

Auntie B's place had not undergone quite such a drastic transformation. A government grant had paid for its re-roofing, provided a bathroom, lavatory and hot and cold running water, but you could still see the old privy at the bottom of the garden. It wasn't called anything either.

There was a pram outside the door. It contained Pixie who waved her fists feebly at Sophie when she peered round the hood. Dee had had to borrow that pram, Tom and Sam having neglected to provide their offspring with this necessity before departing. Apparently they'd brought her down from London alternately in the carry-cot or else slung around Sam's neck in a kind of marsupial pouch.

'You should have rung,' Dee said when she opened the door. 'I'd have collected you.'

'Not worth the trouble. The taxis are still so cheap here I'm surprised that anybody bothers with actually owning a car.'

This was in the nature of dissonance-reduction. Two years ago, Sophie had been re-convicted of drunken driving and had had her licence taken away.

Dee ushered her into the living-room. The table was set for lunch and the television set was on. 'You don't mind, do you?' Dee said, turning the sound up. 'I never miss this. It's brilliant.'

'This' was a product of Asian television called *Empress Wu*. For a while Sophie watched goggle-eyed with disbelief and then, like Dee, began to titter. Characters attired in vague approximations to ancient Chinese imperial dress delivered themselves stiltedly of lines such as: 'Here is a gift of two-thousand-year-old ginseng,' or 'Brother Dick, we must not let down the Lady Mo. Only she can save our country.' The lip-synchronisation was non-existent, the dubbing provided by a variety of incongruous accents.

'That one sounds like Irene Handl as Mrs Puffin,' Sophie gasped. 'I've seen better acting from *sideboards*. God, I thought *our* soaps were bad enough – Oops,' said Sophie. 'Sorry.'

'What do you mean: sorry?'

'I saw your name on those credits last night. Mind you, I've always thought that *that* one was a little more literate than most – '

Dee got up and snapped off the television set. 'I have to *eat*,' she said.

'Well, quite.'

'It's only like lending your voice to sell bars of chocolate,' Dee said. 'Probably less degrading. Certainly less ideologically unsound, given all that unacceptable-face-of-capitalism multinational takeover business.'

Years ago, before Sophie had lent her voice to sell chocolate, she'd lent her name and her presence to various sorts of benefits and protests: Vietnam, South Africa, Chile. Years ago, in the Wilson era, Sophie had voice-overed an election broadcast for the Labour Party.

'Come into the kitchen,' Dee said. 'I can't *yell* at you while I'm getting the lunch ready.'

She took up a tin-opener and removed the lid from a

tinned chicken and mushroom pie, put it in the oven, opened a tin of peas and a packet of Smash.

'Makes a change from haute cuisine at Valerie's, doesn't it?' she said.

'She's feeding me up like a goose for the market. This morning I came down to the full works: bacon, scrambled egg, sausages – '

Dee took a packet of Instant Whip from the cupboard and poured milk into a bowl. 'Well I can see her point,' she said. 'You look as though you could get work on a film about the liberation of Belsen.'

'I told her that breakfast doesn't normally feature in my scheme of things. I have been *known* to take the odd sip at a glass of freshly-squeezed orange juice, but no more than that. She was awfully miffed.'

'She would be,' Dee said. 'She's skint. The bacon and eggs etcetera were probably bought specially in your honour.'

'What will she do?'

'Get a job,' Dee said, instantly whipping with such gusto that strawberry mousse spattered the walls. 'Like the rest of us.'

Strangely, Dee's ready-prepared, pre-cooked repast went down a good deal easier than Valerie's home-made soup and chive-sprinkled scrambled eggs had done. Sophie ate and thought how you always expected Dee to have unmatching china and LMS cutlery and what an out-of-date assumption that was because, actually, Auntie B's cottage was looking quite charming in a thrown-together sort of way. Courtesy of the soaps, presumably. And, no doubt, the chap helped.

They walked past the chap's cottage after lunch. Now *his* really was a *most* desirable residence, a *very* tasteful conversion: rustic brick and hanging baskets and holly-hocks and a pergola smothered in old-fashioned climbing roses. It was the sort of cottage that Sophie saw sometimes in *House and Garden* or *Country Life* when she was

46

waiting to have her teeth capped or her cervix inspected. She'd drool, imagining owning such a place. She always imagined, too, a lifestyle to go with it that featured inglenooked inns and small dinner parties in seventeenth-century rectories, apple-cheeked farmers' wives inviting her to join rural societies and the vicar – a silver-haired handsome old gentleman of extreme erudition – dropping by for a glass of dry sherry and an exchange of Latin quotations.

Then she'd walk out into the fumes of Earls Court or the Fulham Road or wherever and remember that – in these days of severely curtailed public transport – actresses who have no valid driving licence are more or less obliged to reside within reach of the metropolis.

The chap's cottage curtains were closed. The dog kennel outside the door was empty. 'Fred's away,' Dee said tersely in answer to Sophie's cocked eyebrow.

They continued to push the pram towards the sea cop. Dee grumbled, said she'd never been able to see the sense of pram-pushing. After all, the *baby* didn't get any exercise; you might just as well leave it in the garden.

'I think it's for the benefit of the pusher,' Sophie said, throwing back her head and filling her nostrils with the remembered familiarity of that smell: marsh grass, cow dung, alluvial mud, ozone, decomposing shellfish, that sharp, head-clearing aroma that recalled her girlhood more vividly than anything: here I lost my sandal in a tidal pool and my mother smacked me because sandals did not grow on trees; here I walked with the curly-haired boy who tried to kiss me and kept missing my face; here I flung myself in the lee of a sand dune and wept all afternoon because my application to RADA had been turned down; here I came after my mother's death. It was winter, sunset, and the wild geese were skeining across the sky, going home, and it occurred to me then that I'd never really had one, just a succession of flats and then college rooms and then married residences that always felt impermanent, probably because the marriages were.

She took off her sunglasses and looked out over the sea. The tide was at its ebb and the ribbed sand glittered. You could see Blackpool Tower. Local lore, Ferryside Lane intelligence, had it that if you could see Blackpool Tower then rain was due. If you couldn't, that meant that it was already raining. She slipped the sunglasses into her pocket; it seemed a shame to blot out the sun.

'I was wondering when you were going to take those off,' Dee said, braking the pram and arranging the canopy to guard Pixie's eyes from the glare. 'Why do you wear them?' she said. 'Are you afraid you'll be recognised?'

It was a cheap jibe. Everyone knew you had to be a television personality or in a soap in order to be recognised, and Sophie hadn't done a telly since, well . . .

'A woman once stopped me in Waitrose and said, "Didn't you used to be Sophie Stephenson?" '

'Yes, you said. So what *are* you doing these days?'

Challenging gazes met head on. Sophie replaced her glasses in order to give herself the advantage. She said, 'There's a part in a Zeffirelli film in the offing, and my agent's been negotiating for this new *Anna Karenina* production that the Beeb has got in the pipeline . . .'

'No stage work?' Dee said, shifting her glance to the distant horizon and Blackpool Tower.

'Stage work's too exhausting,' Sophie replied. 'I *have* been ill. It was that damned endless run of the Lonsdale thing that probably made me ill in the first place . . .'

That was *ages* ago, Dee thought, nearly two years ago, in fact.

'And how about you? What are you working on? Currently? As Valerie would say.'

Sophie lit a cigarette. Dee very deliberately increased the distance between them, wafted the drifting smoke out to sea. What I am working on currently is, she thought, the painting of the back bedroom ceiling; the mastery of knitting so that I can manufacture some article of clothing for this, my grandchild; and the propagation of some cuttings of pinks that Fred let me have. She said, 'How in the name of God could I be working on anything with *her* to contend with?'

'Why's that? After all you do have the advantage of working at home and you *can* break off whenever it's necessary. And she seems to be an awfully *good* baby,' Sophie said provocatively.

'You really haven't the least idea, have you? You think it's simply a matter of picking up a pen or sitting down at a typewriter . . .'

Sophie had forgotten how touchy Dee could be. She decided upon conciliation, gesturing towards the sand dunes and saying, 'Do you remember – what was it called – the Wide Game? We were divided into two teams and each one had to evade the other and get back to base. Or something. Do you remember?'

Dee debated for a moment whether to stay miffed, then decided against it and smiled and said, 'Yes, I remember. Valerie and Richard were in different teams. She sulked.'

'She thought that girl with red hair and big teeth would take advantage of her proximity to him. What was she called, that girl?'

'Sheila? Stella? Something.'

'What happened to them all?' Sophie said, in a rather silly, dramatic voice. 'All those girls in their dirndl skirts and white Orlon cardigans put on back to front and their Poppet beads, and the boys with the Tony Curtis haircuts?'

'God knows. They grew up, I suppose. Or didn't.'

They walked on. Sophie said that it might be pleasant to do some walking. If the weather held. She could take Pixie, if Dee liked. It would give her a reason. Like having a dog.

'You're most welcome,' Dee said. 'Personally, too much fresh air and I get hay-fever.'

Indeed she was overcome with successive bouts of

sneezing which lasted throughout their homeward journey and all the time she was preparing a bottle for the by-now vociferous Pixie.

'Here,' she said, handing it to Sophie. 'Stop her mouth with it for God's sake while I find my antihistamines.'

'But I can't, I don't know . . .' said Sophie as the child was dumped in her lap. It was so *little*, felt as though its bones might snap at the slightest hint of pressure. She'd once, long ago, played Tess in a television adaptation (another serious bit of miscasting: anything further from the embodiment of bucolic rosiness than Sophie would have been hard to imagine, but the director had owed her a favour). They'd used a real baby. She, who had never been seriously bothered by stage-fright, had sweated and trembled and had to be patted dry while they got the relevant takes in the can.

Cautiously, she cradled Pixie's feathery-fronded head in the crook of her arm. She had a fiercely powerful suck for one so small and fragile: you could almost feel the food coursing through her digestive tract, being transformed, at various stages, into the fuel that would cause the hair to sprout, the muscles to develop, the bones to harden and lengthen.

When she played Tess, Sophie had been obliged to pretend to suckle that baby. It was a scene that took place in a cornfield: she had to open her bodice and put the child to her breast. It had been March, she remembered, and a shrieking wind, but that hadn't been the cause of the goose-pimples that rose on her flesh. The child's mother had eyed her suspiciously and snatched it away as soon as they were done as though her un-maternal qualities were apparent at a glance.

She'd never wanted babies. Certainly not with Constantine. Or any of the others. And besides there was her career to consider. Later on, she and Hawley had thought that their relationship might undergo some magical transformation if they had a child, but she never got pregnant.

50

'I suppose I had one too many abortions,' she'd say, if anyone asked. They all thought she was a hard bitch, and perhaps she was, but there'd been a brief time when she found herself looking into prams and suddenly realising how very beautiful a sleeping child's eyelashes could look when fanned across its cheek.

Pixie pulled rhythmically on the teat. Dee sat down with a box of tissues at her elbow and, in the intervals between blowing her nose, said, 'How does Valerie seem to you?'

'No different from how she always seemed.'

'Exactly. I'd have thought the death of one's husband might just cause a ripple on the surface, wouldn't you?'

'Constantine died, you know,' Sophie said. 'Oh, it was after we'd divorced. I was appearing in that awful revival of *Private Lives* – do you remember? Awful Dudley Page and his corset? And there was this girl playing a maid or something who was friendly with the girl who was living with him then – Constantine, that is. She told me. He'd had a massive cerebral haemorrhage. He was only fifty-three. It was the weirdest feeling. I mean, I'd said, "I hope you drop down dead, you bastard," more times than I can remember, but when it came to the *point* . . .'

'I've never even seen Valerie shed a tear,' Dee said.

'Have you ever seen Valerie shed a tear over anything?'

'No, but then she's never had anything to cry about before.'

She buried her nose in her tissue, but Sophie was still able to detect that unmistakable trace of *Schadenfreude*: Valerie, for whom everything had always gone right, now having to face a hostile world without benefit of partner or money or means of support.

'Perhaps she's had to put a brave face on it for the kids. Stop herself going to pieces for their sake. Incidentally, how will this sudden impoverishment affect them? Are they still at university or have they finished?'

'They finished at the end of last term,' Dee said. 'And it won't, because they were sponsored by – I think it was

British Nuclear Fuels – through their courses. They were guaranteed jobs if their results were good enough – and they were: they both got Upper Seconds, despite losing a father along the way.'

The twins: Stephen and Simon. When Dee was a little girl she'd had paper dolls, propped them against the bottom rail of Auntie B's utility sideboard, christened them, worked out kinship relations between them: Peter and Pamela, she'd called them, Molly and Michael, Stephen and Simon. Whenever she thought of Valerie's sons she remembered those dolls: identically dressed, perfect in every feature, disappointingly unresponsive.

'So where are they now?' Sophie enquired. She suspected that Pixie ought to be upended in some way and patted on the back but was too nervous to attempt it.

'On holiday. Well, working holiday. Camp counsellors in the States. For the summer.'

Sophie tried to ease the teat from Pixie's determined grasp but the suction was phenomenal. 'They always struck me as being totally self-contained,' she said. 'Absolutely complete in themselves. Even Valerie used to hint sometimes that she and Richard felt excluded. Perhaps it's typical of twins. Didn't you once write something along those lines?'

'Mm,' said Dee and got up and wandered round the room. She didn't like to talk about her books, believing that if she discussed the one in progress then it would be blighted forthwith, and as for the finished products – well, they were over and done with once they entered the public domain: she could scarcely remember their themes or the names of the characters.

She drummed her fingers on the table top. She said, 'Quite apart from *her*,' and here she nodded savagely at Pixie who had fallen asleep quite suddenly in mid-suck, 'I'm never going to be able to get any work done ever again anyway. Not if I can't have a fag.'

'So have a fag.'

'I won't. It's a filthy, disgusting, degrading habit. It costs a fortune, it wrecks your health – I had bronchitis three times last year – and there's nobody to look after *me* . . .'

She began to stack together some papers that lay on top of the bookcase. Sophie said, 'There's no one to look after me either. Is that what you're currently working on?'

'It is,' said Dee, and stuffed the papers behind some books. Then she said, 'Sorry, I forgot to ask. You're not married? Currently?'

'Currently? No.'

'Or . . . ?'

'Not "or" either.'

'Oh,' Dee said. 'Just like to get it straight.'

'And what about you? Are you currently married?'

'Don't be ridiculous.'

'Why is it any more ridiculous for you than for me?'

'Because you make a habit of it,' Dee said.

'Twice? A habit?'

'I don't just mean marriage.'

Sophie let this pass. She said, 'According to Valerie, you've got something fairly snug going yourself.'

'Then Valerie knows more than I do.'

Valerie said that the subjects upon which Dee could be drawn were very few in number, but that wasn't true. She'd talk about anything under the sun as long as it didn't touch upon the personal.

Well that was – possibly – understandable, in certain respects. But what was it about her relationship with the chap that it must be kept under wraps? Valerie said he was a widower: free, white and most definitely over twenty-one. Surely there was no need for evasion. Perhaps it was just that secrecy had been practised for so long that it had become part of Dee's way of life.

6

Dee

Pixie's crying woke me from a nightmare. It was the usual nightmare, where I'm on stage and I don't know my lines. I have no excuse, I've had ample time to learn them, but somehow I've not been able to get round to it. The house lights go down, I can see a blur of faces on the front rows, I start to sweat . . .

For once, Pixie's timing was impeccable. Usually, I couldn't wake myself up from that dream. I'd stand there, frozen with fear, trying to open my mouth even though I knew I hadn't the appropriate words. When I was a child, the fear would relax my bladder and I'd wet my pyjamas. That usually woke me up – after the event, of course. I'd force myself to continue to lie on the wet patch hoping that my body heat would dry it out before morning because Auntie B had quite enough to do without extra washing.

Pixie's crying was loud and insistent. I pulled on my dressing gown and rushed through to the other bedroom, although I didn't really understand the need for such urgency: it doesn't matter how long or how loudly she cries because there's no one to hear her but me; Fred is my only near neighbour and he's away.

I got her bottle out of the fridge and put on a pan of water to heat it and thought, while I waited for it to boil, that my reaction was probably conditioned, dated from Tom's babyhood when we lived in a rented room above a not-very-sympathetic landlady. I used to have to make sure that his night-time crying was stifled before ever it began. If he wouldn't stop, I'd put him in his pram and wheel him round the streets of Newcastle. I was scared of what might lurk in the dark mouths of alleyways, scared of the odd solitary figure that I could see in the distance walking towards me, but not nearly so scared as I was of being given notice to quit my room.

The kettle wouldn't boil fast enough for Pixie's liking. I shut the door to muffle the noise, but then I opened it again. What if she were to choke? In my custody. I hadn't applied for it, but that wouldn't make any difference.

It was a warm night, thank goodness. Tom was born in February and all my memories are of midnight vigils, being perished with the cold yet not daring to switch on the fire because landladies' electricity meters were always set so high as to be unassuagable in their appetite for – shilling pieces, I suppose it must have been then; I can't remember. There's so much I've striven to forget but only succeeded in obliterating trivial little details such as whether it was shillings or sixpenny pieces that were required to feed the meter.

Pixie was soaking but I thought it better to feed her before attempting to change her nappy. These disposable things are a godsend. They'd only just come on to the market when Tom was born and were too expensive for my pocket. Ask any mother of a twenty-odd-year-old about her most vivid memory of those early days and if she's honest she'll say nappies steaming dry on a fireguard. No escape from it. I used to leave Tom with a child-minder before he got a place in the nursery and *her* house was redolent with that same smell: soapflakes, dampness, scorching.

I wonder if Tom has dumped Pixie here as a gesture of revenge for those infant years when I was obliged to farm him out. I don't suppose I'll ever know. He certainly won't tell me. There are unfathomable depths to Tom. Even when you think the last of his defences is down, you realise he's faking his frankness in order to get you off his back. I have become secretive because of a need to keep so many things dark, but Tom . . . I wonder about heredity. But wondering about heredity is a totally pointless exercise. How far do you go back?

These nappies are the best thing since typewriters with correction facilities but, despite the nappy and the plastic pants, the sheet's still wet. I'll have to put the machine on again in the morning. I begin to sympathise with Auntie B. And she didn't have a machine. We didn't even have electricity until 1959, for God's sake.

The nightmare sweat began to cool on my skin. I don't wet the bed any more, but that strange theatrical dream will persist. It should be Sophie who has dreams of that sort, but hers is that she can't find the theatre. She knows she has to be in Shaftesbury Avenue or St Martin's Lane or wherever and she gets on a bus or a Tube and finds herself in Catford or Stratford (the East London one, not the birthplace of the Bard). Even if she realises her mistake in mid-journey and tries to rectify her error, the bus or the train that actually said 'Leicester Square' on the front takes the wrong turning and deposits her at Hackney Wick or the Woolwich Ferry.

She's known actors, she says, who have my dream. She knows actors who are violently sick in the wings, actors whose knees shake so vigorously for the first few minutes after their entrances that they can be heard in the back row of the stalls. She's never been affected that way, never been a sufferer from stage-fright. And perhaps that explains why she never quite made it to the top. At school, in the drama classes, on various platforms, speaking verse and collecting trophies, she was considered to be without peer. But later, on stage, it became evident that she lacked that kind of depth and conviction so necessary to inculcate in her audience a willing suspension of disbelief.

She certainly isn't actress enough to convince me that

she still gets regular work, even though she once told me that, once you'd got your break, regular work depended largely on your ability to turn up on time, speak your lines in the correct order and not fall over the furniture.

Perhaps it was her increasing *in*ability to do so that had caused the parts to dwindle to a trickle and then finally dry up. Perhaps there was one late entrance too many. Or perhaps she stopped being able to handle the booze. Valerie talks about 'Sophie's alcoholic period', but she was never that bad. It was just that she took the brakes off during those last terrible years with Harvey Hawley. Whichever member of the acting profession you mention to Sophie she'll say, 'Oh, she's a nympho,' or 'He's a shit.' Harvey Hawley really was. He used to hit her. She once said she'd left her first husband, Constantine, because she was afraid that he might start hitting her. I subscribe to the currently unpopular theory about women who are drawn to violent men: that there's some peculiar personality quirk that makes them want to be used as punchbags. Sophie fled Constantine to the haven of Hawley. And, if I'm not mistaken, there was another angry not-so-young man after him: North Kensington, I remember, a rather nice garden flat, and every mirror in the place cracked from side to side.

(Sophie couldn't pass a mirror without looking into it. The North Kensington man had made sure that all she'd see would be her shattered image.)

A film in the offing, she says, a telly in the pipeline. She can't admit to being unwanted any more than I can speak the truth about my current lack of output, which is due neither to Pixie nor nicotine-starvation, not even worry about Tom's whereabouts, but is the direct result of the well having run dry. For the first time, ever since I pinched that unused accounts book from the components' factory in Gateshead where I was working at the time and wrote all through my lunch breaks and in bed at night, wearing balaclava and gloves, I'm stuck, blocked, parched as the desert.

I brought Pixie's wind up and laid her down again and then unlocked the back door and stood out in the garden for a while, trying to get cool. If Fred had been at home, his dog, Sally, would have barked and then, recognising my scent, stopped and gone back into her kennel. 'No need to worry as long as Sally's around,' Fred said. I said I wasn't worried. It's Valerie who thinks that the night seethes with assorted bogeymen.

Mist was rising from the marshes. Sometimes you can see will-o'-the-wisp. And you can always hear the sound of the sea: either roaring or sighing. People have said: 'Oh this must be an ideal place for you to work; so quiet and secluded.' They may be right but I've worked perfectly well in staff canteens and hotel kitchens and on buses. And in the winter this place can be very bleak: an offshore wind that never lets up, that howls round the house and down the chimney and infiltrates at every point of access. 'A summer house,' Auntie B used to call it when we sat in the stone-flagged kitchen watching the draught lifting the rug in front of the fire, stuffing rags into the gaps in the window frames. She couldn't afford to move. I can, but I don't. Inertia, I suppose. For ten years I seemed to be for ever on the move; now even the *thought* of a furniture van brings me out in a rash.

The peace was suddenly shattered. I went back inside. Pixie, brick-red in the face, was thrashing around in her cot like one demented. I felt her: she was dry. She was certainly fed. I tried to make her more comfortable. She continued to cry. I made crooning noises. She screamed the louder. I picked her up and walked the floor, rocking her. She made convulsive movements as though she would rather have hurled herself to the ground than be confined within my embrace.

Valerie said that looking after babies is like riding a bicycle: you never forget. Well I've forgotten. I don't know what to *do*. And I can feel the panic-frustration rising within me. All this without benefit of nicotine! Has there ever been a case of grandmother-inflicted child-abuse? Just to be on the safe side I put her down in her cot and left the room. Surely Tom must have known that I wouldn't be able to cope? After all the rows we've had? The time he played truant from school for an entire term, the time he dyed his hair blue, the A-Levels he wouldn't work for, the future for which he refused to plan? I'd end up screaming at him and he'd scream back at me. 'You've been a lousy mother,' he'd yell. Has he forgotten? Does he assume that lousy mothers make good grandmothers?

I put Egmont on the record-player and followed it with Leonora and then Coriolan and turned up the volume to capacity but I could still hear her. She sounded so angry. Are people *born* angry? I find genetics terrifying. You can carry yourself like a Ming vase for nine months, you can eschew drink and tobacco and noxious substances and violent emotions and strenuous exercise and still you don't know what may squeeze itself from between your thighs at the end of it.

I lifted Pixie from her cot and pressed her close to my chest. Her wailing reverberated through my rib cage. I said, 'Pixie, Pixie,' cajolingly, but it didn't surprise me that *that* had no effect. Perhaps that was why she was so angry. I'd be angry if I'd been lumbered with a name like that.

I presume she's called Pixie Wyatt. Though I don't know. After all, it is usually the custom to bestow the name of the mother upon an illegitimate child. Or *was*. In my day. I can still remember the pitying look directed at me by the registrar of births and deaths when I furnished the details for Tom's certificate: the shortened version so that he shouldn't be embarrassed by reading: 'Father unknown'.

There had been many pitying glances. All those, in fact, that weren't hostile. People were scandalised, or unkind, or patronising. Patronising was the worst. That's why I tried so hard to impress upon Tom the need to earn respect. He says, 'I don't know what you're on about,' and he doesn't. When he had blue hair and was bunking off school to sit on the bare floor in someone's squat and listen to Joy Division or The Fall and smoke dope (or, if no one had any dope, then dried banana skins or morning glory seeds or Benylin cocktails – anything to make the world go away), his female counterparts were deliberately getting themselves pregnant so that they would be given council flats and thus escape from the unbearable restrictiveness of the parental home.

In the race between Pixie ceasing to cry and dawn breaking, dawn won hands down. Its chorus started to vie for a hearing at about four-thirty. There are two birds in particular which inhabit my garden all summer, blackbirds, I think: raucous, insistent. One calls: 'Frede*rico*, Frede*rico*,' as though mourning some lost love in an obscure Italian opera; the other is more homely: 'Poor Birdie' it cries, over and over again. Goodness knows why. If it's the one I think it is then it's very sleek and well-fed. Their reiterated racket drives me round the bend sometimes. On and on, when I'm stuck between one sentence and the next. I go outside and yell at them, but they don't care. Fred has a bird-table. I have a feeling that they dine in his garden and then return home to annoy me.

Pixie fell asleep at five. By which time I was quite wide awake. So I made coffee and thought: Well, why not take this opportunity to catch it unawares, get started before my brain engages? So I got out the papers from the back of the bookcase, the papers that Sophie had been so nosy about and re-read the pathetically small amount that I'd written during the last few weeks.

Valerie probably thinks that writing a book is like riding a bicycle, something you never forget. I am here to assure her most emphatically that it's not. More like having a baby: in the sense that you have to forget what hell it was at the time in order to contemplate doing it again. And perhaps I haven't forgotten, because I can't do it any more. It won't come. I shouldn't have stacked these papers in the bookcase, I should have chucked them on the fire.

I compromised and shoved them under a cushion and then tried to decide whether to open the bank statement that arrived yesterday and be made aware of just exactly how much there was left between me and penury, or to return to the Soap and address myself to working out the (short-term) destinies of Maggie and Ben and Mr Tovey and Jonathon (or whoever the hell features in this particular episode).

I had a look at what I'd already done. Maggie's still deciding whether or not to have an abortion. She's forty-four and there's mongolism in the family but – wouldn't you know it? – she's Roman Catholic. I hate to question the story-lining, but if she hesitates much longer she won't need to make a decision: she found out she was pregnant in November, as far as I can gather, and it's now May.

One of Sophie's abortions was performed at a fairly late stage. She reckons it was then she got the infection, the one that remained undetected for so long, silently doing its damage. She didn't find out until she actually tried to conceive.

All this was confided during one drunken night after she'd fled the matrimonial home nursing a cracked rib and a split lip. It's always Sophie who flees the nest. I often wonder how she goes on about property rights. Surely she can't have ceded her share of *everywhere* to Constantine and Hawley and all the others before, after and in between?

Well, that portion of my script already completed reads like something from *Empress Wu*, only a mite less intellectual.

I have to do it though. As I told Sophie, I have to eat. Jobs are hard to find these days. As Valerie will soon discover.

I have to do it, but not now. I thought I'd rehearse my

speech instead. I have to make a speech next week to a literary circle. They feed you and then you have to get up and spout about something vaguely relevant. Of course you're so nervous that the meal might as well not feature.

My speech, which is about the incidental joys of a writing career, is typed out in its entirety. Others manage with key words written on cards; I have to memorise every line, like a poem.

While I was pacing the floor and declaiming (fairly quietly in case I disturbed Pixie), I heard the postman at the door. He'd delivered a gardening catalogue and a credit card statement and a postcard with a picture of The Nightwatch on the front. On the back was written: 'Acommodation crisis. No time to get in touch. Now in Amsterdam (see front of card). Back in September. Will ring before then of course. Thanks for looking after P. T and S.'

At least I think that's what it said; the writing grew progressively smaller so that, at the bottom, it was almost indecipherable. T's writing has never been a model of legibility. He can't spell 'accommodation' either. Though, I suppose, given his age and background, he'd be most untypical if he could.

I propped the postcard behind the clock. At least I knew they were safe. At least I knew they intended to come back and reclaim the child. But until September? That's damn near two months. I've a speech to deliver, a script conference to attend, a meeting with my editor. Quite apart from the fact that there's a novel waiting to be written. Sophie has offered to have Pixie, hasn't she? I might take her up on that. I expect she'll very soon change her tune.

7

They hadn't met, all three of them at once, for more than five years, not since the day when Dee had gone to London to see her publisher and Valerie, who hated travelling alone, had seized the opportunity for company – for the journey at least – and treated herself to a tour of South Molton Street. She hadn't bought much, after all; it was a weird time for clothes: everything black and shapeless, more Sophie's style than her own. They'd arranged to dine with Sophie after the theatre. 'It's either a feast or a famine,' Dee had said, making off in the direction of Bedford Square. 'Why is it, that when I'm to be paid for twice, it has to be on the same day?' To Valerie's eternal shame, at dinner, she'd requested a doggy bag and put what remained of her steak into it, together with some gristicks and a plateful of petit fours. It came, Valerie supposed, of years of scratching a living (you couldn't exactly say that Dee was mean but if it was at all possible to wriggle out of paying her half of a bill, she'd wriggle). She hoped that Sophie wouldn't notice and be offended.

Sophie, however, had been too far gone to notice what was going on under the tablecloth. She was downing two glasses to their every one. 'So come on,' she'd said, leaning over the table and sending cutlery flying across the floor, 'what did you think of it? Be honest.'

They'd watched the waiter picking up the knives and

forks because it was impossible for them to be honest. The play had been quite terrible. 'A comedy of manners' it was described as on the billboards, but the only laughter that had been aroused in the audience was that of nervous embarrassment. Sophie, wearing a blond wig, had intoned her lines for some reason as though she were making announcements for British Rail. Worse, in Act Two, she'd had to be prompted.

'It's a disaster, isn't it?' Sophie had said. And tears had started to drip from the end of her nose and into her zabaglione. Then she'd got very maudlin and started asking questions such as: 'How's the old hometown?' and 'Is that nodding Chinese mandarin still in Cresset's window?' and 'Has the Punch and Judy man gone from the Marine Parade?'

'Come back and see for yourself,' Dee had said. But she'd told them that Dirk (Dirk was Hawley; Dee was fairly sure that his real name was probably Derek) wouldn't contemplate anything further north than the boundary formed by the sale-boards of Hotblack and Desiato; he'd had a rotten childhood in Hull or somewhere.

'You're not joined at the hip, are you?' Dee had said.

'No, but . . .'

(They had discovered what 'but' meant that night when they took her home and made his acquaintance.)

Sophie never had come back. Until now. Everything had changed, she said. Everything, that is, that she had had the chance to see en route from the station to Valerie's and then from Valerie's to Auntie B's cottage. It would be nice to have a tour, Sophie said in her best wistful manner, the one she'd used for Blanche Dubois in *Streetcar* at the Phoenix.

'It would be nice,' Sophie said. And Dee, ever one with an eye to the main chance, had said to Valerie, 'Isn't Tuesday Hilda's day? How do you think she'd react to a spot of baby-sitting? Then we could have Our Day Out, couldn't we?'

Valerie said, 'I don't think she'd mind, but you'll have to offer her something. You can't expect her to do it for nothing.'

Dee had grumbled about that. And yet the first words out of her mouth if ever anybody asked her for a favour were usually, 'It'll cost you.' And they weren't always spoken in jest.

The petrol was going to cost them, that was made clear upon arrival. Sophie, watching her approach from the sitting-room window, said, 'She certainly keeps that car of hers in good nick.' Dee's housekeeping might be rudimentary, she might not devote enough time and attention to her personal appearance, but the car gleamed; it was serviced regularly, its oil changed, the air-pressure in its tyres checked, punctiliously. 'You care more about that sodding car than you do about me,' Tom had once yelled. That was a bit of an over-statement but she was certainly very fond of it. It was a symbol; proof of the fact that fate did sometimes recognise that you weren't waving but drowning, and threw you a lifebelt: in 1967, when Tom was three years old, the factory where Dee had been assembling valves closed down and the house in which she had a room was sold and the new landlord gave her notice to quit. She'd found quite the most squalid combined-room that surely was ever offered for rent. Turning on the light in the middle of the night disclosed battalions of cockroaches scurrying for the shadows and there were black – *things* on the wallpaper. Auntie B's poverty had been of the genteel sort and bugs lay quite outside Dee's terms of reference. She'd lifted Tom from his bed and sat rocking him in a chair in the middle of the room, from where she could spot the approach of vermin, dampening his fine-spun fair hair with her tears. On the third day of her residence a letter arrived from a magazine telling Miss Shirley Lawrence (presumably the previous tenant) that she'd won first prize in a competition. First prize was a car.

So Dee became Miss Shirley Lawrence for as long as it took for the presentation to be made and learned, rather late in life, that you can get away with murder as long as you're sufficiently hard-faced.

Her first instinct was to sell the car and use the money to transfer herself and her son to more salubrious accommodation. She ignored her first instinct because she dimly perceived the fact that an opportunity had presented itself. For six weeks she lived on the National Assistance and bread and jam and booked herself a course of driving lessons. She passed her test first time. A fortnight later, primarily because of her gender, she got a job chauffeuring an old lady who had a neurotic fear that any male driver would be bound, sooner or later, to stop the car in the middle of the countryside for the purposes of female violation.

Of course the car that Dee drove today wasn't the one that she'd won in 1967, but what it represented hadn't changed. She'd kept her mouth shut and won a car and learned to drive it and from that moment things had started to look up: the old lady's chauffeuring demands were modest; there was a flat above the garage, a garden for Tom, and time to take out that accounts book misappropriated from the Gateshead factory and scribble down a story, protected by total naïveté from an understanding of what was involved or required, working blind, on the purest of instinct, happy – for the first time in years (ever?) or, at least, not so sad.

It was a smallish, sensible car, Dee's: a Fiesta. Sophie looked at it through the sitting-room window and remembered cars that she'd owned: an MGB, there'd been, a Lotus, an E-Type – 'a man's car,' Hawley had said, but then he'd always claimed that she was either a castrating female or a latent lesbian, or both. She'd been at the wheel of the E-Type when she'd first been done for drink-driving.

Batting down the A4, trying to put the maximum amount of distance between herself and Oxford where, on a surprise visit to Hawley, who was appearing at the Playhouse, she'd found that the surprise was on her in the shape of a girl who'd climbed out of his bed to answer the door.

'Baby,' Dee said, handing Pixie over to Hilda in the manner of a postman delivering a parcel. 'Nappies, bottles, bib, Nurse Harvey's – '

'Nurse Harvey's!' Valerie said, coming in from the kitchen, also carrying a parcel. 'Do they still have that?'

'Obviously,' Dee said. 'What's that you've got?'

'Sandwiches.'

'Oh for God's sake!' Dee said. And so, almost in the same breath, did Sophie.

Valerie sulked, from leaving the house until reaching the town centre – the more you did, the less you were appreciated – and then forgot to sulk when she saw the size of the crowds that lined the streets.

There were police everywhere: on foot, in vans, mounted upon horses. People waved Union flags, had orange lilies pinned to their coats. Dee wound down her window. The smell of ale was strong on the air. Sophie wound hers down too and leaned out and said, 'Oh, a band!' like a little child.

'What is it? What's going on?'

'I haven't a clue,' Dee said, and then she took a hand off the steering wheel and clapped it to her forehead and said, 'Oh yes I have! It's only Orange Day, isn't it?'

'So it is,' Valerie said. 'We should have remembered. We'll be here forever.'

'What do you mean: Orange Day?' said Sophie from the back seat.

'Oh Sophie, I wish you'd stop pretending to have forgotten everything to do with this place. Orange Day. Anniversary of the Battle of the Boyne. July, 1690. Defeat of James II by William of Orange. Assurance of Protestant Succession. Yes? Are we getting there?'

A policeman halted the traffic. They could hear the skirl of bagpipes quite clearly now. Dee looked behind her and said, 'If I'm quick, I can probably turn round and nip back along the Esplanade – '

'Oh, can't we watch?' Sophie said. Two mounted policemen came into view leading a Scottish pipe band. They were playing 'Scotland The Brave'. In Dee's experience, the repertoire of Scottish pipe bands consisted of two tunes; the other one being that mournful thing they played at the Cenotaph on Armistice Day. Behind the band came a procession headed by two children dressed as William and Mary and a bearer carrying on a cushion a representation of what was presumably meant to be the crown of England. The people on the pavement began to cheer and wave their flags and orange streamers.

'Can we?' said Valerie.

Dee sighed heavily, feeling like an adult in charge of two very childish children.

'Oh don't be such a spoilsport, Dee,' Sophie said. 'What's wrong with staying to watch?'

What's wrong, Dee thought, is that you're watching it as you would watch some obscure ceremony performed by Melanesian Islanders or Masai warriors: 'Just a local custom, darling; how quaint'; you have that slightly curled upper lip that I remember from one of your parties that I was once foolish enough to attend. You introduced me to your other guests; you might just as well have said, 'A quaint little friend of mine from way back when I lived in the sticks. You won't have heard of her; she writes novels.'

'It's just that after you've heard "The Sash My Father Wore" for the umpteenth time it can begin to pall,' Dee said.

Band followed band. Pipers, fifes and drums. Elderly ladies and middle-aged women and young girls walked in ranks, each lodge defined by the identical garments they wore. The men wore dark suits and bowler hats, which were removed as the procession passed the war memorial. Little children were dressed as soldiers or flower girls. Huge banners bellied in the breeze. 'Sons of Derry', they proclaimed, or 'No Surrender'; some bore pictures of King Billy; surely England's ugliest monarch?

There was something oddly seductive about the spectacle. 'You can understand,' Dee said, 'why, when they wanted to recruit men for armies, they always used to send a band through the streets. I *hate* this sort of thing; it lays bare one's essential ambivalence . . . Oh, what's *up*?'

Valerie was wiping her eyes. There was ambivalence in Valerie's nature too: nice sensible girl who could always be relied upon to wear her school beret at the correct angle and keep silent in the corridors, whose most oft-repeated remark had always been: 'But it's so silly,' and yet there was a degree of emotional lability more usually associated with the silliest of girls: her eyes would brim at the slightest provocation: bands, horses with broken legs having to be put down, derelicts in doorways – the list was endless.

'I've remembered,' Sophie said, from the back seat, as though they'd been waiting with bated breath for her pronouncement. Talent apart, she had all the other attributes necessary for membership of the acting profession: tunnel vision, a massive ego, and a constant desire for centre stage.

'It was that boy: Sandie Something, the one whose father kept an automatic pistol in his desk all through the war – if the Germans invaded he was going to shoot the whole family – I think he got put away in the end. Anyway, this Sandie and I and some others, we'd been in that horrible pub down by the canal drinking barley wine all evening and we came out and bumped into a group of – followers of this lot, I suppose, and Sandie shouted, "Up the IRA!" They were drunk too, but not as drunk as Sandie. They beat him up, knocked half his teeth out. Poor

Sandie,' she said, doing her mad Tennessee Williams heroine voice, 'he had such a nice smile.'

'Wasn't it Philip Larkin who reckoned that sex began in 1963?' Dee said. 'Well, you'd think, the way the papers go on about it, that violence started around the beginning of this year. And yet, you see, even poor old smiling Sandie was a victim all that time ago. Incidentally, for the record, he got put away too – Sandie. Graduated from smiling to giggling and couldn't stop.'

'Bad seed,' Sophie said, from the back. In her Eugene O'Neill voice this time.

Bad seed. Was there such a thing, Dee wondered. Over the years she had expended a great deal of mental energy debating that possibility.

'Can we *go* now?'

She drove them around the town, through the boarding-house streets. 'I used to live there,' Sophie said, pointing upwards at third floor windows. 'And there. In *that* place, apparently, someone had been murdered. We always thought we could see bloodstains on the wallpaper, but I think it was just awful wallpaper . . . Oh and *there* the light used to go out on the staircase precisely two seconds after you'd switched it on. The entire body of tenants used to hobble round with twisted ankles and barked shins.'

'We always wondered,' Dee said, 'why you moved around so much.'

'My mother was a very optimistic woman. She was convinced that the next place was bound to be better, couldn't be worse at any event.'

She'd thought that about men too. And despite so much evidence to the contrary, never lost faith.

'There's a permanent population now,' Dee said. 'They've shut down Sutton Park and resettled all the inmates into the community.'

Sutton Park was the local asylum.

'Resettlement into the community means, broadly speaking, "You're on your own now, tough shit, get on

70

with it as best you can," ' Dee said, pulling away from the kerb and the curious gaze of what looked like two of the re-settled who were leaning against the front garden wall and drooling slightly.

'So Sandie's probably somewhere round here now,' Sophie said, craning her neck as though there was some possibility that she might catch sight of him.

'If he is, let's hope he's stopped shouting "Up the IRA," ' Dee said. 'OK, where to next, Modom?'

Well, Sophie wanted to see Madame Bertola's Academy of Dance where, at the age of seven, she'd first laced up a pair of tap shoes and known, as soon as the pianist began to play, known with an absolute certainty that performing was her métier. A couple of years later Dee had started lessons. They'd sat next to each other on a bench while they changed back into their school uniforms. Dee had everything brand new: tap shoes, tights, tunic. Auntie B had packed them all neatly into an attaché case and then leaned across to Sophie, who was throwing her stuff willy-nilly into a bag that had W. E. Graham stamped across the flap – lost-property, acquired from the hotel where her mother worked. 'Isn't anybody meeting you, dear?' Dee's Auntie B had asked. Sophie had shaken her head. She'd been ferrying herself to and from the classes ever since she'd started, but from then on Auntie B insisted on superintending her homeward journey. You never knew, she said, delivering her to the front door of the Lamorna Private Hotel, or 17, Marine View, where they moved to the next summer when their rooms were required for holidaymakers. 'For fear,' she said, when Sophie's mother – if she happened to be in – expressed gratitude. She always refused a cup of tea and hurried away. Her old New Look coat didn't quite disguise the bandiness of her legs. Perhaps that was why she was anxious for Dee to learn to dance, in case bandiness ran in the family. Dee never did anything but scowl.

But Madame Bertola's Academy of Dance was now a

video arcade, and the roller-skating rink had been turned into a car-park and the barley wine hostelry down by the canal was a fun-pub. The Kiddies Paddling Pool was reborn as a theme-park and the Gaumont was Safeways.

In fact, just about the only constant was 'J. F. Lamb, Bolts and Rivets' rising, in cast-iron, above Canal Street, and even that was out of date. Valerie averted her eyes from the sign, tried to avert her thoughts from its former proprietor, but that was an impossibility. Richard should never have been expected to take over the firm, she thought. He was never a businessman. He'd had life too easy to be able to handle the cut and thrust. He was too amiable, too – lazy. A picture of him asleep in a deckchair in the garden flashed into her mind's eye. He'd done a lot of sleeping – and procrastinating. 'What, now?' he'd say if she asked him to do something. If she'd had a sarcastic nature, she'd have been tempted to reply, 'No, not now, three weeks next Thursday.' But she didn't have a sarcastic nature. It was what had enabled them to get on well together. In spite of their difficulties.

'Valerie!' Dee said. 'I'm talking to you. I said: Do you have any thoughts about eating?'

Valerie said no, she didn't. Her thoughts had been translated into action; there was a perfectly good packet of sandwiches at home.

'We could drive out to the Hare and Hounds,' Dee said. 'They do quite a nice pub lunch. And quite reasonable.'

Valerie didn't know exactly what reasonable meant in their terms. The picture of Richard asleep in the garden gave way to an image of the ugly concrete façade of the Department of Health and Social Security and the door marked 'Claimants'. To *become* poor, thought Valerie, must be so much more painful than having always been deprived.

Sophie sorted through Dee's tapes. There was Erik Satie and Tchaikovsky's Pathétique and Leonard Cohen's 'Songs from a Room' and 'Blues from the Gutter' by

72

Champion Jack Dupree. 'Nice cheerful stuff you've got here,' Sophie said. She slotted one of them into the machine and turned up the volume. 'Well I've got the TB, and the TB's all in my bones,' sang a rich negro voice. 'The doctor tol' me I ain't got long.'

Dee reached across and switched it off. '*Not* that one,' she said. 'If you don't mind.'

'Then why on earth have it in your car?'

That was the trouble with Dee, Valerie thought: you never knew when you were treading on forbidden territory. How *could* you know? And yet she always reacted as though you had intended deliberate offence.

In the pub Sophie asked loudly and ostentatiously, in her best dark glasses and wide-brimmed hat manner, for a glass of water and took one of her tablets. Not to be outdone, Dee swallowed two aspirins, mentioning sleepless nights and how she needed further aggravation like a hole in the head. Valerie furtively counted the money in her purse and waited for them to come round. They had always squabbled, they always would, but neither had the patience required for sustained sulking.

'Is the old alma mater still standing?' Sophie enquired eventually, bestowing such a dazzling smile upon the waitress that the girl turned to take another look at her. 'I'm sure I've seen her on the telly or somewhere,' she'd say when she got back to the kitchen. She hadn't, but it was a common misapprehension: Sophie could always look like someone you thought you might have seen on the telly.

After lunch Dee drove them to where the old alma mater still stood, four-square, as it had done since 1925, across the fields from the boys' grammar.

'We were let out five minutes earlier, do you remember?' Sophie said. 'So that we wouldn't clash. I couldn't understand their logic then and I can't now.'

Even Good-Girl Valerie, even she had been known to

73

dawdle. She closed her eyes, opened them again and half-expected to see the figure of Richard Lamb running across the grass, coming to an abrupt halt a yard or so away from her, and saying, his eyes fixed on his feet, 'You walking home s'afternoon?'

'Valerie's name's in gold on a notice-board inside here,' Dee said, looking up at the portico where, engraved in stone, were the words 'Suaviter in modo, fortiter in re'. No pupil for the past fifteen years could have told you what that meant: girls' and boys' grammars having, at that date, become mixed and comprehensive.

'In *gold*?' Sophie said. 'On a *notice*-board?'

'Yep. I saw it when I came to a parent-teacher thing when Tom was here.'

Tom, and Valerie's sons, had followed in their mothers' footsteps, had sat in the same desks (except, in Tom's case, that hadn't been as often as the law required), shared the same hymnbooks, no doubt eaten with the same cutlery — but been educated comprehensively (which meant, in the Twins' case, well enough to win them scholarships to Cambridge; in Tom's, hardly at all).

'Only Valerie, among us, is considered worthy of acknowledgement,' Dee said.

She ignored them; she'd heard it all before. She peered across the rugby pitch, the cricket field, could almost see the turf springing back into place in the wake of his running steps. His hair fell over his forehead. He brushed it back. 'Walking home?' he said, without looking at her. They walked on the seaward side of the embankment, the cop. Where lovers walked. He kissed her. Later, he tried to feel her breasts through the wool of her Vyella jersey and her Aertex shirt. Later than that, took her hand and tried to place it upon the tumescence that strained the cloth of his regulation grey school trousers, that bulge from which she hastily averted her eyes. Tried, and kept on trying. Behind a sand dune while the rest of them played the Wide Game, on the sofa in his parents' sitting-room, on beds in halls of residence and student flats and sleeping compartments in railway carriages. Succeeded only on their wedding night. She'd touched it with that mixture of fascination and fear characteristic of a phobic's first close encounter with the object of her dread. Familiarity should have resulted in desensitisation, but in her case that was never – quite – the outcome.

'Would you mind awfully?' Sophie was saying. 'It's only just along the road, isn't it? Of course, if you'd rather we didn't – '

Why shouldn't they? She didn't find the cemetery any more upsetting than anywhere else. She'd visited Richard's grave weekly since he died, since she'd read those letters, staring down at the newly-turned earth, the fading flowers, thinking of all the questions that had never been asked and now could never be answered.

The earth had not settled yet; the yellow sand that had been brought to the surface sprouted dandelions and dockweed. Valerie bent and cleared a handful of couch grass that was already beginning to obscure the lowest line of the headstone's most recent engraving: '21.4.1945–17.3.1988. RIP.'

She'd had to buy a black coat. She could have borrowed something from Dee who always wore black as a matter of course (or Chekhovian principle?) but had felt that that wouldn't be quite the thing. That was before she knew that abject poverty loomed on the horizon.

Dee's Auntie B was buried at the far side of the cemetery, near the wall. The message on her headstone was almost completely obliterated by moss; a small syca-more was growing from the centre of the limestone chippings. How *small* graves looked, Sophie thought, too small to contain the average size person. Auntie B had appeared to be smaller than she was because of her bow legs. Sophie remembered imitating her gait for the delec-tation of their classmates. 'Couldn't stop a pig in a passage,' she'd cried, affecting a kind of nautical roll, drunk with applause. The girls had shrieked. Dee, white-faced, had gathered up her pencil-case and her ruler and her exercise book and left the room.

Sophie had done many things of which she was deeply ashamed both before and since, but that tended to be the memory that returned in the middle of sleepless nights: the intoxicating effect that the exercise of cruelty had produced within her; Dee's white betrayed face. And yet, somehow, it hadn't been directed *at* Dee; it had simply been an attempt to demonstrate that however odd she, Sophie Stephenson, was considered to be, there were others odder still.

'Oh don't be so *silly*,' Valerie, as Form Leader, had said.

It was necessary to count the graves to find where Sophie's mother was buried; there was no headstone. Headstones cost. Sophie hadn't been aware of that. She'd even written out an epitaph and taken it to a stone mason who'd quoted her a price. It was a bad time: *Fighting Talk* had closed after just three weeks, a film had folded, the taxman was after blood, and Hawley was out of work. 'I'll have to postpone it,' she'd said. A postponement of ten years. There'd never be one now.

They retraced their route, past the grave of Auntie B and her parents. 'Room for one more on top,' Dee said. 'Tom'll have to make his own arrangements.'

Naturally. Now there were Tom and Sam and Pixie. A new dynasty, a new grave.

'It'll all be cremation by then,' Valerie said. 'There won't be the land left.'

Richard's sister had suggested cremation. It was the cheaper of the options, but that would have meant nothing, not even a place to visit to ask the unanswerable questions.

Clouds scudded across the sky. A huge expanse of sky stretching low across the flat land: the rugby pitch, the cricket field, the cemetery, the grey sands and the sea. Dee shivered. 'It's going to rain again,' she said and, as if on cue, a few drops fell, splashing over Richard Lamb's marble and Bella Wyatt's moss and the carpet of ground elder that warmed the bones of Gisella Magdalena Stephenson.

Perhaps this was a mistake, after all, Sophie thought. She should have gone to the sun, been *warm* at least. Geoffrey Robinson and his side-kick had a villa in Tuscany. They had *offered*. 'Any time, sweetheart,' they had said. And it would only have cost her her air fare. She hadn't gone because she couldn't face the thought of the performance that would be required of her: the endless smiling, the twenty-four-hour a day pretence. But some sort of a performance was always required, wherever you went.

She looked at her watch. 'How about a swift drink?' she said. 'They're open, aren't they? I can't remember the weird hours that you've got up here.'

'Same as yours,' Dee said. 'Yes, why not?' She'd had a drink at lunchtime without craving a cigarette as accompaniment. If she'd done it once, she could do it again. Full-time sobriety was tiresome.

'What about Pixie?' Valerie said.

Psychopaths who were lacking a voice of the conscience ought to be supplied with a Valerie. 'Why don't you adopt her?' Dee said.

'But Hilda . . .'

'We will find a telephone and ring Hilda and say, "Look, dear, would you mind holding the fort for a little while longer?"' said Sophie, setting off for the cemetery gates with a determined stride. Once an idea had occurred to Sophie it must be executed forthwith. Besides she was getting that funny pain and she needed to sit down, preferably with a very large gin in front of her.

The Orange People had colonised every pub in the town centre and a great many on the outskirts as well. It was raining steadily by now, forcing them indoors. They left mounds of debris in their wake: cans and bottles and crisp packets, chip papers and polystyrene fast-food containers, rosettes and streamers and flags.

'They won't have got as far as the Grosvenor,' Dee said, beating another motorist to the only free parking space for miles and smiling regally in response to his gestures of frustration. 'It's too expensive anyway.'

But apparently it wasn't because they had. They walked into a wall of sound: a burly tattooed man with his hat on backwards was playing the accordion with inebriated zest, a group of people were engaged in community singing – to a different tune, by the sound of it; cacophony otherwise known as popular music blared from loudspeakers. 'Don't worry,' Dee said, as they quailed. 'There's a bar upstairs.'

'Where's the loo?' Sophie enquired of her. 'I need the loo quite urgently. Get me a gin, would you?'

To Valerie's immense relief, upstairs was fairly quiet. She gathered her courage preparatory to approaching the bar. It was her turn. She *hated* having to order drinks, but in the event Dee did it, bringing back, in stages, a gin and tonic, a glass of lager and a mineral water. It wasn't fair: Dee didn't need confidence; she had Fred to go to the bar for her, Fred to inspect her house for lurking burglars when they came home late at night, Fred to hail taxis and deal with headwaiters and threaten unsatisfactory tradesmen.

She sipped her Perrier and caught sight of her reflection in the mirror behind the bar. She wasn't bad-looking. Women in far worse condition married again.

But second husbands would expect the same privileges as those their predecessors had enjoyed. You couldn't start again from scratch: snatching your hand away, averting your eyes, praying that when you got used to it, it would seem less of an ordeal.

'Where's she got to?' Dee said. 'Her ice is melting.' And at the same moment a woman with a flushed face and a drooping orange lily pinned to her lapel came panting up the stairs and looked around the room and then approached them and said, 'Are you the ones that's got a friend in the toilet? She says can you go down there. I don't think she's too grand.'

There were several ladies in the Ladies: washing their hands, combing their hair, painting fresh mouths on to their faces, but only one of the cubicle doors was closed. Dee rapped upon it. 'Oh thank God,' she heard Sophie say faintly. The women paused in what they were doing and turned to look. They made knowing faces at one another: one over the eight, no doubt. Early yet, but perhaps she, like them, had been at it all day.

Sophie slid back the latch and Dee pushed open the door. 'Sweet Jesus!' said one of the women, looking from the person sitting on the lav – who appeared to be perfectly sober – down to the floor which was covered in blood.

8

Sophie

Oh it's lovely to be pampered, to lie beneath a duck-down duvet with a hot-water bottle at your feet and have Valerie bring in a soft-boiled egg and buttered toast. I can't remember the last time I was pampered like this – apart, perhaps, from the early days with a man – unless I'd paid for the privilege.

It isn't really necessary. It looked worse than it actually was. Just like a bad nosebleed. I'd stopped haemorrhaging soon after they got me to the hospital. They gave me a shot of something or other. Now it's just the normal flow, just like one has at that time of the month. Except that it's not that time of the month.

The whole episode was *deeply* embarrassing. I thought Dee was going to pass out. I don't know whose face was the paler: hers or mine. It was the bystanding women who rallied round. They pooled their resources and fed the Kotex machine on the wall until they'd emptied it of its stock. They asked Dee did she have any sort of rug in the car and if so to go and fetch it. One of them had a hand-towel in her bag out of which she fashioned a napkin. Swathed thus, I managed to make it out to the car and thence to the infirmary, leaving a red trail in my wake: on the staircarpet, the pavement, Dee's back seat. My dress has had it, my lovely Jean Muir. It would be that one, wouldn't it? I've just a few decent garments left and I have to go and haemorrhage all over one of them.

It certainly wasn't necessary to call out the doctor. Valerie did that, expressly against my wishes. She kept saying, 'They said, at the hospital, call your own doctor as soon as you can.'

'He isn't my own doctor,' I said. She said he wasn't hers either; he was a locum, and I'd just have to make do.

The casualty doctor looked about twenty-two, the locum perhaps a year or so older. He'd grown one of those little moustaches that they grow under the mistaken impression that it adds maturity. He pressed and prodded me a bit in the womb region and then asked how old I was. I gave him the official version, which is my real age minus five, and then remembered that he was a doctor not a theatrical producer and amended it.

'You're a bit young,' he said, 'for your hormone levels to be disturbed like this.'

I said that I sincerely hoped so. But my flippant tone was obviously not at all to his taste because he frowned and said, 'A *bit* young, given the average age, but the beginning of the end of a woman's reproductive life can start as early as thirty-five.'

I've always been absolutely determined not to fall foul of the menopause. Not for me: the sweats and flushings and floodings and the changes they herald: the sagging structure, the wrinkles, the hair thinning on the scalp as it thickens on the upper lip. Not likely. Not if I have to have hormone replacement therapy until it comes out of my ears.

Though I read somewhere that HRT can give you cancer.

'You haven't, by any chance, been sterilised?' he asked me, this little boy with a moustache and a medical degree.

'No,' I said. I said that would have been like taking coals to Newcastle – but in reverse, if he saw what I meant. I don't think he did.

'You *have* been going for your smears regularly?' he said sternly.

I said, 'Absolutely. Practically on a daily basis.' I couldn't resist it. He was so young and so pompous. Besides, the more serious everyone else is, the more flippant I tend to become. It's a great character defect. It's been responsible for the demise of many a beautiful friendship.

'How long are you staying?' he said, getting out his prescription pad.

'I'm not sure. Two – three weeks. It depends.'

On several things, among them: whether I can get my head together, as they say these days.

'Well, when you get back, be certain to make an appointment with your own doctor for a thorough check-up. And, of course, should this occur again, while you're here, don't hesitate to call me.'

He put the prescription on the bedside table and it was then he noticed the two bottles of pills that had been partly obscured by Barbara Pym and Ellen Terry. 'What are these?' he said, in the manner of a policeman who's just discovered illegal substances on someone previously thought of as clean.

'It's Tagamet. I have ulcers.'

'Does it help?'

'I'd be worse without it.'

He picked up the other bottle. 'So why do you need these then?' he said, squinting at the label. 'Are these prescribed?'

I nearly said, no, I'm part of an international drug ring, but I wanted to get rid of him so I said yes, they were prescribed. They even had a label that said 'Boots the Chemist' to prove it. I thanked him very much for visiting me. I gave him a smile. He paused at the door. He said, 'Excuse me, but do I know you from somewhere? Your face is awfully familiar.' And then light dawned and he said, 'You're not an *actress*, are you?'

82

'No,' I said. 'But I know the one you mean. Other people have mentioned that I look rather like her. But I think, actually, that she's dead.'

'Haven't seen her for quite a while, now I come to think of it,' he said. 'Funny, isn't it, how these people suddenly disappear from view? Now, Mrs Hawley, remember what I said: straight to your own doctor when you get back, and any problems in the meantime . . .'

My doctor is called Mr Patel. There are four of them at the Health Centre and three of them are called Patel. I can't always understand what he's telling me, but on the last occasion he took great pains to articulate as clearly as possible.

I used to go to Mr Roger Llewellyn-Jones just off Wimpole Street. He had beautifully-cut suits and the whitest fingernails I've ever seen. Probably still has, but I can't afford to contribute to his tailor's bills or his manicurist any more.

I remember that I'd take myself off there with the most trivial of complaints: ear-wax, piles, urticaria, as well as my troublesome guts. It was he who arranged the termination of the first of my pregnancies – put me in touch with the clinic, that is; he didn't actually perform it. I couldn't imagine those beautiful hands dabbling in gore.

I'd found out that I was pregnant just a week before my agent called to say that Adrian Bailey wanted me for Rosalind. I didn't have a qualm. I could scarcely feel the pavement beneath my feet as I walked along the Marylebone Road towards the salvation that was Mr Roger Llewellyn-Jones. He'd put his fingers together and made steeples and looked at me over the top of them. He had a twinkle in his eye and just the exact degree of sub-flirtatiousness required for attracting the sort of female patients to keep him in Savile Row suits and gold-plated nail-clippers. The chance of a lifetime, I'd said. *Mine*, at any rate. 'Yes,' he'd said. 'I quite understand.' It didn't occur to me that my chance of a lifetime meant the sacrifice of another's; it never does, until afterwards.

The other two operations were performed on the National Health and were far from pleasant experiences. Especially the last one. As a result of the last one I got Pelvic Inflammatory Disease. PID, they call it. Undetected, it can block your tubes. It did mine.

PID, HRT – all those initials. STD – I once had to go there too. In the days when it wasn't accepted that clean unpromiscuous people can catch nasty bugs just as easily as their dirty, indiscriminate counterparts. 'I'd have *died* first,' Valerie had said, years later, when I happened to mention it to her (at first she'd thought I was talking about telephones). 'I'd die before I could bring myself to go into one of those places.'

We say it all the time: 'I'd die before I'd . . .' Lately I've been totting up the number of experiences and events to which death would be preferable. They are actually very few in number.

Valerie knocked at the door. She'd brought me the paper (the *Telegraph*, naturally). I somehow expected there to be letters too. I was quite disappointed. Which must mean that I'm going round the bend because if no one knows where you are, you can hardly expect to receive letters from them.

'You won't mind a scratch lunch, will you?' Valerie said. 'Only I've to be at the Job Centre at a quarter to two.'

I wondered what they'd make of her, find for her. Nothing, probably. Which is a great pity because Valerie is a born employee: conscientious, industrious, and not given to answering back.

'Soup and sandwiches?' Valerie said. And I said, 'Fine,' but, like the doctor, she lingered, stroking the bedcover until all the pile lay flat in the same direction. 'Sophie,' she said, and I thought, oh, oh, what's coming?, but all she said was, 'Do you know Bennett's Hotel?'

'No, I don't think so,' I said. And then I remembered. 'Oh yes I do. It's in Mayfair, isn't it? Curzon Street? Around there, anyway.'

I'd had to meet an American film producer there once. I'd expected the stereotype: shiny suit, cigar, philistinism on a grand scale; he was reserved and scholarly and overwhelmingly polite, as it turned out. I still didn't get the part though.

'Very plush, is it?' Valerie said.

'Mm, pretty plush. Why,' I said, 'is someone taking you off there for a dirty weekend?'

It's my tongue, not my womb, that ought to be amputated. Even Dee wouldn't have said anything as crass as that. But Valerie didn't appear to have taken offence. She said, 'I just wondered. I'd heard someone say they were thinking of staying there,' and went downstairs to make the sandwiches.

Dee rang while she was out. She said, 'I've had to scrub the car seat with upholstery cleaner. How are you? Do you think you'll be all right by tomorrow?'

I said, 'Dee, your concern is overwhelming. I think the worst is over now. Why, what's happening tomorrow?'

She has a script conference at the television studios and Pixie needs a minder. 'I'd ask Fred,' she said, 'but he's got an auction or something tomorrow afternoon. Anyway, Valerie'll be in, won't she?'

Poor Valerie. Unless she gets herself fixed up with a proper job pretty soon she's going to find that an unpaid one will be thrust upon her.

'By the way,' Dee said, 'what is all this about? You're not starting the whatsit, are you?'

'When you start the whatsit it gets less not more.'

'Not necessarily,' she said. She's a mine of information when it comes to medical matters. All the writers I've met are. Though I suppose it may not be just morbid curiosity; it may be necessary research.

There was a theatre page in the *Telegraph*. I turned it

over unread. It was bound to be filled with accounts of brilliant productions and stunning performances – it always is when you're out of work. Though I'm not actually out of work. That is to say, I could probably have been in work if it wasn't for being ill: I had that Canadian tour lined up.

'Have you given everyone my number in case you need to be contacted?' Valerie had asked when I arrived. She's read enough books and seen enough films to know that actors have a very deep and meaningful relationship with the telephone. I'd nodded, but nobody has Valerie's number, no one connected with me, at any rate. Who would there be to ring? My agent? The Canadian tour was the first proper thing in more than a year.

It's more a case of me ringing them these days. And I've had a bellyful of that: the insincerity, the lies and evasions and excuses, the unreturned messages left on answering machines. Such a gradual falling-off; I can't pinpoint the exact date when it started: that Australian/English co-production that they decided to re-cast? *Fighting Talk* that closed practically before it opened? – largely because of that bastard Finnegan's review: he's always hated me. 'It would be fair to say,' he'd written, 'that Miss Stephenson no longer acts but rather trots out her (very limited) repertoire of mannerisms whenever she takes the stage these days.' 'I hope he gets cancer,' I said to Dirk. Dirk replied that he had a point: I was getting a bit Bette Davis, only minus the charisma. (I don't think that actors, as a body of people, are nicer or nastier than any other cross-section of the population; not all of us glory in our colleagues' downfalls or take understudies, praying the lead will break a leg. Not all of us are unable to sustain marriage to a fellow-actor because professional jealousy is stronger than personal affection, but that's how it was with Dirk. He started off quite sweet, but I was successful when he wasn't and that ruined him.)

He'll be happy now, having observed my career going

downhill fast. He'll be saying in pubs, at parties, anywhere he can annexe an ear: 'She just got found out, that's all. You can fool some of the people some of the time . . .'

I should have kept off the booze. I shouldn't have turned down that provincial tour. I should – oh how I should – have turned down Douglas Parry's wretched play which buried everyone concerned with it. There are all sorts of reasons to explain my decline: fashions change in acting, influential friends move on or die, faces cease to fit. Oh, there were things I could have done: one-act jobs in rooms above pubs that paid peanuts, tours of schools and arts' associations, seasons in Zimbabwe or somewhere, but I'm too old for all that piling into a van and eating in motorway services and dossing down wherever you can. In 1969 Adrian Bailey wanted me for Rosalind.

There's an article about Montreal in the *Telegraph*. I'd have been in Montreal in a few weeks' time if I'd been well. It's often the way: the minute things start to look up in one direction, they take a swift plummet in another.

Still. Every day, in every way, I am getting better and better – give or take the odd haemorrhage. During our last meeting, Dr Patel asked me if I'd experienced any unusual bleeding. He had to repeat himself and not entirely because of his accent: he was not looking at my face when he spoke but my private parts, and his voice was somewhat muffled. He straightened up and said that he was making me another appointment with the gynaecologist. I said, 'I spent most of last year with my knees bent up around my ears – and not for the purposes of enjoyment.' He smiled. 'Then you'll be quite used to the position, won't you, my dear?' he said.

I'm getting used to the terminology, the initials: cytology clinic, D and C, squamous cells, colposcopy, lasers, cryo-thermy and diathermy, cone biopsy, erosion, cervix, chronic inflammation. I am word-perfect on the little speech they make as you are putting on your knickers and pulling down your skirt: no tampons, they say, for six weeks, and no sexual intercourse. All in all, if you're bleeding and then recovering from treatment and then having your normal period, there isn't much chance of squeezing in the odd act of sexual intercourse.

I obeyed Dr Patel. I went to see the gynaecologist. There were about a hundred women in the waiting-room. After two and a half hours I was ushered into a cubicle and told to undress. Three-quarters of an hour after that I climbed on to a couch and splayed my legs and presented all my vulnerability to the scrutiny of a bleary eye. It was bleary and weary, sick of looking at women's things – you could tell. Its owner unscrewed his speculum and said, 'We had you in last year, didn't we? Why didn't you come back for a check?'

'Nobody told me to.'

They were cutting back, he said. As a result, administrative errors occurred all the time.

He'd made me bleed simply by poking around in there. Sexual intercourse, I thought: some chance.

'We'll let you know,' he said.

Next morning I entrained for Valerie's.

Letters. Are there any on my doormat? Apart from bills? (Well, John Wainwright's doormat, to be precise. He's in Australia till Christmas so he's lent me his flat. The Lord be praised. Otherwise I really would be in the clarts.) Are there any bearing the legend: 'Middlesex Hospital, Department of Gynaecology and Obstetrics' at the top of the page? Any written in a large and slightly backward-sloping hand (sign of a bad character, that)?

I will not think about those things: it, him, I will *not*. The reason I came here was so that I need not think about them. Oh, and to recover from my virus of course.

9

The prospective buyers whom Valerie showed around the house compared it unfavourably with every other house they'd inspected. Salisbury Road had had a jacuzzi, Western Avenue a swimming pool and en-suite bathrooms, and out by the Links they'd had a tennis court.

Sophie overheard these remarks as they moved from room to room but kept clear. She'd have been bound to say something rude and thereby might have jeopardised a sale. Although Valerie said that so many of them were just timewasters. You got a sixth sense after a while, she said.

Valerie was very polite. Principally because she knew of no other response to comments such as: 'We've never cared much for all these pale colours and wishy-washy furnishings, have we, Monica?' And, 'I wouldn't call this a utility room; more like a glorified glory-hole.'

'I've had worse,' she told Sophie after they'd gone. 'People who insult your taste and talk to each other as though you weren't there. Surely you must know what I mean? You've sold houses, haven't you?'

Sophie had never actually sold a house. There were houses – and flats – that must have *been* sold. She vaguely remembered a cheque arriving from Constantine's solicitors for half the sale price of something or other: the Chelsea mews house, that was it. And *that* was a long time ago, before house prices got out of hand. Since then there'd been short leases and rented accommodation: she'd never managed to get her foot on the bottom rung of the property market ladder at the time when there were killings to be made or, at least, insurance for one's misfortunate phases.

'Do you think they'll make an offer?'

'Yes, I think they might,' Valerie said. Monica's husband had had a tape-measure and made a big point of checking dimensions – usually a sign of serious intent. If they did, then there'd be another terrible decision to be made. She'd turned one offer down already. She'd had some justification because it was a thousand below the asking-price: something about damp patches in the attics. But this one might be impossible to reject.

'I don't want to leave.'

It was the first time she'd admitted it, to herself or anybody else.

'Perhaps you'll get a job,' Sophie said encouragingly, 'a really good one, and then you won't have to sell.'

'It would have to be a really good one.'

The woman at the Job Centre had been very pleasant, had asked a great many questions and taken an equal number of details and heaped leaflets upon her. She was now registered for employment, available for work. She had a code number and an insurance card. She had information about training schemes and enterprise allowances and job clubs. After a year out of work she would qualify for vocational re-training.

'A year out of work?'

The woman's sympathetic smile implied that this was not inconceivable. Meanwhile, there was the possibility that she might be a candidate for income support. That was a matter for the DHSS, of course.

It was at that precise moment that Valerie had been seized with a blinding fury. How she hated him: for his laziness, his deceit, his lack of acumen. Most of all she

90

hated him for dying. No, most of all she hated him for making her dependent upon him.

At home she read the leaflets. There seemed to be one for every conceivable contingency, and yet none of them fitted her case.

'It would be easier to find a rich husband,' she said to Sophie. Sophie, after yesterday's faux-pas about dirty weekends at Bennett's Hotel, trod carefully. Rich husbands, she said, by and large, seemed to prefer rich wives. Incidentally, Sophie said, while we're on the subject: I didn't intend for you to keep me for nothing. Here, Sophie said, take it, yes, take it. And Valerie, who was only beginning to learn to silence the protestations that sprang automatically to her lips, eventually took it. 'Where are you going?' she asked. Sophie had put on her jacket and was doing a very professional job in brightening up her pallor.

'Just to the shops.'

'You shouldn't be *up*,' Valerie said, 'let alone *out*.'

'I told you, I'm all right. It's finished. I have no legitimate reason to languish.'

She rang a taxi and went to Sainsbury's and bought steak and cheese and fruit and vegetables and tins of Baxter's soup and eggs and bacon and a gâteau and nuts and smoked salmon and a couple of bottles of Beaune and a bottle of gin and some tonics. Then she went to the cash machine outside Lloyd's bank and asked for a balance and was pleasantly surprised to see those magic initials: 'CR'. Then she thanked God for residuals.

'Tell you what,' she said when she got back, 'we'll surprise grumpy old Dee when she gets back even grumpier than usual from her script conference . . .'

'How do you know she'll be grumpier than usual?'

'I don't. But there's a fair possibility: prostitution of her artistic integrity and so forth . . .'

'Do you think Dee's a good writer?' Valerie said unexpectedly. They hadn't talked about Dee's writing for years, ever since they'd gawped awestruck at the reviews for her first book.

'Lots of people do.'

The backs of various book-jackets bore testimony to these opinions. Words such as 'perceptive' and 'insight' and 'skilful' and 'evocative' were to be found there.

'But do *you*?'

'I'm not much of a reader,' said Sophie, side-stepping. 'Except in the line of business. Why do you ask?'

'I've always found them rather cold – clinical,' Valerie said. 'As though they were accounts written by somebody completely uninvolved and standing a long way away.'

'That's what writers are supposed to be, aren't they: detached?'

'Yes, but her books give you the impression that she's surveying a lower form of life under a microscope. Oh, maybe it's me,' Valerie said. 'I was only a thick scientist, wasn't I? I'm not qualified to comment. I'm sorry, what were you saying?'

Sophie leaned over Pixie's carry-cot and tickled her under the chin. Pixie gurgled and then smiled. 'She smiled!' said Sophie, in wonderment. 'She smiled,' Sophie repeated. There was no doubt about it. How flattering it was when a baby who cried for everyone else singled you out for a smile.

'You were *saying*?' Valerie said impatiently. Valerie had had babies and knew all about smiling and wind.

'I thought we could do a meal tonight. Nothing fancy. Just steaks and so on. Cheer us all up. Including your grandmother,' she said, turning her attention once more to the baby who followed the movement of her hand with huge eyes that were as blue as Dee's had once been.

'As we all know, she doesn't like cooking – '

Sophie didn't mind cooking; it was eating that she found bothersome. But other people seemed to enjoy it.

'We could invite him, couldn't we? It's a bit short notice but still . . .'

'Him who?' said Valerie, somewhat less than enthusiastically; she knew upon whom the cooking would inevitably devolve.

'*Him*. Frank. *Fred*. Whatever he's called. The Merry Widower. I take it they do socialise *à deux*?'

'Depends what you mean by socialise. They go to the theatre and the cinema and eat out and so forth, but I don't think they socialise in the sense you mean.'

She meant socialise in the sense that she, Valerie and her late husband Richard, had socialised, which entailed couples from the same socio-economic grouping dining in each other's homes and playing golf and attending functions arranged by the professional or local associations to which they belonged.

'Do they sleep together?' Sophie asked. She made a rabbit out of her handkerchief and waggled its ears at Pixie. Pixie's smile widened. A sound that could, quite reasonably, have been described as a chuckle issued from her depths. A fan, Sophie thought, a fan.

'I don't know,' Valerie said. 'I suppose so. People *do*, don't they?'

'I can't imagine Dee in bed with anyone,' Sophie said. Pixie's fingers closed tightly around her own. 'But then, I find, one can't really imagine anyone . . .'

Valerie could imagine Sophie. All too clearly.

'What's he like, this Fred?' Sophie asked. Pixie gripped the forefinger of one of her hands; with the other she stroked the baby's hair. It gave you the strangest feeling, as though something inside you might be going to melt.

Valerie had never been any good at supplying satisfactory descriptions. Fred seemed very pleasant, she said, judging by what little she'd seen of him. He was retired from the army and now ran a bookshop in County Road – antiquarian stuff, mainly. He'd moved to Ferryside Lane about two years ago and had, presumably, taken up with Dee because of her proximity, her available status and their shared literary interests – even though Dee always pulled a face at that word and pronounced it: 'literatewer'.

'What's he look like?'

'Clean,' Valerie said at length. 'You know, like they do in the army. As though they only stepped out of the shower about five minutes since. Funny really, when you remember Dee's tidemarks.'

They put Pixie in her pram and took her for a walk, recalling Dee's childhood lack of scrupulosity in the matter of personal hygiene. Understandable, perhaps, Valerie said, when you remembered that the plumbing in Auntie B's cottage had consisted of one mains cold water tap.

'Nonsense,' Sophie replied. 'Auntie B was fanatical. Were you never there on washdays? Scrubbing-boards and dolly-blue and starch by the bushel. No, it was just that Dee was a slob.'

They walked down to the shore, past the golf club and the fog bell and the lifeboat station, walking towards the pinewoods down a lane which became a track and then petered out into a pathway. Here stood the remains of what had once been the Wayside Café: only a wooden shack, even then, with a leaking verandah, upon which were placed a few tin tables and chairs – if it rained you were quite liable to get your tea diluted; now it was completely dilapidated: a graffiti-daubed shell, with a rusted enamel sign advertising Black Cat cigarettes still precariously attached to the rotted timbers.

Prompted by association, Sophie lit a cigarette and perched herself on the wooden rail that enclosed the verandah. She said, 'What do you think I am – a teenager?' and Valerie looked blank for a moment and then remembered and smiled.

'It's all I *can* remember,' Sophie said, swinging her legs. She wore jeans, Levi Red Tabs, Valerie noticed, with envy. Sophie would be able to wear jeans when she was seventy, jeans and extravagant fur capes and Marlene Dietrich trenchcoats and wide-brimmed straw hats. Sophie had been able to wear crotch-skimming mini-skirts and dramatic floor-trailing crushed velvet gowns, *Irma la Douce* leather berets and *Jules et Jim* caps and six-inch stacked Cuban heels and the widest flares in creation; boob-tubes, Sophie had been able to wear and long overcoats and spiv shoulder-pads, Doc Martens and tons of fake jewellery. Sophie had always looked just right in everything that she, Valerie, had never dared to attempt because she suspected she'd have looked completely wrong.

'What were we doing here?' Sophie asked. 'Do you remember?'

'Yes I do. We'd been to a sausage sizzle on the beach – a youth club thing – and Auntie B would never let Dee come home alone along here . . .'

'She wasn't alone. We were with her. How old were we, for heaven's sake?'

'Thirteen, fourteen. I don't think she considered we'd be much protection against mad-eyed rapists.'

'And she would?'

Auntie B in her old coat with its pinched-in waist and dusty velvet lapels (a coat bought when she was a different shape. Or a coat bought originally for someone else whose shape was different?), Auntie B with her bow legs and her bad feet and her perpetual frown, self-appointed bodyguard to defenceless young girls. Perhaps she'd have *frowned* assailants away.

'Anyway it was only about nine o'clock and this place was still open and she asked us if we'd like a drink of pop.'

'Dee didn't want to stop, did she?'

Dee, being mortally ashamed of Auntie B, never wanted her to be exposed to anyone else for longer than was strictly necessary.

'She certainly didn't want pop. None of us did.'

Coffee bars were opening by the minute then. If you were chic, you paid sixpence and sat all evening behind an espresso.

'We went to the counter and ordered three coffees. And then we remembered Auntie B was paying and asked if she wanted one too. She said, "What do you think I am: a teenager?"'

'It wasn't espresso, surely? Not here?'

'No, it was Camp Coffee in a bottle, made with water that had gone off the boil. Not chic at all.'

Sophie climbed down from her perch and they resumed their pram-pushing. 'Where does this bring us out at?' she said. 'I've forgotten.'

'By the old aerodrome. It's a squash club now. Why do you forget everything, Sophie?'

'I don't know. Maybe I've got Alzheimer's.'

Alzheimer's was the worst, worse than *anything*. Far better dead than alive with Alzheimer's or – think of other ghastly illnesses – Multiple Sclerosis, Motor Neurone Disease, Parkinson's. Dee's Auntie B had had Parkinson's. That was when Dee had returned from her self-imposed exile and done her duty. No one could find fault with her on that score.

'She used to meet Dee out from everywhere, long after it was necessary. Dee used to be mortified,' Sophie said. 'I remember that she even used to take me home if I happened to be unescorted – which was most of the time. She was kind, in her way, wasn't she? On Dee's ninth birthday she took us to Uncle Eddie's Kiddies' Party in the Marine Pavilion and bought us knickerbocker glories.'

Sophie had sung 'Sur le pont d'Avignon' and executed an appropriate little dance and won first prize in the talent contest. Auntie B had tried to persuade Dee to enter too, but the only prize that she might conceivably have won would have been the trophy for the most accomplished display of glowering.

'I think she was sorry for me,' Sophie said, stopping to empty sand from her shoe. Valerie walked carefully, keeping to the path, but Sophie's was an erratic, weaving process.

'Why?'

'Because I had to fend for myself so much. Odd, really: Auntie B feeling sorry for me and then I'd go home and tell my mother when she came in that Dee's auntie had seen me home, and she'd say, "I feel so sorry for that child." I could never understand why. I mean, I knew they were as poor as we were, but at least Dee didn't have to live in rooms; at least she didn't have a mother with boyfriends.'

Auntie B didn't go 'out to business'. She stayed in for it: treadling away all day and half the night sometimes. She sewed for her livelihood: curtains and frocks and dirndl skirts, evening gowns and confirmation dresses and choir-boys' surplices, boleros and swagger jackets and day-dresses for many of the ladies who lived at the other side of town (including Valerie's mother). The cottage in Ferryside Lane was always strewn with fabric and bits of Butterick paper patterns and pins and bias-binding and loose threads. She sewed until she shook too much to get the cotton through the eye of the needle.

Sewing didn't attract the same sort of stigma as going out to business. And Dee might have been poor but she was as well-dressed as any but the most filthily-rich of her contemporaries. So Sophie never could understand why her mother said, 'I feel so sorry for that child.'

Valerie steered the pram around the corner of the squash club and pushed it uphill past what had once been the Emily Ashton Excursionists' Day Nursery and was now a pizza parlour, towards the Marine Pavilion and the ghosts of Uncle Eddie and all the children who had entered his talent contests and won bars of nut-milk chocolate.

'When did you first find out?' she said.

'About Dee? About her parentage?'

Sophie stopped at the mouth of an amusement arcade and fed an old-fashioned, non-electronic machine with a penny and won three. 'I suppose I'd have been about – sixteen. Dee and I had had a row and I'd called her a bastard. It was what they'd call now my buzz word of the moment. My mother was furious, told me that on no account, must I ever use that word to describe Diana. And after a lot of prevarication told me why. I never knew who else knew and who didn't . . .'

'I overheard my mother talking to the vicar's wife. I could only have been twelve or so. They were talking about an American soldier.'

'*My* mother said it was a man who couldn't marry her because he was already married. I remember thinking at the time how coincidental that was because my mother was involved in exactly that situation herself.'

'I think,' Valerie said, 'that the theories they put forward had more to do with their own attitudes than the truth.'

'Did anyone know the truth? Apart from Auntie B, that is?'

'Well Dee must have done, sooner or later. Surely?'

'She's never, ever, talked about it to me,' Sophie said. 'Not even when we've been plastered. Has she you?'

'No.'

Not that Valerie had ever been plastered. In Dee's company or out of it.

'You know, American soldier or married man or who-ever – I could never credit it,' Sophie said. 'Auntie B! I can't still, even now. It must have happened during the black-out.'

'I don't suppose she always looked like that.'

Sophie drew contemplatively upon her cigarette. 'Funny,' she said, 'how coming home brings things back. I haven't thought about that business for years.'

She'd used the word 'home' quite inadvertently. But supposed, on reflection, that it wasn't entirely inappropriate; at least, there was nowhere else likely to compete for the title.

'Oh *what* a big yawn,' she said, as Pixie opened her mouth and then her eyes and slowly began to focus upon her unfamiliar surroundings. 'Do you think Pixie's *short* for something?' she asked Valerie. 'I mean, I imagine it could be a drawback in later life: what if she wants to become a senior civil servant or a high court judge: "Lord Justice Pixie Something-or-other"! What possible chance would she have of being taken seriously?'

But Valerie thought it highly unlikely that anyone with Tom for a father and Dee for a grandmother would be drawn towards that kind of career.

At home, while Valerie peeled potatoes and blanched vegetables, Sophie took a lavish and leisurely bath. She washed her hair and set it. She anointed her skin with lotions and applied scent to her pulse points. She borrowed another lamp from Valerie's bedroom and plugged it in, together with her own, at each side of the dressing-table mirror. The light still wasn't ideal but she did the best she could under the circumstances, diving into her make-up case, choosing, discarding, pausing continually to assess the effect, watching her face take shape in the same way that a blank canvas is gradually transformed beneath an artist's hand. She was observed in these manoeuvres by Richard and Valerie in a photograph frame. They'd made a handsome couple. In Sophie's experience, very good-looking young men often went off. Richard hadn't.

In the kitchen Valerie sweated onions and hulled straw-berries and warmed Pixie's early-evening feed. 'Leave it,' Sophie had said. 'I'll do it when I come down.' How very typical of Sophie that was.

She came down a few minutes before Dee arrived. She looked stunning: dark, slender, vivid, in a flame-coloured dress. She couldn't resist doing herself up for a man, any man, Valerie thought sourly. But this time it might be a wasted effort.

Dee didn't say that Sophie looked stunning. Dee raised an eyebrow and said, 'Why are you got up like a dog's dinner?'

Sophie had decided upon Noël Coward mode. She posed

within the doorway. 'Dee, darling,' she said, 'this is how I always look.'

'Except for when you're wearing my car rug,' Dee said, 'which, incidentally, I've had to send to the dry cleaner's.'

'Well I'm sorry. I didn't *plan* on bleeding all over it, you know.'

She narrowed her nostrils, exhaled thin plumes of smoke, quite deliberately, in Dee's direction. Dee waved it away and said, 'There's no need to *choke* me. By the way, I was in the canteen at the studios and Winifred Frobisher came and sat opposite me. She's guesting, you know, on the series. She was enquiring after you. Said you and she were together in rep somewhere or other. Said she hadn't seen or heard of you for so long that she wondered if you'd pegged it.'

Sophie produced the sort of smile that could probably turn the milk. She said, 'Old Winnie. It was a knocking bet – as they say – that she'd end up in soaps. What's she playing?'

'A sort of bag-lady who breaks into the community centre and dosses down and starts a fire.'

'How very appropriate,' Sophie said. 'When we were in rep she used to carry this whopping great handbag around with her everywhere she went. We wondered why until one day somebody noticed that it contained a half bottle of gin. And apparently it wasn't her weak bladder that was the reason for her nipping off to the loo every five minutes.'

'At least she can make a fair stab at acting,' Dee said. 'Some of them . . . well let's just say it's pretty apparent that God intended them for some career, any career other than the stage.'

'Sometimes,' said Sophie, 'the problem is the impossible, unspeakable, speeches that are put into our mouths. They get in these novelists, think they're injecting a bit of class, forget that people in novels speak an entirely different form of dialogue.'

Valerie, whipping cream, said, 'If you two have quite finished fratching – '

'Fratching, Valerie?' said Dee.

'*Fratching?*' said Sophie.

'Yes, fratching. Goading each other, niggling. You know perfectly well what I mean. It's time you grew up.'

'I am a grandmother,' Dee said sadly. 'What could be more grown up than that? Speaking of which, I suppose I'd better take her off your hands. In the sitting-room, is she?'

But she seemed in no hurry to leave. 'Mm,' she said. 'That smells good. You certainly do yourselves proud, you two, don't you?'

'If it was just us two it'd be beans on toast,' Valerie said. 'This is partly for your benefit.'

'So get yourself back home and spruced up and return forthwith with your consort,' said Sophie, who'd vanished briefly and returned with a glass in her hand. 'And *don't* say it's too short notice. You must make the most of me while I'm here.'

'My consort?' said Dee.

'Yes. Himself. I'd like to meet him. And anyway it's time we injected a little male company into our midst. All this we-three stuff is getting to be unwholesome.'

'I'll *ask* him . . .' Dee said.

After she'd gone Valerie went into the hall and came back with her purse and opened it and took out a pound and said, 'I don't usually gamble but this is a certainty: one pound says she'll come back alone.'

'What makes you so sure?'

'Instinct. Dee needs to compartmentalise everybody. There's you and me that she's known for ages. And there are the telly people. And the publishing people. And there used to be the other parents when Tom was at school. And now there's Fred. And we all have to be kept separate.'

'But why?' said Sophie, who, in the days when she'd

101

enjoyed a more energetic social life, had liked nothing better than to invite the most disparate groups of people to her parties in the hope that, thereby, blandness might be avoided.

'Perhaps it's because she's totally different with different people,' said Valerie, who often surprised herself with the odd flash of perspicacity.

Dee was back within the hour. She'd changed into rather a nice dress and put on some lipstick, but she hadn't brought Fred with her. He had a previous engagement, she said. He sent his apologies. Maybe another time . . . 'Mm!' she said when Valerie brought in the food. There was enough for four. She ate Fred's portion as well as her own. It seemed a shame to let it go to waste.

10

Valerie

On the way back from the Job Centre I passed the railway station and, on impulse, called in for a timetable of the London trains and that night, after Sophie had gone to bed, I read it, working out an imaginary itinerary. Richard always used to tease me, said that I'd plan for a trip to the shops as though it were a round-Britain tour. Sometimes my excessive forethought irritated him: my car rugs and flasks of tea, my travel-sickness pills and boxes of tissues and spare sweaters. 'Let's just *go*,' he'd say. 'All this forward planning – it spoils the fun.'

We are as we are. In my case, cautious; in his, lackadaisical – and also, it would seem, completely and utterly false.

Melissa is sixteen. I've thought and I've thought, trying to recall how things were sixteen or seventeen years ago. Richard's parents were still alive then. And mine. The Twins were just starting school. Our car was a Triumph Stag. Or was it a Rover? One year we had a holiday in Cornwall; the next, in Corfu. Richard broke his wrist playing badminton. I had a card from Sophie saying that she was married and wasn't it a hoot? That winter there was a severe gale and several tiles were blown off the roof and came crashing in through the conservatory.

Everything else is forgotten. Whether Richard was away

from home more often than usual or not, whether he was more moderate in his sexual demands, whether it was obvious that he wished to be elsewhere.

The thing is: to keep busy. To rush from one activity to the next without pause for thought. But somehow, no matter how frenetically I clean and shop and mow the lawn and help to organise the tombola for the Parklands Ward Conservatives and write letters of application to employers who rarely even do me the courtesy of replying, my thoughts keep returning to the one track. Waking up in the morning, closing my eyes at night – and most of the hours in between – I think of all my fool's paradise years, all the stupid, innocent assumptions I'd made about the stability of my marriage, my status in Richard's eyes – and in the eyes of all our friends and acquaintances. Once, at a committee meeting of the League of Hospital Friends, I thought I saw a few of them going into a huddle and then rapidly ceasing their conversation when they noticed me. I may have been wrong. It's so easy to become paranoid when all your certainties have been shown up for delusions.

At least I can relax a bit with Sophie. And Sophie provides the perfect excuse for not being brave. For example, it was my turn today to host the monthly meeting of the Housewives' Register. 'Oh God,' Sophie said, when I mentioned it, 'you're not filling the house with women?' as though women were some alien species, particularly dangerous when encountered *en masse*. So, with a certain sense of relief, I rang up and made my excuses.

Sophie usually saunters down at about ten o'clock. She wears this marvellous peignoir thing: all lace and embroidery (she wore it when she was in *Hay Fever* and she bought it afterwards, or they let her keep it or something). It's magnificent but, despite the splendour of her attire, she still looks pretty dreadful in the mornings: chalk-white face, dark circles under her eyes, little puckered lines visible around her mouth, from which – invariably – droops the first cigarette of the day; there's always a trail of ash from her bedroom door and all the way down the stairs.

I'd had my breakfast hours ago, but felt obliged to make gestures towards the toaster and the grill. She just shuddered and spooned coffee into a mug and, while waiting for the kettle to boil, lit another cigarette. She seemed dazed. It's the pills, I suppose. She takes sleeping pills as well as pills for her stomach and some others called Fortral – there's quite an array on the bedside table.

'So what's on the agenda for today?' she said.

'Well – nothing in particular, actually.'

If ever I have anyone staying I'm driven by a compulsion to lay on a feast of entertainment, as though the mere pleasure of my company could not possibly be enough. I suppose it's because I'm always convinced that other people's boredom thresholds are much lower than my own. Sophie's is low, I know. I get the impression that Sophie expects life to be one endless party and I, who am unused to playing hostess unaided, will be unable to provide constant distraction.

She'll get bored and she'll leave. Go back to London and those parties of hers and all the bright brittle people I'd met at that one I'd been to when Sophie was telling everyone about the crabs.

I'd only gone because Richard was tied up on business and I didn't want to spend the evening alone in a hotel room. (It's like a knife between the ribs when I think how it never even *occurred* to me that he might not be telling the truth.)

'In that case,' Sophie was saying now, 'I thought I might collect Pixie later and take her for a stroll.'

I said, 'I thought you didn't like babies.'

'I don't, particularly. But it gives me an excuse for fresh air and exercise.'

She finished her coffee and went upstairs to take yet another bath, singing 'Falling In Love Again' in an accent reminiscent of her mother's. I made some pasta for lunch and wondered if she'd stopped falling in love by now. Surely the day must come when it all begins to seem a little repetitious?

And surely, after years of picking the wrong men, some note of caution must sound, some alarm bell, among all the others that start to ring?

Though that may be an over-statement. Sophie has had – consorted with – a great many men. Too many for them all to have been wrong. It's just that the ones she's actively chosen to occupy the centre stage of her life have – to the best of my knowledge – been as wrong as could be: the first husband, Constantine, twenty years older than her, a sort of poor girl's Svengali, sweetness and light as long as she walked in his shadow – once she started getting recognition on her own account, his ego just couldn't cope; the second husband, Hawley, who sponged off her yet resented her success; the man in North Ken who smashed all the mirrors; the Lebanese ('that black man', my mother called him) who was not just unpleasant, but actually criminally unpleasant; the wretched Jeremy who was always displaying his wonderful physique and who couldn't decide which sexual orientation to opt for ... One could go on.

I sometimes wonder what it must be like to have had a lot of men. Not just sexually. From what I've heard, in that respect, it's usually more of the same. Richard and I met when we were young and there was no competition. For either of us. I was pretty when I was young. Only Sophie came close – and Sophie wasn't Richard's type at all.

I loved him. I loved his sleepy smile and the grace of his movements. I loved the equability of his temperament, his sunny-natured refusal to foresee trouble ahead, his often misguided optimism. I loved the way that his hair grew from a widow's peak on his forehead and sprouted up above his shirt collar, his crooked tooth and his air of injured innocence when I pushed his hand away. I loved him when I first met him and I loved him twenty-eight years later when he lay lifeless beside me. I loved everything about him – except for the strength of his sex-drive.

I once thought about going for therapy, but it wasn't that I was physically frigid, or non-orgasmic, or any of those things that they talk about at such length in the magazines. I could be aroused and I could be brought to climax. It was just that I preferred not to be. It seemed such a waste of time.

I could never make sense of my reactions: my shrinking from a man whom I loved and desired. I was forced to conclude that something had gone very wrong at an early age. My mother's fault, possibly, for teaching me to cringe away from physical contact. Physical contact, in terms of germs, could be lethal.

Dee once recited a verse by Philip Larkin, her favourite poet. I must say, until I actually saw it on the page, I thought she'd made it up because I wasn't aware that you could use those sort of words in proper poetry. The opening lines, the ones I remember, were: 'They fuck you up, your mum and dad. They may not mean to, but they do.'

I don't know whether Dee meant to imply that Auntie B had done that to her – in my opinion, it'd have been a miracle if she hadn't – but I don't see much point in blaming. Auntie B, because of the prevailing social climate, was obliged to explain Dee away with lies; no doubt this caused Dee great identity-confusion. My mother warped my developing sexuality. Sophie's father up and left, almost, but not quite, before she was old enough to remember him; perhaps that explains Constantine the father figure and all the other men who proved themselves incapable of constancy. This is how things are: we are done to and thus we do – or don't do – to others; blame somehow seems irrelevant.

11

Dee missed a great deal of what was going on around her because she was busy being curious about unrelated particularities; odd facts: whether there *were* still tribes in New Guinea living Stone-Age lives; what television programmes they received in Ulan-Bator; whether Alma Rattenbury really *did* have a hand in her husband's murder. She would question, probe, ferret out every last detail on a subject that intrigued her; and yet the doings of those closest often appeared to be of no interest at all. Valerie had once asked her whether Fred had any family and she'd said, 'He's got a son in Australia – or it may be a daughter.'

Sophie's curiosity was of the more conventional variety: she collected Pixie from Auntie B's cottage, where Dee was doing a very little typing and a lot of staring out of the window, and wheeled her into town, down Church Street, past the railway station and round the corner into County Road and then, parking the perambulator where she could keep a wary eye upon it, she entered 'F. E. Browning. Books'.

Bookshops had never had the effect upon Sophie that they used to have upon Dee who, when young, had had to be dragged away from them, kicking and screaming, because, once in, she couldn't be persuaded to leave until every volume had been inspected, either cursorily or – if it looked promising – in depth. It was an addiction as besetting as drink or cigarettes: one sniff of printer's ink or binding glue and her heart would beat wildly, her pupils start to dilate.

She'd been weaned off it the hard way. Books were no longer objects of worship, lifeblood of master-spirits, but rectangular parcels that arrived, periodically, to be re-read and found seriously wanting; that occupied, briefly, shelf-space in W. H. Smith's before W. H. Smith's gave itself over almost entirely to travel bureaux and knitting-wool. The best way to get over book-fever, Dee maintained, was to write books.

F. E. Browning's was the sort of bookshop that has boxes outside containing quantities of uniformly-bound sets of Dickens and Guides To Good Housekeeping and Histories of The British Empire, and a room at the back wherein the serious stuff – the stuff that makes the money – is kept. In between was a very respectable selection of current fiction (including, naturally enough, a couple of Dee's books) and great heaps of coffee-table fodder. Sophie was the only customer (or, rather, non-customer) on this July afternoon – not the weather for bookshop-browsing, and the holidaymakers would buy their beach paperbacks from the supermarkets or the newsagents on the Marine Parade. She flicked through art books and gardening books and she read the first page of a biography of an actor who had been an unpromising contemporary of hers at LAMDA but who now, on the strength of his Welsh Valleys' accent and brooding Celtic gaze, was responsible for the placing of a great many bums on cinema seats.

A girl stepped forward and asked if she could help. Sophie switched on the most endearing version among her repertoire of smiles and said that she was just looking. She continued to do so, whilst listening for voices from the back room. She couldn't ask if Mr Browning was in in case he was. She dipped into Plato's *Philebus* and *Teach Yourself Esperanto* and got quite engrossed in a large paperback called *Be Your Own Diagnostician*. She stayed so long that she thought she might be obliged to buy something. And then her perseverance was rewarded: the phone rang and the girl picked it up and listened and then said, 'I'm afraid Mr Browning isn't in this afternoon. He's gone to a book-sale,' and Sophie was able to make her getaway without having to open her purse. 'Foiled,' she said to Pixie, who was looking about her in a most intelligent way while sucking mightily on a teething-ring.

Pixie hadn't cried once, not since being collected. And she didn't cry during the homeward journey either. Sophie informed Dee of this with more than a trace of smugness in her tone.

'It's extraordinary how many people speak to you when you're wheeling a pram,' she said.

'I hope you're not going to tell me that they think she's yours,' Dee said.

As a matter of fact, one old gentleman had said exactly that. Though Sophie, vain as she was, suspected defective eyesight.

Dee wore glasses now, for reading and writing. She took them off and rubbed her eyes. She said, 'Put the kettle on, would you? I'm flogging a dead horse here with this bloody script.'

She talked about it while they were waiting for the tea to brew. She was always loath to discuss work in progress but scripts didn't count. Particularly this one, which was drivel. 'I mean to say,' she said, 'what on earth can I add to every other account of abortion that we've seen on the screen lately? And, God knows, there have been plenty.'

'Well, it's a new *angle*, isn't it – her age, and the fact that it's a late operation? As well as the Roman Catholic business.'

Dee blew across the surface of her tea. 'But it's unreal,' she said. 'Nobody has religion to that extent, these days, surely? Apart from a few peasants and the kind of headcases who'd never find themselves in that situation anyway. I find it impossible to make all this crisis of conscience stuff sound remotely convincing, all the agonising . . .'

Perhaps Dee had never agonised. Neither had Sophie, much, until now.

'I just want not to have to do it. It's damaging my brain,' Dee said, rubbing her head furiously as if to attempt to soothe that organ. 'And they're all such twerps, discussing these cardboard cut-outs and their terrible dilemmas as though they were real – or even convincing. And *don't* accuse me of intellectual snobbery. I'm the one without the education, remember?'

Dee had been due to take her Advanced Level examinations when she disappeared. She had been expected to do well. Sophie tried to remember the story that Auntie B had concocted to explain her departure: something about going to help out some distant relations in Cornwall who had illness in the family. She'd even given them an address. She and Valerie had written a couple of times but, naturally, because the address probably didn't exist, had received no reply. They were involved in preparing to leave home themselves anyway. And, besides, it wasn't long before people started putting two and two together. Girls who became prematurely pregnant were usually sent away from home until after the event. The difference in Dee's case was that she didn't come back for ten years.

'I wouldn't care,' Dee was saying, 'if I could tell them where to stick it and get on with some proper work. But there's nothing *there*. It's gone. I don't think it's ever going to come back.'

This had been said so often before that Sophie did not feel the need to acknowledge the remark.

'Would you hear my speech?'

It had always been the other way round: 'Would you hear my lines?' With Dee acting out all the other parts.

At least then she hadn't needed to pace while she

declaimed. 'You won't be able to do that on the night,' warned Sophie.

'This is just to *remember*,' Dee said impatiently.

'Well you'll have to *remember* then.'

'No I won't. I'll have the speech in front of me in case I go blank. Now, can we continue?'

Hearing a speech was apparently different from hearing lines. 'There are two common misconceptions in existence about the business of writing,' Dee began. 'The first is that writers can write only when the muse is upon them; the second, which usually stems from the pronouncements of writers themselves, is that writing is a business like any other: you start at nine and finish at six, with an hour off for lunch – '

'No, hold on,' Sophie said. 'It's: "stems from the writers themselves" – there's no "pronouncements", and it's not "nine", it's "nine-thirty".'

'Oh for heaven's *sake*, I'm allowed to paraphrase. I don't have to be word *perfect*.'

'I remember doing a Ben Rowley play once,' Sophie said, 'a telly. He sat in on every session and woe betide you if you said "a" for "the" or stuck in an extra "and" somewhere – '

'Yes, very interesting,' Dee said. 'Now, if you wouldn't mind . . .'

Memorising the speech took precedence over everything else. Sophie wondered at Dee's priorities – she was being paid very little for the engagement – but realised that her obsessiveness had nothing to do with remuneration but was in direct ratio to the degree of her anxiety.

'There are techniques,' Sophie said – helpfully, or so she thought – 'breathing – '

'Breathing, bollocks,' Dee replied. 'It's not breathing I need, it's beta-blockers.'

The venue for the dinner was a hotel some twenty miles away. Fred was to take her and collect her afterwards because of her need to tranquillise herself with alcohol.

On the afternoon of the evening when the speech was due to be made, Sophie volunteered to get her ready.

'Left to herself,' she confided to Valerie, 'she'll go looking like a cross between Naomi Jacob and Virginia Woolf. Now eccentric might be all right; bizarre is not . . .'

While Dee stood by, stiff with nerves, her wardrobe was ransacked. 'But you have some nice things!' Sophie said, holding up an embroidered chiffon dress.

'Don't sound so surprised. Actually,' Dee said, 'I'd thought of wearing this.'

'This' was a black velvet suit.

'In July?'

'Well, perhaps not . . .'

'This chiffon's lovely. What jacket would you put with it?'

'This?' said Dee, picking out a grey quilted peasant coat.

'Good God, no. It would *ruin* the effect. What you need is one of those beaded jobs, you know: black, jet, something like that. Have you got anything like that?'

'No,' said Dee humbly.

'You see,' Sophie said, 'it's not what you've got, necessarily; it's how you assemble the total look . . .'

Valerie, who usually bought her total look ready assembled from Windsmoor or Jaeger (or rather, used to do, she realised with a pang), recognised that she had little to contribute and went downstairs to feed Pixie.

It was finally decided that the chiffon dress, enhanced with a black scarf of Sophie's, would do. 'Right!' Sophie said, and brought a lamp to the dressing-table and sat Dee down in front of the mirror and proceeded to make up her face.

She rubbed and patted and drew and painted. Dee kept darting sideways to drink from a glass of vodka and tonic; she had to measure – and time – the amount of her alcoholic intake absolutely precisely in order to arrive at the requisite degree of anxiety-quelling inebriation at the exact moment when the chairwoman rose to her feet, banged her gavel on the table and announced their distinguished guest.

'Hold *still*!' Sophie said, busy with eye-liner. Dee remembered the teenage parties for which she had been got ready by Sophie, remembered sitting in the bedroom of whatever flat Sophie and her mother happened to be living in at the time while Sophie spat in flat black boxes of mascara or teased her hair and manufactured kiss-curls with the tail of a comb. This operation always had to take place at Sophie's because Auntie B disapproved of make-up. She also disapproved of Dee's going to teenage parties, though she need not have worried because Dee generally spent most of the evening skulking in the kitchen and then left early and alone. 'Don't *glower*,' Sophie used to say. 'It puts people off.' Dee felt that her glowering was a kind of test, a form of quality control: if young men were not able to see through it to the attractive personality beneath, then they were not worthy of making her acquaintance. Also she was agonisingly shy and glowering protected her from having to make the kind of small talk that others seemed to master so easily and she found such a strain.

Sophie had said, 'Hold *still*!' then, while she coloured and prinked and teased. Valerie had never been present at these sessions. Obviously Valerie had been in no need of transformation. Anyway, Valerie had had Richard.

How Sophie had encouraged her, soothed her, cajoled her, attempted to bring her together with the most unthreatening of the young men. 'This is Andrew,' she would say, or 'Mario,' or 'Colin,' or 'Anthony,' and Andrew or Mario or Colin or Anthony would, respectively, attempt to draw out the girl who seemed so ill at ease and who looked at them either fearfully or as though they were less than the dust.

'There!' Sophie said now, with one final, keenly-critical scrutiny. 'You'll do.'

And there was no doubt that she did better than she had done as a teenager. Dee had needed to grow into her looks, needed the confidence of success to dare to throw back her head and un-hunch her shoulders and allow her mouth to relax into a smile.

Of course, the vodka helped. Had it not been for the vodka, Sophie suspected, she and Valerie would have been banished with Pixie as soon as their services were no longer required. Or else Dee would have left them to their babysitting duties while she walked the hundred yards or so to Fred's cottage. As it was, she picked up the phone and dialled Fred's number and said, 'I'm as ready as ever I'll be, if you want to come and get me.'

Sophie went out into the garden to smoke a cigarette. Consequently, she was obliged to introduce herself to F. E. Browning when he brought his car to a halt outside Dee's front gate.

('What an appropriate name,' she had said to Dee, 'for a literary gent.' 'I don't know about that,' Dee had replied, 'it's the name of a gun.')

He wasn't what she'd expected (although she wasn't quite sure what that was).

He smiled and extended his hand. 'You must be . . .' he said. And she said, 'I'm Sophie Stephenson.'

If this meant anything to him in terms of world fame, he didn't let on. Perhaps Dee had coached him. Dee found recognition difficult to cope with. She never confessed to being a writer unless obliged to do so. She said that such a confession usually elicited one of two responses, each in the form of a question, for which she could supply no answer; one was: 'What sort of books do you write?' and the other was: 'Should I have heard of you?'

F. E. Browning simply shook the hand of Sophie Stephenson, of whom he might or might not have heard. A firm handshake, but then you'd expect that. Also the erect carriage and – as Valerie had mentioned – the impression of extreme cleanliness. What she hadn't expected was the limp, and the stick.

Fifty-ish, tall, well-proportioned, nice eyes, skin that held a hint of years of the kind of bronzing that you don't get from an English sun, that sort of fair hair that greys so gradually that you can scarcely tell that it's happened, a mouth shaped for smiling – Sophie was observant and always trusted her first impression. Not that that necessarily stopped her from flying in the face of her better judgement.

'What's the condemned man doing?' he asked, consulting his watch. 'Eating a hearty breakfast?'

'Drinking a fairly hefty aperitif, actually.'

'Ah yes. Of course. Alcohol as medicine.'

He smiled fairly quizzically as though not quite sure how much should be said, how conversant Sophie might be with Dee's *modus operandi.*

'I was in your shop the other day,' she started to say, conscious that she was looking at him appraisingly – he was quite a handsome man and handsome men elicited a certain sort of response from Sophie that was as reflexive as a knee-jerk – and then Dee came through the door and his attention switched instantly to her and Sophie realised, just as instantly, that as long as Dee was around, the charms of any other woman, however endearing, would count for nothing.

'You look splendid,' he said. 'They will be quite bowled over – the ladies in hats. What on earth have you got in that great case?'

'My speech – and my emergency supplies.'

She opened it and showed them the bottle of vodka. And then she got into the car and said, 'I am going out. I might be gone for some time.' Before she could change her mind, Fred accelerated away from the kerb at a lick.

'You didn't tell me he was a bit of all right,' Sophie said accusingly to Valerie. Valerie was washing up the tea things. She said, 'I didn't think he'd be your type,' and handed Sophie a tea-towel.

'Oh be still, can't you? Come and sit down and have a drink.'

But Valerie shook her head and continued to potter:

putting away the crockery, plumping the cushions. It was as though she was afraid to be still.

'He came as quite a surprise. From what you'd said I'd expected cavalry twill and a toothbrush moustache. Incidentally, what caused the limp?'

'He had a riding accident.'

'Was he in the cavalry?' Sophie asked, her face alight with the 'goodness-how-romantic' look that tended to appear in response to the sort of information likely to reinforce her somewhat stereotypical thinking.

'No, I don't think so. But anyway the accident happened after he'd left the army, Dee said. I expect he'd retired from it. He'd be about the right age for that, wouldn't he?'

The right age for Dee, Sophie thought; there being a gap of some eight years or so between them. The right sort of gap – as long as it was in the right direction.

Valerie seemed not to be terribly interested in Fred. Valerie seemed to have something else on her mind. She sat down on the edge of the sofa which had an Indian shawl thrown over the back of it and began to fiddle with the fringe: stroking it, plaiting it, knotting it into tassels. 'Sophie,' she said, 'do you know of any cheap hotels in London?'

'With or without bugs?' Sophie said. 'By the hour or for the night?'

'Seriously. Somewhere that's decent and cheap.'

'I don't think there's any such thing,' said Sophie. 'Hotels are a hell of a price. Particularly when they've bunged on that single room supplement. We are talking single rooms, are we? Why? Are you thinking of going?'

'I may need to go down,' Valerie said. 'On business.'

'Goodness, how grand that sounds. Anyway, why do you need an hotel? You can stay in my flat. Well, the one I'm borrowing. No problem.'

But from the look on Valerie's face, one might have supposed that she'd been done a disservice rather than granted a favour.

12

Dee

I remember experiencing a muted sort of orgasm and then immediately falling fast asleep. Like a man. Terribly rude. I slept so soundly that I never even heard Pixie crying nor Fred getting up to attend to her. I dreamed the stage dream again and woke shouting. Fred said, as he always does, 'It's all right. Hush,' and stroked the damp hair away from my forehead. Poor Fred; it seems he'd spent most of the night laying cool hands on fevered female brows.

'What time is it?' I said. I usually keep the curtains open so that I can tell, but when Fred stays they need to be closed. Obviously.

It's only recently that he's started to stay the whole night through. Originally, I used to kick him out after the act. One night, as he buttoned his shirt, he said, 'I feel like a whore's client.' I took his point. But, all the same, sharing my bed took some getting used to.

He picked up his watch from the bedside table and looked at its luminous dial. 'Quarter to seven,' he said.

I raised my head gingerly from the pillow. It throbbed. I remembered odd, disconnected bits about the previous night: Fred taking Sophie and Valerie home and then going to see to Sally and then coming back and saying, 'I'll let you get to bed. Can you make it unaided?' and putting out a hand to steady me and me getting very amorous and

119

asking him to stay. But most of it was a blank: the speech, the vote of thanks from the literary ladies, the journey home.

'How do you feel?' he said now.

'Pretty much like hell.'

He whispered, because of Pixie, though I had discovered that she could sleep through the 1812 and yet wake up when there wasn't a sound to be heard.

'What day is it?'

'It's Sunday.'

'Oh shit!' I said, meaning that because it was Sunday I could have had a lie-in. (Though I don't work office-hours, I feel that I have the right to a lie-in on a Sunday like everybody else.) And then I remembered that since the advent of Pixie, who was quite unable to differentiate Sunday from any other day, there was no longer any such thing as a lie-in.

She was quiet now though. Fred said, 'Do you feel too terrible?' and stroked the side of my face.

'Too terrible for what?'

He said, 'We have some unfinished business. Well, mine is, anyway.'

Despite my hangover it was a not unattractive proposition. Sex with Fred has always been a good, and comfortable, experience. For me, a rare combination.

Perhaps it's because Fred's so straightforward. I used to think that I'd find lack of complexity unendurably dull, but actually it's a relief after other men with their games and their deviousness, other men who leave you wondering what that comment, that look, that gesture, actually meant.

I don't have to guess with Fred. His history – as recounted to me – seems pretty straightforward too: an army family in whose footsteps he followed despite a passion for books; an early marriage and a daughter; service in almost every far-flung outpost of the Empire where Britain still maintained two squaddies and a flag;

his discharge, followed closely by his wife's death and his daughter's emigration to Australia. She wanted him to go too, but she has a family of her own now and anyway he was nostalgic for rain and twilight and the smell of old books.

He moved into the cottage up the road and, soon afterwards, I had to ask for his help because all my lights had fused. After that, he took to calling in occasionally to see if I needed assistance with the sort of jobs that women are supposed to find difficult. It was obvious from the start that he was lonely for female company. It became obvious that he missed sex: he'd had a good marriage and was used, as they say, to getting it regularly.

Though he didn't make a move in that direction for some considerable time. In fact, I believe it was I who made the first move.

In bed he was less tentative. I liked his love-making; it suited me. There was something so entirely wholesome about it: he seemed able to negotiate that fine line that separates delicacy from coarseness, and capable of arousing a reciprocal degree of desire in me.

He was, in short, the best I'd had. So when he turned to me, although my head was aching and the room tended to spin round if I opened my eyes too suddenly, I welcomed him.

I came, and then he did. He smiled and I smiled. He kissed my damp forehead, cuddled me. I started to doze.

But one cannot remain too long in Arcadia. Sometimes sex is merely sugaring the pill. For, after the proposition, the proposal.

There are many ways of turning down an offer of marriage, but eventually the gamut is run. I'd said that we hadn't known each other long enough. He'd replied that he thought two years, at our age, was long enough to know whether we were suited. I'd said that I needed time to think. He'd said how much. I'd said that I wanted to enjoy my freedom since Tom left home for a little while

121

longer. He'd said how long: Tom had never been at home for more than a few months at a time since he was seventeen. I'd said that I wasn't the marrying kind, that I was too set in my ways/selfish/afraid that I wouldn't be able to cope with constant proximity.

'You lived with Tom for seventeen years,' he'd said. 'For a time, you lived with Tom *and* your aunt.'

'A husband's different,' I'd said.

'Why? I'm house-trained. I don't need nursing. And I promise not to play electric guitars at full blast until all hours of the morning.'

'Can't we leave it?' I'd said. 'For now?'

My objections were always qualified. I was scared that he might issue an ultimatum, put me on the spot.

But this morning I was feeling too rough to be bothered wrapping up my response in any sort of politeness. I wasn't regretful, or rueful, or tender; I simply said, 'Oh Fred, give it a rest, will you?'

He rolled away from me and sat on the edge of the bed and reached for his shirt. His leg was paining him, I could tell that from the merest hint of a wince, which is all the reaction he allows himself.

'Fred . . .' I said, and held out a hand, but he moved ever so slightly so that it failed to make contact. I always tried to imagine how I would feel if I kept asking someone to marry me and he kept turning me down, but the concept was so alien that I was incapable of such a tremendous feat of imagination. I wanted to tell him that my response was due to me, not him, but I could never find the words.

'Bring your washing round,' I said placatingly, as he felt under the bed for his shoes.

'I did it on Friday,' he said. 'Thank you all the same.'

(In truth, he's a better ironer than I am. He can also sew on buttons and darn socks: they teach you in the army. He can also cook better than I can. The proposals do not stem from a need to equip himself with a housekeeper.)

122

He dresses in an orderly fashion, very rapidly. I suppose that's a legacy from the army too: right sock, left sock, left shoe, right shoe, belt clasped, tie knotted, jacket shrugged on. He can be finished and ready to go while I'm still groping for my slippers.

He's not rushing off because his nose has been put out of joint. He has to go home in the mornings to let Sally out. He could bring her with him, but she's a guard dog and there have been burglaries in this area since it was gentrified. Fred has some nice things: heirlooms, and souvenirs of his travels.

He also has quite a thriving little business and an army pension and some family money too. Fred is kind and good-looking and sexy and considerate, and if he were to put one foot – even his bad one – inside a singles club, or send his particulars to a computer-dating agency, he'd be snapped up before you could say compatibility.

I heard the front door close behind him as I got out of bed. There had been years and years of my life: punctuated by rotters and bores and other women's husbands, when I'd prayed for a Fred to come along. There had been no ambivalence then.

I looked in on Pixie. She was sleeping. Fred, like Sophie, seems to have a knack with her. But after all he has had a child of his own and he strikes me as the sort who'd be a highly-participative father. I often amuse myself when I'm struggling to put words on paper by building up a picture of Fred's marriage from the odd details he's disclosed. I see him taking Caroline's little hand in his large one, lifting her on to his shoulders, tucking her up in bed at night. Lawns, I see, and a pony in a paddock, Christmas trees with fairy lights and Fred dressed up as Santa Claus.

The facts are probably not like that. Being posted abroad, Fred was very often an absentee father, and Caroline was at boarding school from quite an early age. But one thing's certain: Fred's experience as a young parent would have been very different from mine.

He never said whether he'd be back for lunch. I'll have to ring him. He has a tendency to sulk after being turned down. I wonder if my time is running out, whether I'm becoming complacent. I wish I could make him understand that my independence has been too hard-won for me to relinquish it without a good deal of thought. 'Trust me,' he says, as though it's just as simple as that. I wish I could. More than that, I wish I could tell him why I can't.

I felt that a walk might clear my head. Unlike Sophie, I always suffer for my indulgence. Sophie can swill it down and wake up next morning with no ill effect and start all over again. Perhaps that explains alcoholism.

But they say it's not so simple. Nothing's simple: not the reasons for alcoholism, nor why some women are attracted to men who abuse them, nor trusting people. And I must stop seeking certainties when I know full well there are none.

Fred says: 'I know what I want. I want you. I love you. I'll look after you. I'll try to make you happy.'

Now *that* would be no small achievement.

I wanted to go for a walk, but I didn't want to have to go to all the trouble of waking Pixie and changing her and feeding her and arranging her in her pram, so I took a chance: I just walked out of the door and locked it behind me and trusted to luck that she wouldn't choke or smother or scream so loudly that some passer-by would call out the fire brigade.

Not that there were many passers-by, particularly at this time in the morning. Mist was still rising from the marshes and there were all sorts of muted sounds: rustlings and little crepitations as the tide gradually receded and the grasses began to dry out and tiny creatures advanced towards the shoreline in search of sustenance.

There was also the muffled sound of gun-fire farther away, over towards the headland – a duck-shoot, I supposed – and a dog barking: probably Sally; Fred usually took her along the coastal road first thing in the morning.

So I deliberately turned my steps in the opposite direction; I didn't want to bump into him – not just yet.

I stopped feeling guilty quite quickly. I may have compounded being a bad mother with being an even worse grandmother, but the air was good and I could feel the faint caress of sunshine on my face and all the poisons of the night before were being exhaled from my lungs and exuded from my pores as my circulation woke up and my walking attained a rhythm. I realised why I stayed put in Auntie B's cottage: it was the chance to walk along the shore before the world was awake. All the time I was away from it, I missed the sea, the knowledge of its just being there; when you can see the sea there's always the feeling that you can escape.

It's crazy, I know. I can't even swim, I get sea-sick, and marsh vegetation, in full bloom, gives me hay-fever.

Nevertheless I've always walked on the beach, ever since I can remember, with Auntie B's warnings ringing in my ears: beware of drowning, stinging insects, being cut off by the tide, losing your way in the mist, quicksand, strange men – the most dangerous of all.

I used to walk here and hide behind a sandhill and cry because I loved Richard Lamb and Richard Lamb loved Valerie.

It was behind that sandhill, as I wept for the lifetime of loneliness that I saw stretching ahead of me (I used to take Tennyson along on those walks; reading Tennyson intensified the poignancy of my unhappiness: 'Dear as remembered kisses after death, And sweet as those by hopeless fancy feign'd On lips that are for others; deep as love, Deep as first love, and wild with all regret.'), that Auntie B's direst prediction came to pass and I encountered a strange man and, instead of taking to my heels in accordance with instruction, I let him take a handkerchief out of his pocket and wipe my eyes and offer me a wine gum.

This morning I walked as far as the fog bell and stood for a little while looking out to sea. From the corner of my

125

eye I could see St Wilfred's. The man who had had it built – a Liverpool ship-owner – was, apparently, derided at the time, warned that it would sink into the treacherous sand. But it's standing still, a hundred and fifty years later. It's been known as St Wilfred's ever since it was turned into a boys' school at the end of the last century, although I can only ever remember it as a sanatorium.

It hasn't been a sanatorium for twenty years. Apart from brief spells as a home for wayward boys and a geriatric hospital, it's lain empty, and it's disintegrating fast. They've boarded up the doors and windows and put a fence around it but that doesn't stop squatters and vandals and winos from availing themselves of its amenities.

I used to walk along there when I first came back, but once I tripped over what appeared to be a bundle of rags clutching a bottle of VP sherry, and another time a group of youths who had climbed on to an out-house roof rained a hail of cans down on me, so now I keep my distance. It isn't as if – whatever anyone likes to pretend – places are invested with memories. Places are places and the memories are all in our heads.

I thought: I'd better get back in case Pixie has woken up. Like Valerie, I wondered how Sam could have so nonchalantly left her to my mercies – tender or otherwise, for all she knew. Young and terrified as I was when Tom was born, I knew from the first moment that I would not allow anyone to separate me from him. I'd been in one of those unwed mother homes – in the Yorkshire Dales; Wuthering Heights, it was known as locally, and just about as cheerless – and the plan was that at the end of six weeks Tom would be handed over and placed for adoption while I would return home and tell my story which, I seem to remember, had something to do with Cornwall and sick relatives.

Instead, as soon as I was able to walk, I walked to the nearest railway station and used part of the most recent five pounds that Auntie B had sent me to buy a ticket to whatever happened to be the nearest city. I was terrified of being caught and brought back and, because of my age, thrown into a home for young-girls-who-were-in-moral-danger, or whatever they had in those days. A city would allow me to go underground, as well as providing me with work.

But Sam's position is not really comparable with mine. She's in what they call a stable relationship, well, a relationship anyway. Pixie has a father who recognises her existence, although he may not be married to her mother.

I retraced my steps, climbing up on to the sea wall, which has been re-built since my girlhood. It was just a raised embankment then, a footpath, barely wide enough for two people to walk abreast. Sometimes I try to remember on just how many occasions I walked two abreast, rather than solo, along it: six, ten, two dozen? At the time, I wrote an account of each of our meetings in my diary. I noted everything down in the most meticulous detail: what the weather was like, what he wore, what I wore, our conversation, word for word. But that diary got lost during one of my many moves and though I can remember a great deal, there's a lot that I can't. Sometimes it all seems so remote that, if it were not for Tom, I'd think that I'd dreamed it. In fact my dreams are much more vivid than my memories: an eighteen-year-old girl discovered in tears behind a sandhill by a man who had a clean handkerchief and a packet of wine gums, a few walks along the embankment, cups of tea in the Wayside Café, assignations in the lee of the dunes while the red flags fluttered and the gulls squabbled over their tideline spoils and once, late in the evening, while Auntie B paced Ferryside Lane (she'd have rung the police, except, thank God, nobody had a phone in those days), the mist rose and first the sea and then the shore became shrouded, obliterated, and the fog bell began to toll.

One summer.

13

Simon and Stephen wrote to their mother from America, enclosing a photograph of themselves. Valerie showed it to Sophie. 'Good-looking boys,' Sophie said.

And they were, like their father before them: clear-skinned, dark-eyed, slim – and identical still. At school they'd been distinguished by pinning on different coloured badges to their uniforms. They were responsible little boys who never dreamed of swapping them over. 'Bill and Ben, The Flowerpot Men,' Tom used to call them. And no wonder. They were so often held up to him – despite being some three years his junior – as examples that he should emulate. While Tom was discussing the meaning of life and rolling joints, they were getting A grades; when Tom was playing truant and riding around on a lethal motor-bike and being thrown out of pubs, they were gaining their Duke of Edinburgh awards, and their prefects' badges. It had been obvious from the beginning that the Twins – more astute than their father, more confident than their mother – would never put a foot wrong.

'When will they be back?' Sophie asked.

'The beginning of September,' Valerie said, with more conviction than she actually felt. The camp finished at the end of August; their jobs awaited them in mid-September; she assumed that they would come home in the meantime. She hadn't yet got out of the habit of making assumptions.

'You must tell them to drop in when they get to London,' Sophie said, not meaning it. (She hadn't a clue, anyway, where she'd be by the time they got to London.) She'd said the same to Tom years ago when she'd met him in Brixton. He'd taken her at her word, called round to – Notting Hill, it was then – and touched her for a few bob.

She hadn't begrudged it. Things were really dodgy, he'd told her: they'd been ripped off by an unscrupulous manager; a record deal had fallen through. 'You won't let on to my old woman, will you?' he'd said. 'I get enough flak from that direction as it is.'

'Well perhaps if you were to keep in touch a bit more regularly . . .' she'd said, but realised that that was tantamount to asking a river to run backwards. She hadn't let on anyway.

'Yes, I will,' Valerie said, stifling the shudder that arose automatically whenever the word London was mentioned.

Ambivalence had given way to action with Dee's announcement that she needed to take a trip to London to describe to an importunate editor a book that had no substance, neither in the corporeal sense nor yet in the imagination. Almost before she knew what she was saying, Valerie had interjected: 'I'm going to London on the third. Perhaps we could go down together.'

Once the decision had been made, arrangements seemed to be put in train with alarming rapidity; and the intervening days sped by. I can always not go, Valerie told herself as she bought her ticket, looked through her wardrobe and tried to decide what was the most suitable garment to wear for meeting one's late husband's mistress; I can always not do it, right up to the last minute: until I step on to the train, put my foot over the threshold of Bennett's Hotel, introduce myself to the parties involved.

'What would *you* wear?' she asked Sophie.

Well, none of these, Sophie felt like saying, as she rattled the clothes along the rail. Safe clothes: suits and floral dresses and skirts and jumpers, in muted colours, classic lines.

'What about this?' she said, lifting out a pale blue suit, removing its plastic cover. All Valerie's clothes were covered in plastic.

'Or the grey dress?'

It must be my function now, Sophie thought, to assess people's wardrobes and advise them on the most suitable apparel for the occasion. A desolate thought flashed into her mind: all those never-quite-made-it actresses that she remembered from years ago: dressers, they'd become, or – if they could sew – wardrobe mistresses in provincial reps.

'I'll take both of them,' Valerie said. She generally took two of everything anyway: Richard always went through the cases after she'd packed them, discarding extra tubes of toothpaste and spare towels, as well as most of the pharmaceutical supplies she'd included in the event of there not being a convenient chemist.

'It is just one night that you're staying?' Sophie said. There was extra this and extra that and three books.

'Yes. Look, you don't mind me using your flat?' Valerie said, in a last-ditch attempt to find an excuse for calling the whole thing off.

'Not in the slightest. You can give the place an airing.'

Sophie had heard other people talking about the need for houses to be aired, but had rarely lived in one place long enough to understand what was meant by the term.

Not that she hadn't, in her time, been houseproud: in that first house in Chelsea with Constantine: Art Deco, they'd bought – you could still get hold of the genuine article quite cheaply then. Who'd got it? Where had it gone? And then there was Highgate when she was married to Hawley. (She'd always felt that, with Hawley, she should have lived in Hilldrop Crescent; he hadn't found that funny.) A journalist and a photographer from a colour supplement had come round to Highgate. She'd been photographed among what were, purportedly, her favourite things: 'Sophie Stephenson At Home'. (Actually, when she'd found out that it was in the offing, she'd rushed around junk shops acquiring objects and subsequently invented histories for them.)

That article had appeared because of her success in *Hay Fever*. 1982. She remembered the photograph: the Kenzo dress, the Ferragamo shoes. Possibly the last time she'd really looked, and felt, good. There'd been money then, and how they'd spent it, she and Hawley: clothes, restaurants, holidays, booze – as well as all the House Beautiful bit. I should have stuck to comedy, Sophie thought. It was my forte. My mistake was diversification.

'Is there anything you want checking while I'm there?' Valerie was saying. 'Heating, or bills paid, or anything?'

'I think John has all the bills paid from the bank,' Sophie said vaguely. 'As for the heating, I wouldn't know. I just flicked a switch when I left . . .'

'I'll look,' Valerie said. 'They say you should put it on from time to time, however briefly, so that the pump doesn't seize up.'

Richard's pump had seized up. There, on the matrimonial bed. She was still unused to the idea that all of it was now available to her, still kept meticulously to her side, still woke and reached out a hand expecting to feel him beside her.

He'd always slept deeply. 'Like one dead,' she used to say, as a joke. She thought now that the comments we make in jest often turn out to be oddly prophetic, almost as though some foreknowledge, too terrible to be taken seriously, is contained in them.

If he hadn't been such a deep sleeper she might have suspected – on that night of March 17th – that all was not well. As it was, she'd had no reason to suppose there was anything amiss, would never know at what precise moment – while she dreamed a gentle, unsymbolic dream – the last breath was exhaled from his body.

'Myocardial infarction,' it had said on the death certificate. 'He wouldn't have known about it,' the doctor had said. She suspected that he said that to comfort her, but certainly Richard's face, apart from a slight blueness round the lips, had looked quite peaceful, as though he too might have been experiencing some pleasant, insignificant dream.

She put sanitary towels into her suitcase. Her period was a week away but she had no doubt that stress would precipitate it.

'That reminds me,' Sophie said, catching sight of them, 'I must get some.'

'But I thought you'd just finished . . .'

'Yes, but my period's due,' said Sophie, unthinkingly. And then she realised what she'd said and continued rapidly: 'I remember reading somewhere that girls in dormitories menstruate in synchronisation. Maybe that's what's happening here. I told you it was time we had some male company . . .'

'Sophie,' Valerie said, 'you *are* all right, aren't you?'

'What do you mean?'

'I mean that haemorrhage that you made so light of and those pills you're forever taking and the amount of weight you've lost . . .'

'Shall we talk about our operations?'

To make a joke of it, that was the thing. There wasn't anything that couldn't be joked about.

'I've never had an operation,' Valerie said. 'Have you?'

'Only the usual sort of thing.'

'What's the usual sort of thing?'

Valerie wasn't suited to playing the Grand Inquisitor. At any moment she would lose her nerve, suspect that – horror of horrors – she had failed in politeness.

'Surely you must have had them: those scrapings and freezings and so forth?'

'No.'

'Well everyone else I know has. You know: when you

get a funny smear and they haul you in and muck about with your cervix . . .'

In Fred's shop she'd found herself drawn irresistibly towards the gynaecological section of *Be Your Own Diagnostician*. She could recall a passage from it word for word, could have recited it as fluently as she'd once recited, 'On either side the river lie Long fields of barley and of rye': 'Cervical cancer is probably a sexually-transmitted disease, as it is unknown in virgins. A virus is thought to be implicated, which may be passed from partner to partner. Therefore women who have had many sexual partners are at greatest risk, as are those who began sexual activity at an early age.'

No one, no book, ever told you how many was many. Sophie's mother had had a fair number of boyfriends who were no doubt sexual partners also. But in those days nobody made the connection. You just reached a certain age and things went wrong. Her mother was having a bit of trouble and they persuaded her to have a hysterectomy. Within six months she was dead.

Valerie unlocked her case and put in another pair of knickers. Sophie wasn't secretive. Not like Dee. Sophie used to kiss and tell, and tell. The only secrets that Sophie used to keep were other people's, never her own.

'If you put anything else into that case,' Sophie said, 'you're going to need Pickfords.'

14

Sophie

They've gone, thank God. I thought they never would. Dee just came in, dumped nappies and bottles and several little tins of baby food, and then went to the car and came back carrying Pixie and dumped her too. She said, 'I'll be back about ten. If there's any sort of a crisis give Fred a bell at the shop.' But Valerie had screeds of instruction to impart: what to say if estate-agents rang, or the bank manager, or somebody who might want to give her a job; where the stop-cock was situated and the fuse-box; which latches to drop if I went out and which keys I would need to take with me if I wanted to get back in.

You'd have thought, from the nervy way she was carrying on, that she actually had an assignation in Bennett's Hotel with a lover whose reliability was somewhat in doubt.

There's never been one. I sometimes wonder what it must be like to have slept with only one man. Surely it must be like eating the same meal every day or reading the same book? At least Valerie won't get cervical cancer.

But what am I saying? Like it used to tell you on the posters in the clap clinic: 'All it takes is you, him and one other.' And we, all of us – Valerie included, presumably – knew about Richard's proclivities.

It was gloriously peaceful after they'd left. 'Just you and me, Pixie darling,' I told her. She chuckled as though

134

pleased at the idea of it. She often chuckles when we're alone together.

'So what do you fancy doing?' I said. 'Shall we go out and pick up a couple of men and get them to show us a good time?'

Her smile widened at that, as though she considered it to be a pretty good suggestion. I had to make it clear that I'd only been joking: I wasn't in any condition for picking up men and she was still very young. 'Now you wouldn't want cervical cancer, would you?' I said.

I bet it's not true. I bet the BMA have had pressure put upon them to issue a statement to all the researchers involved in the field that the results must be made to fit the hypothesis: cancer is caused by promiscuity. I bet it's an M. Thatcher edict, part of her return to Victorian values bullshit. 'I bet there are virgins all over the place with cells at the neck of their wombs undergoing the most sinister changes, even as we speak,' I said to Pixie.

I wheeled the pram on to the train at Parklands and off it at the terminus. I may have had to forfeit male attention now that I am no longer young and lovely, but a pram does the trick: you get plenty of assistance with a pram, no matter what you look like. I thanked my helpers and Pixie made gurgling noises and tugged at the brim of her sun-hat.

She likes being with me. And that's not some form of self-delusion which may be common to childless women of mature years whose wombs have decided to shut up shop. I know she likes being with me; I can see her eyes light up whenever I approach. And it's not just cupboard-love. Dee feeds her and cares for her, therefore if her eyes light up for anyone it ought to be her grandmother.

Almost without noticing it my steps had led us to County Road. Automatic walking. Prompted, no doubt, by there having been such a dearth of male companionship these last few weeks.

I've no husband any more, nor even a lover – not now

– and, quite honestly, no desire to fill the vacancy, but I do miss male company.

Fred was nice and what was more – this time – he was in. But I knew that anyway, didn't I? Dee had said so. 'If there's a crisis,' she'd said, 'give Fred a bell at the shop.' I didn't see why I needed a crisis.

He was looking through a catalogue and drinking coffee from a mug that said 'Capricorn'. He said, 'Hello,' and started to get to his feet. I gestured to the mug and said, 'If you're typical, you won't thank me for interrupting you.'

'Typical of what?' he said, combing his fingers through his hair.

'Typical of your astrological sign.'

'Am I?'

'If you're a Capricorn.'

'Am I?' he said again. 'I haven't a clue.'

'No, you're not,' I said, suddenly certain. 'You're April, aren't you, or May?'

Taurus, I was sure: sturdy, persistent, obstinate.

'April,' he said. 'Yes, how did you know?'

'Clairvoyance,' I replied. And then I became aware of just how stupid and affected I sounded. Somehow I had got myself locked into a set of conversational responses typical of the essentially superficial style of living that had been my existence for so long now: idiotic dinner-party chit-chat: how much is your house worth; who's doing what to whom; what's your sign?

'I felt like company,' I said. 'And I couldn't think of anyone else.'

Fred, I can tell, is a gentleman of the old school. The big clock on the wall opposite says eleven-forty-five; there are no customers in the shop and the girl is on top of a ladder flicking a duster desultorily along the shelves. He double-checks the time with his watch, closes his catalogue and gets to his feet. He says, 'Would you allow me to buy you some lunch?' in exactly the same way as he'd make the offer to an elderly aunt or a schoolgirl niece.

'I'd be delighted,' I said, 'but what about Pixie?'

'Oh,' he said, 'there's a wine bar down the road where they welcome babies with open arms.'

They didn't. But neither did they object. They even heated up her bottle and her little tin of disgusting-looking mush that Fred and I took turns to spoon into her mouth. He said, 'Look out!' as she spat back what had been shovelled in all over my Jean-Paul Gaultier blouse.

'They do that,' he said.

'You don't say?' I dabbed at the stain with my napkin. I said that it must be a law of life that if one's wardrobe consisted of a very few designer labels and the rest from Oxfam, it was invariably the designer labels that got sicked over or spat on or bled into.

'Perhaps you should wear an overall,' he said.

His clothes looked to be of the rather old, very expensive sort in shades of what Hawley used to refer to scornfully as Gieves and Hawkes greige. Hawley was my age but had somehow got himself stuck in a young Marlon Brando time-warp: tee-shirts and buttock-straining jeans; it can look a bit daft when you're going bald and your broad leather belt is required to act as a corset.

I'd expected Fred to be the abstemious sort. But he ordered a bottle of Chardonnay (they had – for a wine bar – quite a good list; I was used to their London counterparts which usually offered a choice between Ribena and anti-freeze); perhaps Dee had told him that I liked a drink. 'She's a bit of a piss-artist,' Dee might have said.

He leaned back in his chair and raised his face to the sun. (We had taken our food and drink outside on to the terrace and I had uncovered Pixie so that she could kick her scrawny little chicken legs with abandon.) 'Make the most of it,' he said. 'Probably just about all we'll get this year. You can't blame people for taking off for foreign parts, can you, even if it does entail sitting in an airport for the best part of three days?'

'You must have seen plenty of those,' I ventured. I was going to say 'Foreign parts' but that always sounds anatomical to me, so I amended it to 'countries'. He struck me as one of the few men who could don khaki shorts and those knee socks they wear with them, and a bush-hat, and not look utterly ridiculous.

'A fair number. I thought, when I was abroad, that I'd be happy to watch the rain if it lasted all summer, but it's surprising how little is too much. I suppose,' he said, 'that somewhere there's an ideal climate. My daughter's in Australia. In Queensland. I write to her complaining of the rain and the cold and she writes back saying come over here where it's so hot that even the flies have sunstroke.'

'And will you? Go over there?'

He wound his spaghetti round his fork, opened his mouth and captured it neatly. When he'd chewed and swallowed he said, 'For a visit, yes. For good – I don't know. There's something horribly drastic about saying Goodbye England.'

I never feel that about places, only people. But I suppose, being a soldier, he thinks in terms of Queen and Country.

He moved his bad leg gingerly until it was in a more comfortable position. His stick was propped against the wall behind him. 'Were you in the cavalry?' I asked, remembering about the riding accident and wanting to have my dashing, galloping major image of him confirmed.

He put his head back and laughed. 'No,' he said. 'Education corps, actually. Does that dim my lustre a bit?'

It was impossible not to laugh too. I said, 'Yes, it does, a bit. I'm sorry. I just thought – your leg.'

He'd been staying with friends in the country who kept horses, he said. Stupidly, he'd claimed to be more competent in the saddle than was actually the case. They'd gone for an early-morning canter. His horse – not the placid creature that he should have been riding, but a nervous thoroughbred – had been startled by a car back-firing, had bucked and reared and thrown him. His leg had been broken in several places and all the bolts and screws and metal plates known to orthopaedic surgery were not sufficient to restore it to its normal functioning.

'So I'm a cripple,' he said.

'Isn't that a bit strong?'

'No. It's an accurate description. Would you rather I called a spade a digging implement?'

Yes, I thought, I would, any day of the week.

We emptied the bottle. The sun beat down. Pixie kicked her legs and burped and gently regurgitated a little food. Fred took off his jacket. He said, 'In this weather, one could be very tempted to play hookey.'

'Could one?'

'One could. If you're not busy,' he said hesitantly, 'and you don't mind keeping cripple's pace, we could drive down to the nature trail and go for a stroll. How does it sound?'

When I was younger I met a few men like Fred. The sort who stand by the wall at parties and seem to be rather glum until you coax a smile out of them and it's the kind of smile that can illuminate the whole room. They're very courteous, that sort, but very reserved; they help old ladies on to buses and lend you their blindingly-white handkerchiefs, but find it difficult to express their feelings. I used to think that co-existing with those sterling old-fashioned virtues would be the very worst kind of male piggery: 'My wife'; 'Where's my dinner?'; 'Why are you three minutes late?'

It's only now that I realise my error, realise that it's when one's youthful charms have faded that one starts to appreciate the masculine protection on the street-side of the pavement, the door held open, the hand at one's elbow.

(Well, Fred would have put his hand on my elbow, I'm sure, if he hadn't needed it to lean on his stick.)

'Dee will just about now be making up the story of the novel that she's supposed to be in the throes of writing,' he said, as he drove us along the coastal road.

He looked at his watch. 'On to her nth glass of wine and getting more fluent by the minute.'

Of course, as I ought to have realised, he'd decided to prolong our contact so that he could talk about Dee. What greater pleasure can there be – apart from actually being together – than for the lover to be able to mention the beloved's name?

He waved away my assistance when we reached our destination, propped himself against the car and managed to lift the pram out of the back. It took him twice as long as it would have done if I'd lent a hand, but I supposed that such stubbornness was the only way he had of asserting his independence.

It was cool and fragrant in the shade of the pines. I pushed the pram and he limped along beside me, keeping a wary eye out for tree roots and rabbit holes. When we reached a clearing we stopped so that I could have a cigarette and he could rest his leg. I said, '*You've* not just given up, have you? I shan't be subjecting you to terrible torment if I smoke this?'

He took my lighter and lit the cigarette for me. He said, 'It's so long since I gave up that I've forgotten the pain. Poor Dee. She's really suffering, isn't she? I often wonder whether she nips into the loo in the middle of the night to have one.'

So he wasn't in *that* sort of residence then.

I said, '*I'd* do that, but Dee wouldn't. She has a strong will.'

He propped himself against a tree and took the weight off his leg. 'You've known her a long time, haven't you?' he said.

'Since we used to swap copies of the *Sunny Stories*.'

'So you might know what it is I have to do to get her to marry me,' he said, looking past me and into the distance, obviously hugely embarrassed.

'Is that what you want?'

'Very much.'

'And, I take it, she doesn't?'

'She doesn't trust me,' he said. 'That seems to be the top and bottom of it.'

'Dee doesn't trust anybody.'

'But *why*?' he said explosively. 'Just what *is* the problem, that it can blight her life like this?'

Personally, I couldn't see that Dee's life was particularly blighted, but he obviously thought so. He said, 'I love her dearly, I'd do anything to help, but mostly she keeps me at arm's length. It isn't as if we don't get on well together – in every way,' he said, rather rapidly, as though I might be about to enquire whether bed was the problem. 'Everything's fine and then I take one step too far and she retreats at the speed of light . . .'

All my life people have bored me rigid with their confidences. It isn't that I'm sympathetic – I'm not. Nor am I particularly discreet. I must just have that sort of face.

Dee's history wasn't confidential. Once upon a time it was common knowledge: the woman who sat treadling morning till night in the cottage in Ferryside Lane who brought up as her niece a girl who was really her daughter.

I told Fred. I trusted my instinct with him, believed that he had her best interests at heart.

'Incredible, isn't it,' I said, 'in the light of now? But then – well, you can imagine – small town, shame, scandal . . .'

He was very quiet, digesting it. Eventually he said, 'Christ! What we do to each other!'

I hoped I'd done the right thing, and not the wrong thing for the right reasons. I said, 'You *won't* let on, will you?'

He shook his head. He said, 'Poor Dee. I thought it might be something to do with Tom – his father . . .'

Pixie, who had been watching, fascinated, the changing patterns on the ground made by the sunlight filtering through the trees, suddenly looked at him as though she recognised her father's name. I said, 'Now that really *is* on the official secrets list.'

15

'Liverpool Lime Street, Runcorn, Crewe, Stafford, Rugby, Milton Keynes, Bletchley, London Euston.'

These were the stations listed on Valerie's timetable. Unfortunately – despite her fervent wishing that it would – the train did not stop at all of them. Valerie wished for protracted halts, points' failures, full-scale derailments – anything to delay her arrival.

She'd read about calming techniques in magazine articles on stress: deep, rhythmic breathing was supposed to help (it didn't), as was breathing back one's own exhaled carbon dioxide from a paper bag. Though how you were supposed to produce a paper bag and start breathing into it in the middle of a crowded train compartment, heaven alone knew. She'd brought sandwiches, therefore she had the necessary equipment, but nevertheless . . .

Dee, as usual, had made scathing remarks about bringing sandwiches, but wasn't averse to eating her share of them. She went along to the buffet and brought back a bottle of house wine. She needed some Dutch courage to see her through her forthcoming interview. Dutch courage was a mutual requirement. To Dee's surprise, Valerie accepted a glass instead of refusing it, and another one after that. Nervousness, Dee surmised, at the thought of making her way to the further reaches of the Old Brompton Road without a guide or a party of native bearers.

'God, this is a boring journey,' Dee said. She knew it by heart: the chemical works on the banks of the Mersey, the glimpses of brightly-liveried narrow boats on the canals, the Ovaltine factory, the endless stock-brick suburbs of North-West London. Known too well, it offered her no scope for the exercise of the imagination. Dee preferred new routes, places half-seen, around which could be woven all kinds of supposition. There wasn't much to be got from the Ovaltine factory or the knowledge that you were passing through Kensal Green.

Valerie sat quiet, attempting to conceal the physical manifestations of her extreme apprehension. If only her travelling companion had been someone other than Dee! The previous night she'd tried to prevail upon Sophie to accompany them. Sophie, with unarguable logic, had said, 'But who would look after Pixie?' She'd also said that she had no desire to see London for a little while yet and forbade Valerie to tell anyone where she, Sophie, was presently holed up. 'I don't want to be pestered,' she'd said. 'If anybody should ask, just say I've gone abroad.'

The train slowed at Primrose Hill and came to a halt some way outside Euston. 'It's going to be late. I knew it would,' Dee said, in the self-satisfied tones of the vindicated pessimist. 'Unless they get their act together pretty quickly.'

Valerie knew, with an equally bleak certainty, that it would be got together, and of course it was. They were disgorged into the station before Dee had finished her second sentence of complaint. She strode away along the platform, throwing comments over her shoulder: 'I've forgotten what it was I was going to *say*. Oh God, I remember now and I think I'd prefer to forget . . .'

Valerie, hauling her unnecessarily heavy suitcase, panted in her wake. Reaching the main concourse, she called, 'Couldn't we share a taxi?' but Dee, shouting, 'See you tomorrow – or whenever,' stepped on to the Underground escalator and disappeared gradually from view.

144

The best calming technique, better than deep breathing or paper bags, was to tell yourself that you were safe right until the very last moment. This enabled Valerie to queue for a taxi, to announce her address to the driver and to sit in the back of it as it turned towards Bloomsbury (silly Dee, preferring to pay on the Tube when she could have had a lift for nothing) with some semblance of composure.

(In fact, Dee had opted for the Tube because she knew it would get her there in half the time. She sat opposite an elderly Indian gentleman with a dark grey face who was reading *Lace*. He looked as though he'd got hold of the wrong book. She was reminded of her early childhood when, able to read before she was capable of making sense of the text, she'd plucked from the bookcase a novel called *The Girl in the Tube*. She'd taken the title literally, assumed it would be a fairy story, was most disappointed to discover that it was grown-up stuff: nothing more than a girl travelling on a train. Auntie B had snatched that book from her. She didn't know why. But that was just another puzzle in her infinitely puzzling existence.)

Valerie hadn't known quite what to expect of Sophie's new address. The neighbourhood to which the taxi conveyed her seemed nondescript: wide, traffic-choked roads, coalyards, a cemetery, some nice property, some not, a council estate – one somehow never expected to find council houses in Royal Boroughs.

But it turned out to be a very pleasant flat: spacious and tastefully decorated. If it hadn't been for the layer of dust that lay undisturbed on every horizontal surface and a pair of grubby sheets on the unmade bed and – judging by the smell – a dead body in the kitchen, she would have been quite reassured.

She picked up a lot of mail from the doormat – later she would sort it and take Sophie's back for her – and followed the dreadful smell to its source: half the contents of a carton of milk, that had been there, she supposed, since Sophie left.

She went downstairs and disposed of it in a dustbin at the back of the house, looking up at the windows of the other flats, behind which there seemed to be no sign of life. Flat dwelling, she thought, as she climbed the front steps, read the names above the entryphones: it's what I shall have to get used to: proximity, confined spaces, and the determined privacy that is bred of proximity and confined spaces. No longer any Hilda limping along every Tuesday and Friday to break up the day; all my things having to be disposed of because there won't be room enough for them in a flat.

It was too frightening to contemplate. Everything was too frightening to contemplate, everything but the very next step: searching for clean sheets and making up the bed, working out the controls on the central-heating boiler, searching the cupboards for the staples that Sophie said she had left there, only to find that she hadn't and therefore having to venture out again, map in hand, to seek a grocery shop.

A Pakistani gentleman sold her some provisions. She turned the wrong way when she came out of the shop and soon found herself in unfamiliar territory, wandering somewhere between a cemetery and a railway line. Every single passer-by looked like a potential rapist; she could hear her heart beating, feel the sweat beads forming on her upper lip. She forced herself to pause and look at the map. Eventually she got her bearings.

There was a big mirror in the hall inside the flat. She looked into it and wiped away the sweat – and the tears – from her face. If I can't even get myself to a corner shop and back again, she thought, how, in God's name, am I to accomplish what must be accomplished?

(Dee, seated behind her second gin and tonic in a charming little French restaurant in Soho Square, smiled sweetly and said, 'I always find that this is the trickiest time of all: when one is just approaching the mid-point of a book. Most people think that *starting* is the problem,

146

but *starting's* a piece of cake. I could start a dozen novels as of now. No, it's that crucial time when you realise that although you've done a lot, there's still more than that to do . . .'

Her companion, an editor wise in the ways of authors both self-deceiving and devious, blinked her eyes to stop them glazing over and thought: 'I must remember to collect my dry-cleaning on the way home.')

The best time to catch a hotel guest, Valerie supposed, was just before dinner, during what, nowadays, they called the Happy Hour. A singularly inappropriate description in this instance. The obvious course of action: to ring the hotel and make an appointment was not open to her. She must simply dress herself to look as appropriate as possible and venture forth.

It had taken her all afternoon: getting herself ready. She'd tried to eat some bread and cheese but every mouthful made her retch, so instead she'd bathed using Sophie's very expensive bath oil and then stood for a long time in front of the mirror trying on the outfits she'd brought with her. The suit? Too stern. The grey dress? Too prim and fussy. The clothes she had travelled in? Creased.

She was searching for an iron when she stumbled upon the drinks cupboard. For once, she had no compunction about helping herself, recognising, as did Dee when faced with some daunting public engagement, that alcohol was the only possible enabler.

She washed a glass and filled it with gin. For some reason she imagined gin as being slightly less lethal than any other of the spirits available. She pressed her skirt and drank her drink. Like Dee, she knew she must monitor her consumption down to the last sip: too little and she'd never go through with her plan; too much and she'd fall over.

Bennett's Hotel was, as Sophie had said, situated in

Mayfair. Valerie wasn't keen on negotiating the Underground and she couldn't have hailed a taxi to save her life. Her salvation occurred by chance: while ringing TIM to make sure that her watch was keeping time she noticed, written on a pad by the phone, the number of a minicab firm. She rang and booked one for five-forty-five.

That left an hour to fill, an hour to twitch and tremble and sweat and palpitate and ration the gin. Seeking for distraction, she began to open drawers and cupboard doors – normally she'd have been horrified at the idea of abusing someone's hospitality by rummaging through their belongings, but there was nothing normal about this situation.

Clothes, men's and women's, hanging in the wardrobes, invitations to various functions: first nights, parties, private views, on mantelpieces and stuck into the frames of mirrors. Notes scribbled to unknown persons and fastened to the fridge door: 'Pay milkman'; 'See you in the Lamb and Flag at 8.30'; 'Back in half an hour'. A few photographs: a young, rather flashily-handsome man dressed in Shakespearian costume, another that had 'To Dearest J' scrawled across the bottom of it. A cupboard crammed with scrapbooks filled with press-cuttings – all referring to John Wainwright. (Where was Sophie's life – apart from that exhibited by a few clothes and trinkets and a phial of 'Joy' on a shelf in the bathroom? Scattered throughout Chelsea and Highgate and North Ken, no doubt, left behind in the headlong flight from one wrong man towards another.)

She switched the radio on and then off. Ditto the television. She activated the cassette that was slotted into the video recorder: 'Prick Up Your Ears', fast-forwarded it and then wound it back. She hesitated a moment beside the phone and then did the same to the answering machine and heard what was, presumably, the voice of John Wainwright, delivering himself, in very fruity tones, of the information that he was unavailable but would be happy

148

to deal with any queries upon his return. There was a message from a television repair man, a double-glazing salesman, an insurance broker, someone called Pamela who said, 'Hi darling. I'm back in Maida Vale. Call me just as soon as you can,' and a man with a faint accent: Irish? who didn't identify himself before saying, in a very angry voice: 'What the hell are you playing at? I come back this morning to find all your things gone. I'm off to Dublin tonight, back mid-August, they reckon. I'll see you then.' There was a pause and then the voice said, 'I'm sorry.'

One of John Wainwright's boyfriends, no doubt. A lover's tiff. Though you'd have thought that John Wainwright would have at least told him that he was going to Australia. Unless of course that was why he'd gone to Australia . . . Valerie suddenly became aware of what she was doing, blushed for shame, and re-set the machine.

The cab was fifteen minutes late. While waiting for it, she swigged gin from the bottle, aware that there was another calm, perfectly sober self watching this spectacle, horrified.

(Dee, who had added the best part of a bottle of Nuits St George and a couple of brandies to her pre-prandial gins, was back in Bedford Square, firmly convinced by now that the imaginary novel which she had described so confidently was actually halfway to being complete. Gripped by a kind of *folie de grandeur*, she heard herself saying, 'Definitely by October. At the latest.' She burped gently. She had mopped up the alcohol with onion soup, a large helping of duckling with sauce bigarde, masses of vegetables and a vast wedge of Normandy flan, as well as two bread rolls and a plateful of after-dinner mints. Dee believed in eating her publisher's money's worth whenever she got the chance, being only too well aware of the saying concerning free lunches.

'I think I've taken a new direction,' she said. 'At least that's how it feels . . .' Tomorrow she would wake up and recall the gist of this conversation and close her eyes again, hoping that it had only been a bad dream.)

Valerie walked down New Bond Street. She walked stiffly, like an animated doll, her arms tight in to her sides, her eyes fixed straight ahead of her. There were steps at the entrance to Bennett's Hotel. For one awful moment she thought her limbs intended to disobey her and carry on walking rather than making a right turn to mount them. The liveried doorman standing at the top tipped his hat to her; she avoided his eye, believing that he might divine her purpose and turn her away.

But as soon as she'd pushed through the swing doors she found herself face to face with another one. The place was awash with footmen. Dodging between them she made her way to the reception desk and waited for attention behind a group of noisy Americans with innumerable pieces of luggage.

Dee had said, of her literary luncheon engagements: 'I can just about cope with my knees knocking and my hands trembling; it's when I open my mouth to speak and this breathy little squeak emerges that I know I'm done for.'

It was a breathy little squeak that emerged from Valerie's mouth when she finally engaged the receptionist's attention. 'Mrs Hilliard?' she said – almost.

'I beg your pardon?' said the receptionist, who was possibly the grandest person alive and had been blessed with a very long nose the better for looking down it. Valerie cleared her throat and repeated herself.

It was only by chance that she had a name to proffer. In one of the letters Ba, relaying information about Melissa's equestrienne achievements, had inserted a verbatim quotation: 'First place in the dressage section, with ninety-three marks, Melissa Hilliard'. Presumably the girl had taken her mother's married name. Valerie had immediately thought of the miniature painter. Inappropriately, she was sure: Ba was certain to be large, vivid, dominating.

Without a name, this expedition could never have taken

place. Valerie, waiting for the receptionist to check through arrivals on her computer screen, wished profoundly that Ba had not inadvertently included in her letter a handle by which she could be grasped. Valerie, hanging on for dear life to the edge of the desk, began to realise how close she was to collapsing into a heap on the floor. Consequently her immediate reaction upon being told that Mrs Hilliard was not due to arrive until the following day was one of drenching relief. She almost skipped through the revolving doors, smiled at the commissionaire, strode buoyantly past the jewellers' shops and the fine art dealers towards Green Park Tube.

It was only when she was actually seated on the train that it dawned on her that she had to decide whether to go through the ordeal again tomorrow or bow to fate and join Dee on the evening train north.

(At that precise moment Dee was scanning the shelves in the Euston Station branch of John Menzies. There was no example of her work on display. This was not surprising. Her energies of late had been dissipated in producing drivel for women's magazines and garbage for television soap-operas. But things were about to change. She positively *seethed* with ideas. She chose a biography of Oscar Wilde for the homeward journey, fiction would have been too distracting; fiction was always too distracting – and one felt that there might be the danger of subliminal influence – when one was working on one's own novel.

With her alcoholic intake topped up by two cans of lager bought on the train, she was quite able to ignore the fact that there *was* no novel.)

The gin had a delayed reaction. Its effect didn't become felt until Valerie had, after a wearisome walk and numerous checkings of her map, reached the flat. She stumbled on the stairs, had difficulty in getting the key to turn in the lock, felt vomit rising in her gullet, only just managed to make it into the bathroom and even then had to opt for the nearer washbasin rather than the further lavatory bowl.

She ran water for a long time afterwards, splashing her face, trying to clear her head. Tears mingled with the tap water that ran down her cheeks. 'Oh Richard,' she said. 'Why did you die?'

She dozed for a few minutes in a chair and when she woke she couldn't remember why she was where she was, and then light dawned: it was unfinished business that had brought her to London, and before she could change her mind she got up and went to the phone and dialled her home number and told Sophie that she would be staying another night.

('She's staying another night,' Sophie told Dee when she came to collect Pixie. 'I wonder why? She was practically monosyllabic on the phone.'

But Dee wasn't interested. Dee smelled of British Rail house wine and gin and tonic and burgundy and Courvoisier and Kestrel lager. Dee, as always when full of drink, was expansive, bonhomous, rather loud. 'Ssh,' said Sophie, 'you'll wake Pixie.'

Dee sank down on to a sofa and kicked off her shoes. 'I really think,' she said, 'that it's going to be all right.'

'I really think that I ought to call you a taxi,' Sophie said.

'No,' Dee said. 'Call Fred. It'll be cheaper.')

I shan't sleep, Valerie told herself. The effect of the drink was wearing off. It left her with a pounding headache, an upset stomach and an inability to keep warm. She turned the heating to maximum and took the duvet from the second bedroom to add to her own. (The Valerie married to Richard would have felt guilty about adding to somebody's gas bill; the Valerie betrayed by his death was certain that she would never be able to come to terms with the person she was becoming: a person who vomited into washbasins and rummaged through other people's possessions and rang TIM without leaving a ten pence piece beside the phone.)

I shan't sleep, she thought. But she did. She was fast asleep and dreaming that the house was on fire when she was woken by the bedroom door opening and the squeaking of the floorboards at the threshold and saw a dark shape silhouetted against the light from the hall.

There wasn't even the feeblest breathy squeak to be got from her paralysed vocal cords. The only movement of which her body seemed capable – and that involuntarily – was the thunderous beating of her heart.

There were women all over the capital raped and murdered in their beds. One read about it daily. It had been foolishly optimistic to assume that she might be spared such a fate. Paralysed, she awaited it.

'Christ, it's like a Turkish bath in here,' a voice said – strangely, it seemed like a familiar voice – and then the light was clicked on and the owner of the voice looked towards the bed and – obviously startled at what he saw – took a step backwards.

'I thought you were Sophie,' he said, the owner of the voice: a youngish, dark-haired man wearing jeans and one of those light linen jackets with the sleeves rolled up (so *scruffy*, Valerie had always thought).

Gradually her heartbeat slowed to its normal rhythm. If this man knew Sophie then he was hardly likely to be a nocturnal marauder – or at least an unknown nocturnal marauder. 'Where *is* Sophie?' he said. He had a slight accent. An Irish accent. She suddenly realised why his voice seemed familiar; it was the voice she'd heard on the answerphone tape, the voice that had announced its intention of returning in mid-August, the voice that had sounded at first angry and then apologetic.

Valerie had been about to say: 'She's staying with me,' and then remembered Sophie's parting instruction. 'I'm not sure,' she said. 'Abroad, I think, at the moment. She said I could borrow the flat when I came to London. Oh,' said Valerie, struck suddenly with a thought, 'You're not John Wainwright, are you?'

153

'Do me a favour,' the young man said. 'Do I look like John Wainwright?'

'I don't know what John Wainwright looks like.'

He approached the bed, stopped as soon as she gathered the duvet around her. 'It's all right,' he said. 'I'm not some nutter. My name's Dominic Roche. I used to live here. With Sophie. I've been in Ireland for the past few weeks. I've just got back. I expected her to be here. Look, I even have a key.'

He opened his hand and showed her. She looked down at it and then up at him. He was very good-looking and, for some reason, this reassured her; she didn't know why, good-looking young men were every bit as liable to be rapists and murderers as their less prepossessing counterparts.

'Should I know *you*?'

'I doubt it.'

She explained her connection with Sophie, told him she'd been unaware that Sophie was sharing the flat with someone else, apologised for startling him, said that Sophie might have warned her.

He sat down on the edge of the bed. He said, 'Well actually it's me who ought to be apologising to you. She'd have no reason to warn you. We split up, you see – a while ago. She maybe wouldn't have expected me back. You don't know where she is now?'

Valerie lowered her face until most of it was concealed by the duvet. She had never been able to lie without the accompaniment of a blush. 'No, honestly,' she said. 'Abroad, that's all she told me.'

'But you *have* seen her?'

'Yes,' said Valerie, after some thought.

'And she was all right, was she?'

'Well, apart from the virus . . .'

'Virus?'

'Yes, she's still recovering from it. Apparently it's what stopped her from going on tour. To Canada.'

154

'That's what she told you?' asked the young man, searching through his pockets until he located a packet of cigarettes and a box of matches. He said, 'That's where I'm off to in the morning.'

'Canada?'

'Right. Christ,' he said, wiping a trickle of sweat from his forehead, 'do you *need* this heat?'

She shook her head and he got up and presumably went into the kitchen to turn it off. She took advantage of his absence to don her dressing gown.

He reappeared in the doorway, carrying a big hold-all. He scratched the top of his head and said, 'Look here, is it all right if I crash in the next bedroom for the night? It's a bit late to go seeking accommodation – I've not fixed myself up with anywhere else yet. No point till I get back from Canada. I really thought she'd be here, you see.'

What could she do but nod her head in agreement and hand him the second duvet? What could she say in response to his request for her telephone number but give it to him? He said, 'I'll be back in about a month. D'you think I could have your number in case you hear from Sophie in the meanwhile? You know what she's like, don't you: just ups and leaves without a word to anyone? But she might get in touch with you, mightn't she? I really need to talk to her.'

Reluctantly, she wrote her name and number on a page of the notebook that he held out to her. Although in about a month she might well be residing elsewhere. And chances were that Sophie certainly would be.

16

Valerie

So Sophie has – or had – what they call a toy-boy. It didn't surprise me: women like Sophie always go for older men when they're young, and vice-versa. Anything to be different.

Anyway I was too bound up in my own concerns to be particularly interested. I just didn't fancy facing him across the breakfast table and continuing to lie on the subject of Sophie's whereabouts.

But by the time I woke he'd left. There was a letter and a note on the kitchen table. The letter was addressed to Sophie. The note said: 'If S turns up, could you give her this? Cheers. D.' The envelope was barely stuck down, but after yesterday's appalling lapse of standards, I wouldn't have been tempted to read the letter if it had lain face up in front of me.

I put it in my handbag in case I should overlook it before I left. I was pretty sure that whatever transpired before I left I wouldn't be thinking straight by then. I sat drinking coffee and contemplating the day ahead, dreading the thought of having to go through all the gin-drinking and screwing up of my courage once again.

To distract myself, I began to flick through a heap of old copies of *The Stage* that I'd found in a magazine rack. They were very old copies. One had in it a review of the play that Dee and I had seen Sophie in the time she got drunk and burst into tears in the restaurant. It had been an awful play and it was an awful review. I think that actors and writers must have some kind of extra layer of skin to enable them to cope with the criticism, even though Dee maintains that they actually have one *less*.

Eventually, when I'd read them cover to cover, I began, once again, to get myself ready. I felt quite calm. I couldn't figure out why I felt so calm until it dawned on me that I had convinced myself that Ba wouldn't be at Bennett's Hotel today either, that our meeting was fated not to be.

There was a different receptionist on duty at Bennett's Hotel, but stamped from the same mould: equally grand, equally long-nosed. Her vowels let her down a bit though. I noticed that when she picked up the phone and intimated to Mrs Hilliard that there was a lady – a Mrs Philips – desirous of meeting her, down in the foyer. ('Your name?' she had said, and I knew I couldn't say 'Lamb' or Mrs Hilliard might just stay forever holed up in Room 307, so I gave her my maiden name instead – presumably their intimacy had not extended to him telling her *that*.)

'She'll be down in a moment,' the receptionist said. And it was then that the fantasy evaporated, the fantasy that had enabled me to make it to the hotel: the certainty that Mrs Hilliard wouldn't be there, had no existence outside the pages of a few crumpled letters. I went to pieces: my heart pounded, my pulse raced, my limbs seemed to take on some spastic life of their own: jerking wildly in the most complete dissynchronicity. I recognised it, even as it was occurring, as a panic attack, but was powerless to stop it or avert attention from its manifestations. I heard the receptionist saying, 'Are you all right?' in the most unwilling sort of way, as though if I wasn't then that was just my hard luck, and then something merciful must have intervened because I believe I fainted.

Almost forty-eight hours with nothing but a little toast and a lot of gin – it was enough to make anyone faint; I had the justification already trembling on my lips when I came round. I came round in a little room furnished in the style of the French Empire unhappily married to the wilder shores of Chinoiserie: there were screens and stools and prie-dieus and lacquered cabinets and dragons and geishas vying with stripes and scrolls wherever the eye came to rest. I was lying on a chaise-longue and I was covered with a dark green blanket that was monogrammed in gold with the initials: 'BH'. In my confused state I assumed that this stood for Barbara Hilliard – the woman who sat at the end of the sofa, at my feet; it wasn't for quite a while that I realised it would be 'Bennett's Hotel'.

She was holding a brandy glass, this woman, and when I opened my eyes she held it towards me, but I shook my head.

'Feeling better?'

She had a very faint Australian accent, but I knew – from the way she looked – that it must be her, before ever she spoke.

'They've sent for a doctor.'

'Oh no,' I said, 'no.'

'Don't worry. Apparently there's always one on call.'

In an establishment of this splendid sort, I supposed there would be.

'You went out like a light,' she said wonderingly.

I couldn't look at her, not directly. I had to assemble a composite picture from the details gleaned from successive covert glances stolen when she looked away from me to put down the brandy glass or to check whether the doctor was on his way: smallish, dark-haired, round-faced, brown-eyed – a pretty woman. Not the Ba of my imagination at all. In fact, she looked rather like me.

The doctor arrived. He listened to my heart and my chest and the pulse at my wrist. He examined my eyes and measured my blood pressure. Then he asked me if there was any reason for my anxiety. I explained about not having eaten for a long time, pretended that I'd always been a fainter. (Mrs Hilliard had tactfully retired to the other side of the room and was examining a mock Ming vase with seemingly rapt attention.) He said. 'If I were you, I'd have a light meal and then a little rest.'

He stood up to leave. For an instant I was afraid that he might want payment, but apparently it was all part of the service.

The service was very good. No sooner had he spoken, it seemed, than a light meal (compliments of the management) was wheeled into Room 307, whither I had been persuaded to adjourn for my rest. (She walked in front of me, Barbara Hilliard. It was like walking behind myself.)

There was an omelette on the trolley, so fluffy that it barely registered weight on the fork. There was bread and butter cut so thin you could see daylight through the slices. There was cherry conserve and mineral water and China tea and anchovy toast and a bowl containing a luscious example of every kind of fruit that I knew and some that I didn't.

I made a valiant attempt but I might as well have been presented with a packet-soup, bought-pie, instant-mashed-potato Dee meal for all the appetite I could bring to it.

I gagged on every mouthful, but the more I attempted to eat, the longer I could postpone telling her my business. I saw her glancing – discreetly as she thought – at her watch. She'd obviously been in the process of unpacking when called downstairs; there were clothes draped everywhere, young clothes, some of them: skimpy, shapeless, brightly-coloured.

'Better?' she said.

My throat felt as though it was full of toast crumbs, though I hadn't eaten any of the toast. I had to clear it and clear it before I could make myself understood. And even so it was a croak that emerged: 'Is your daughter not here?'

Her eyebrows shot up. She said, 'My daughter? She's with some friends at the moment. Why? Do you know her?'

I knew that she had gained ninety-three marks in the dressage competition, that she had a gift for languages, that she had three male siblings of some sort or other. I knew that she had been conceived during some wholly insignificant time in my life. While I was, presumably, peeling potatoes and wiping noses and pushing the Twins on the swings in the park, somewhere, my husband was fathering a child upon the woman who sat opposite me, her composure now just ever so slightly disturbed.

I had stopped being nervous. I felt instead a most unexpected and peculiar fondness, as though for a co-conspirator. After all the months of pretending for strangers, I was now in the company of a woman with whom – whatever else – I had something in common. I said, 'I'm Richard Lamb's wife.'

And then, before she'd finished reacting to that information, and not exactly intentionally – for I had no real desire to be cruel, I said, 'Richard's dead.'

Her eyes opened so wide that the white was visible right round the iris, her face burned with a flush of embarrassment, her mouth opened as though there might be some appropriate response, but no sound emerged.

But power is only of use to those capable of exercising it. I heard myself saying: 'I'm sorry, I didn't mean to blurt it out like that.'

She clasped her hands in her lap, lacing the fingers together so tightly that her knuckles showed white. 'When?' she said at length, looking not at me but at her knotted fingers.

'In March. He had a heart attack.'

'And how long had you known – about me?'

She was scarcely able to manage more than a whisper. In all my long imaginings I never thought that I would have the upper hand, never saw myself as otherwise than the last-to-know wife of a philandering husband: humiliated, ridiculous. It never occurred to me that I might have had an existence in her head too, that every time she wrote his name on one of those envelopes she could possibly be fitting an appearance to me, a personality, a history, thinking of me as a rival rather than a pathetic little creature, unable to hold on to her husband's affections.

I said, 'Only since he died. I found – or, rather, I was given – some of the letters you'd written to him.'

'Oh God,' she said, 'I wasn't to know he'd *die*.' She was blaming him as I had blamed him: not so much for his infidelity as for the inconsiderate manner of his death.

'It said in your last letter that you were coming to London with – your daughter. That's why I came here.'

'Why?' she said. Her hands had been clasped together so tightly that she was having difficulty in unwinding them.

I looked away from her and through the window on to a vista of brick walls and drainpipes (an expensive hotel, but one of the cheaper rooms; I remembered the money-box on the mantelpiece: 'Melissa's European Odyssey'); I found it altogether disconcerting to look at her because it felt as though I was looking into a mirror and I kept losing my certainty as to who was the betrayer and who the betrayed. (Sophie once told me that when she had an affair with a married man she always felt guilty: a great weight of social opprobrium on her shoulders – and yet when her husband had an affair: Constantine, it was, she felt guilty then too, and ashamed, as though the whole world was looking and laughing her to scorn.)

Why had I come? Because otherwise nothing would ever be resolved: I would spend the rest of my life trying to put a face to her. Because, in a funny way, I felt I had a responsibility to inform her of his death. Because she was the only person with whom I could be perfectly honest.

'Because I need to know. Tell me. Please,' I said.

In different times, a different culture, this might have been the stuff of farce: wives, mistresses, illegitimate children, revolving doors and trousers falling down; Sophie's play, the one in which she wore a blond wig and forgot her lines, the one for which she got the terrible review, had dealt with just such a set of circumstances. But that play hadn't been funny and neither was this.

She went to the fridge and took out a miniature of whisky, Mrs Hilliard, my Antipodean almost-doppelgänger, opened it and poured it into a glass and drank deep. '*What* do you need to know?' she asked.

'Everything.'

I could tell that she wasn't a drinker any more than I was by the flicker of distaste she displayed every time she sipped her whisky. She sipped and spoke, very evenly, without much inflection.

'I used to work in public relations, arranging conferences, that sort of thing. In the Midlands. We organised one for some engineering firms. That's where I met him.'

'When?'

'Summer, 1971,' she said. She covered her eyes with her hands and said, 'Oh God, do you really want all this?'

'Yes, I do. If you wouldn't mind.'

('You, you're too polite,' Sophie says. As if there's some merit in being otherwise.)

'We couldn't see each other often, obviously. The odd weekend. Sometimes he'd steal a day mid-week. Or I would.'

(The odd weekend? But it was *I* who took the odd weekends, took the Twins to see my parents who'd moved, by then, to Yorkshire. Richard drove us there and then returned home to catch up on work. I got the picture now: hotels booked all in a flurry at the last minute, meetings at motorway service stations, couplings when he didn't even take his watch off – lazy Richard, dashing hither and thither, dressing, undressing, shaving as he drank his coffee, driving down A roads and B roads at full throttle. 'I knew Constantine had been up to no good when I looked at his mileage,' Sophie said. 'She lived in the wilds of Essex or somewhere.' Such squalid stratagems, I had thought.)

162

I moistened my lips. I said, 'Who else knew?'

She looked at me then, surprised. 'A couple of my girlfriends,' she said. 'That's about all. It was hardly broadcast material. Oh, you mean, on his side? No one, I should think. He wasn't one of those awful swap-tales-of-conquest-with-other-awful-men-in-bars sort of men, was he?'

'Wasn't he?'

'Well,' she said, 'you should know.'

'How long did it last?'

'A year or so. Until I found out I was pregnant.'

'You mean, he *dropped* you?'

She almost smiled. I suppose because of my shocked expression. She said, 'No. He wasn't *that* sort of man either – I don't think. I just knew it would be for the best if we packed it in. He wasn't going to leave you, no matter what. And I didn't fancy being either a part-time mistress or a poor brave abandoned girl. I met John while I was pregnant. He *did* want to marry me despite the cuckoo in the nest. Immediately after Melissa was born I followed him back to Australia.'

'He must have been remarkably tolerant.'

'Not really,' she said. 'He was a widower with two sons and he wanted a wife for himself and a mother for them. Another baby was neither here nor there really. We get along just fine,' she said. The way she said it made you think that she felt he was just as lucky to have met her as she was to have fallen in with him.

'What I don't understand is why you went ahead and *had* the baby. Unless . . .'

'You think I got myself pregnant to blackmail him? No. I'd have been on a hiding to nothing. I just sort of let things drift until it was too late. Started feeling maternal, I guess. It certainly wasn't because I hoped that by presenting him with another child I'd lure him away from the ones he already had.'

'You knew about them?'

'Well of course. He was a very proud father.'

'And me too?'

'Well . . .'

(Oh God! What? What had she known? How had he described me? *When* had he described me? Post-coitally? To be known by those who are unknown to you, those who, though they have never met you, carry your fate in their hands, as fragile as an egg – it's the worst sort of helplessness.)

'He wasn't disloyal. You were his wife and I – wasn't.'

She looked at me again: a long, level stare, challenging me not to believe her. I thought she might be going to say: 'After all, I wasn't the only one, was I?' I prayed for her not to say it.

She said, 'I don't suppose I'd have married him if I could have done.'

'You didn't love him?'

The ultimate wickedness: to take another woman's husband on a whim. Without even the excuse of what they call love.

'Oh I loved him all right,' she said. 'You couldn't not love Richard. He was very lovable.'

'And do you still love him?'

'It doesn't survive sixteen years apart – love.'

'But you wrote. All those years . . .'

'I wrote because he wanted me to write. And because I reckoned he did have the right to know how his daughter was getting on. I wrote maybe twice a year. And on Christmas and her birthday he'd send money and ask me to buy her something nice.'

'What did you tell her?'

'The truth. I told her the truth: that her father was married to another lady. I told her what I knew which actually wasn't very much, told her he'd felt it best if she had the chance of a proper family life, you know . . .'

'No,' I said, 'I don't know. I've no experience whatsoever of such things.'

My hostility lit a reciprocal spark. She said, quite nastily, 'It's not some Shakespearian tragedy, for heaven's sake. Melissa hasn't spent sixteen years pining for the father she's never known. Your marriage presumably survived. I'm happy. She's happy. You're happy – '

Then she realised what she'd said. 'I'm sorry,' she said, looking down into her empty glass. 'Was it sudden?' she said.

'Very.'

'I can't imagine him dead.'

'No,' I said. 'Nor can I.'

There was silence between us for minutes. The trouble was that neither of us knew the form or procedure; there ought to be a handbook for such encounters.

Eventually I said, 'This trip – weren't you afraid that your daughter might want to look him up? Or, seeing that you'd suggested meeting him, figure out who he was?'

'He'd always said he wanted to see her. I wasn't sure about it, I must say. When I didn't hear from him, I assumed he'd changed his mind . . .'

(Would they have slept together? For old time's sake? Would she have found some excuse to get Melissa out of the way and joined her body to his on one of these twin beds? How did old lovers behave towards each other after a gap of sixteen years?)

'But even if he had come and they'd met I knew he'd be discreet . . .'

'Why? Because he was such a good liar?'

(Coming back from my parents' house on Sunday evenings: 'Did you get your work done?' 'Yes, most of it. Thank goodness.' Kissing me on the cheek, lifting the boys into the air, swinging them above his head until they shrieked with delight . . . when, every time, he must have just finished washing this woman's smell from his skin, her secretions . . .)

I had started to cry. I hadn't cried properly since the day of the funeral because I knew that if I started, I might

165

never stop. 'Don't,' she said. 'Please don't. Look, what can I do?'

Tell me that it never happened. At least then I need only be angry with him for failing to provide for me. Incompetence was easier to forgive than infidelity. Wasn't it?

'Please don't,' she said again. There are some people who can't cope with tears. Richard was one of them. He'd stand on his hands, console, clown, promise you anything to stop you crying. Like most selfish, self-indulgent people, he couldn't bear to be reminded that his actions might have repercussions involving others.

I wiped my eyes. I said, 'If I hadn't come, you'd never have known, would you? You'd have carried on writing, wouldn't you? Twice a year.'

She shrugged. 'Possibly. For a while. And then I suppose I'd just have assumed that was that.'

She didn't even seem grateful for the enlightenment. How could something that meant so much to me mean so little to her? 'And what about your daughter?' I said. 'What would you have told her? That her father just couldn't be bothered to keep in touch any longer?'

It was all so casual, random, accidental; these people who caused such hurt to others for what didn't, in the end, mean very much for themselves.

'I don't know,' she said. 'John's Melissa's father. She's never been particularly curious about the real one. It was all a long time ago. He was only her *biological* father, after all. Apart from one brief glimpse just after she was born, he never even *saw* her ... Look, I know it must have come as a terrible shock to you. Especially in the circumstances. But, if you think about it logically, if I hadn't got pregnant – well, what would it have mattered: one brief affair against all the years of your marriage? Honestly?'

'Is that how you would feel if it were *your* husband?'

She didn't reply. She didn't need to. It was written all over her face: her certainty that *her* husband would never be tempted to stray from a wife as satisfactory as she was.

166

'When is your daughter due back?'

She glanced at her watch. 'Any time now,' she said. 'She couldn't wait to have a look at the sights with some friends she made on the way over. You know what kids are like . . .'

She looked uneasy. And I knew that mere vulgar curiosity must not be allowed to over-ride my need to leave before she arrived.

'I wouldn't have had this happen,' she said, Mrs Hilliard, that more successful version of myself, as she showed me to the door with a scarcely-concealed eagerness. 'Not for the world.'

I had started to cry again on the way down the stairs. The young girl that I passed looked at me curiously. Not just because of my tears, but because I was staring at her. I was staring because she was the absolute image of Richard, much more like him than the boys were. Even if I hadn't known of her existence, such was the resemblance that it would have struck me, made me wonder if I'd stumbled by chance upon some long-lost relation of his.

I stared at her until she'd disappeared from view. She'd go into Room 307 and she'd say, 'I just saw this weird woman. She looked at me like she'd seen a ghost.'

17

'I had this brilliant idea while you were away,' Sophie said. 'You say you don't want to leave this house, right? Well, why not have it converted into flats – it would make two perfectly adequate flats – then you could sell one and live in the other? It came to me while I was wheeling Pixie down the road the other day: most of the houses this size that aren't being used as schools or old people's homes have been turned into flats. What do you think?'

Valerie said, 'I have absolutely no desire to fill my house with strangers, and even if I were willing to do so, where am I supposed to go while this conversion is taking place?'

Sophie could have said, 'Well, Dee has a spare bedroom . . .' but there was no point in saying it, because the first part of Valerie's response had made reply to the second redundant. She might, however, have continued to push the idea, had not Valerie cut her short by going upstairs to bed.

She would have been happy to discuss that plan, or any other, or anything at all, so long as it meant she didn't have to think about other things: the encounter with Dominic that Valerie had reported on her return, the letters she had brought back with her.

Valerie had seemed strangely lacking in curiosity about Dominic; she had merely said, 'A friend of yours called round on Wednesday night. He nearly frightened the life out of me. He left this for you. Oh, and there were these too . . .'

Junk mail, most of it. A bank statement. A communication from her agent containing a couple of cheques (praise the Lord!), a query as to whether she was yet fit for work (though no mention of any work that she might be fit for). And a letter from the mad fan who wrote regularly whether in mental hospital or out of it. There was a postcard from Sydney from John Wainwright. There was bumf from the Edinburgh Festival and some theatre workshop or other and a reminder from the dentist that she was due for a check-up. And there was Dominic's letter and one from the Middlesex Hospital.

She set herself a test: to see how long she could hold out before opening them. Valerie handed them over at lunchtime on Friday. She put them on her bedside table next to Ellen Terry and Barbara Pym. Saturday passed, and Sunday. On Monday morning she transferred Dominic's letter to her coat pocket. At three o'clock on a wet Tuesday afternoon, in a shelter on the Promenade, while Pixie sucked contentedly on her plastic ring and made the little triumphant grunts that indicated she was in the process of filling her nappy, she succumbed to temptation. The other letter, the one from the hospital, remained on the bedside table. As time went on the temptation with that one was *not* to open it. Tomorrow, she promised herself; I'll open it tomorrow.

She read Dominic's letter quickly and then slowly. But by then an obviously deranged person had sat down beside her and was making no bones about his intention of sharing the letter's contents so she didn't get to take it in properly until she'd delivered Pixie back to Dee who was sitting at her desk in novelist mode rather than that of churner-out of soap-opera episodes. (There was a difference: something about her expression which was rather vacant as though listening for astral voices – Sophie found

169

it reminiscent of Pixie's when she was engaged in evacuating her bowels.)

Dominic had written to say that he was sorry for his behaviour, that he'd been an insensitive pig, a selfish brute, that these past weeks away from her had made him realise just what she meant to him, that he would be in touch as soon as he got back from Canada. Surely, he had written, they could get it together? Surely love was enough?

She wasn't sure whether she was glad or sorry that he'd written. She'd been furious at first when Valerie had told her about giving him her phone number, but realised that after he came back from Canada they'd be bound to bump into each other sooner or later.

'I'm really, really sorry,' he had written. Like a child. He was a child still, in many ways: the desire for instant gratification, the need for constant distraction, the conviction that absolution followed upon confession as surely as night followed day: coming home with the smell of some young actress upon him, saying, 'There's no need to get so het up about it; it didn't mean a thing.'

They were unsuited. Quite apart from the age difference. He needed someone of the same type as himself: someone as happy to be uncommitted as he was.

And she didn't need him. If she needed anybody it was a mature man, a man who would cosset her and nurse her through whatever she had to go through and understand, intuitively, about women's problems. Someone like Dee's Fred perhaps.

If she needed anybody.

The pain started in the taxi going back to Valerie's. Stress, she supposed. Bloody Dominic! She fished out the tablets from her handbag; she had thought, during these recent quiet, calm, Pixie-wheeling days, that she might not need them again.

'Valerie!' she called, going from room to room. Valerie was in bed. Again. She knocked at the door, opened it. 'Valerie?' she said. 'I thought you were out. Didn't you hear the phone? It was the estate agent. He wants to know what you intend to do about some offer or other. I asked him to ring back later. Valerie?'

Ever since returning from London, Valerie had more or less taken to her bed. At first Sophie had said, 'What's up, Valerie?' And then it occurred to her that perhaps she was witnessing the breaking down, at long last, of Valerie's defences, the beginning of a natural period of mourning. So she stopped asking and started making a great many cups of tea which she carried upstairs (though she very often brought them down untouched).

But Sophie was not cut out for letting things take their natural course. Sophie's temperament inclined her more towards jumping into the midst of things with both feet. After a week she said, once more, 'Valerie, what *is* up?' and put on the light and gazed upon a most unprepossessing spectacle: pretty, neat Valerie, who had always been so meticulous, now with her hair gone lank and greasy, her big brown trustful eyes small and red from weeping and encircled with dark rings, her nightdress sweat-stained and crumpled.

She looked a wreck.

'What is it?' Sophie asked again.

'Nothing.'

'Right. I'm calling the doctor.'

'Don't be absurd.'

Sophie began to flick through the phone book. Valerie began to cry. 'Why,' she said, 'can't you just leave me?'

Sophie had aimed for, but never quite achieved, that piteous note in her Ophelia with the RSC. God, that was years ago! She hadn't been invited back for another season. It wasn't that she couldn't do Shakespeare; there'd been her Rosalind for Adrian Bailey; it was just that she wasn't Ophelia in a million years and she'd been too young and inexperienced to know it. A bad agent, a bad piece of miscasting . . . Sophie thought: if I really persevere, I can probably date the decline in my career to the time when I recited Mary Had a Little Lamb on the platform at infant school.

'I can't just leave you,' she said to Valerie who was making choked little whimpering noises into the duvet.

'Why not?'

'Because you look terrible, you haven't eaten properly for a week, and because I don't know what to do for you.'

'You don't have to do anything.'

'OK. Fine. I'll just leave you to starve yourself to death. Idiot!'

'Oh yes. I am an idiot. I've always been an idiot, haven't I?'

Sophie settled down at the side of the bed suspecting that some kind of unburdening was imminent. Valerie would reach for a tissue and wipe her nose and say again, 'Please, just go away and leave me alone,' meaning: 'Coax it from me, this secret that causes me to lie in bed all day, turning my face to the wall.'

'You won't tell Dee?' Valerie said at length, after a lot of tears and a lot of tissues.

Sophie didn't tell Dee for almost a week. She told her then only because she was starting to get seriously worried. Unburdening, Sophie had always believed, led to catharsis and catharsis meant healing and recovery, but in Valerie's case, this normal pattern of events did not appear to be taking place. Indeed, she had said herself: 'I thought that by going to see her – Barbara – it would somehow be resolved, made right.'

'Cancelled out?' Sophie had said.

'Yes, I suppose so. But how could it be?'

And Valerie had pulled the damp sheet over her face.

So worried was she that Sophie made a point of taking the Fortral with her whenever she went out and looked through Valerie's medicine cabinet, but there was nothing more sinister contained within it than the odd aspirin, indigestion tablet and preparation for the treatment of vaginal thrush.

'You must give me your word,' Sophie said to Dee, 'that you won't let on to her that I told you. I'm only telling you because I'm afraid she might do something silly.'

'Top herself?' Dee said with her customary delicacy. 'Valerie's not the type.'

'What is the type?'

'Oh, your hysterics, attention-seekers, impulsive people,' Dee said with a careless confidence, choosing to forget a time when life had seemed just too difficult to contemplate continuing with it, and one's personality characteristics, whether hysterical, impulsive or otherwise, had been entirely irrelevant.

It wasn't, after all, Sophie told herself, as though she was *really* breaking Valerie's confidence: Dee had known all about Richard's womanising for years. The only surprise was the child. Dee said that the child put a different complexion on it.

'I don't see why.'

'No, you wouldn't,' Dee said, drawing mongol faces in the margins of her manuscript. 'You've never had one.'

'I *mean* that the infidelity's as real whether or not it results in a child.'

'Anyway,' Dee said, 'you're worrying unnecessarily. You don't tell me that all these years she never suspected what he was up to?'

'*You* didn't know about this Barbara?'

'No. But there was that woman in Wellington Road. And before that the one who worked in the office at the Prudential Insurance. And remember that time in London – where was it we saw him with that girl?'

'L'Escargot. Upstairs.'

He'd been so engrossed that he'd never even noticed them. The girl had looked utterly besotted. Young girls, Sophie had thought, had always found him attractive and would continue to do so. It was only when they got older that they realised that the looks disguised a lack of depth, a want of resonance. Richard was perfect for being in love

173

with when you were young; the ideal candidate for a brief encounter. Dee, who had once been a young girl in love with Richard, had looked across to his table and endeavoured to recall just what it was about him that had caused her to mope and pine and weep behind a sand dune. She could only conclude that it was because he was the one that everybody wanted. She could have set her sights lower: the boys to whom Sophie introduced her at those teenage parties, but they were also-rans and if she couldn't have the best then she didn't want anybody at all. No one had known about her passion for him, least of all Richard himself.

'I think he must have been carrying on from the time they got back off their honeymoon,' she said. 'Although I wasn't around then, so I don't know.'

There were other things she didn't know, Sophie thought, among them the fact that Richard had been carrying on since well before returning from his honeymoon.

She changed Pixie, powdered her bottom and laid her in the pram. 'Phie, phie, phie,' Pixie said. At least, the sound that emerged through the bubbles she was making resembled the last reiterated syllable of Sophie's name – at least, Sophie thought so.

She walked to the children's playground amongst young mothers, sat beside them on benches as, prams parked, they watched their older children stumbling about in the sandpit or climbing on to the swings. They looked at her a little curiously: she was clearly on the old side to be Pixie's mother and yet not old enough to be taken for her grandmother. Sophie rather relished the ambiguity; the enigmatic pose was one that had eluded her thus far: she had always been too impatient and impulsive to allow anyone time to wonder about her.

The sun came out. She put on her dark glasses and sat smoking a cigarette and watching the mothers and the children and wondering if it would ever have been possible for her to have enjoyed so-called normal life: marrying young, producing babies, being content to keep house and await some man's return to it.

As Valerie had done. An unenviable lot, Sophie and Dee had always maintained. They had scoffed at Valerie's play-group, coffee-morning, school-run, supermarket, golf-club way of life. But there had been times: playing to empty houses in the provinces, reading some snide review, being asked: 'Should I have heard of you?' when they couldn't keep the envy from contaminating their scorn. Valerie might be married to a man who did not keep himself wholly unto her, but despite his philandering, he respected the duties of partnership: when Valerie had good news, she could share her rejoicing; when she needed to cry, there was always a shoulder available.

And perhaps Richard's philandering had been Valerie's fault, Sophie thought, closing her eyes against a jag of pain beneath her ribs. (If she ignored it, it might go away.) But she only had his side of the story, and the allocation of blame depended upon whether you believed that one of the obligations of marriage was a commitment to conjugal relations: if the wife wouldn't do the business then who could blame the husband for straying?

Valerie had certainly refused to do the business before marriage. Valerie, according to Richard, had been grossly under-sexed. They had discussed Valerie's lack of libido at length. In fact, Sophie probably knew more about Valerie's sex-drive than she did herself.

While Pixie slept and snored in the summer sunshine, Sophie remembered another summer some twenty-five years ago. It was the summer at the end of which Dee had suddenly and inexplicably disappeared and she, Sophie, had first developed her stomach ulcer.

They'd told her to take a term off school, to rest. The exams were over, so she wasn't missing anything import-ant in the scholastic sense. But she missed the company. During the day, at least. The hotel where her mother worked was full of holidaymakers so *she* was scarcely ever home. Valerie, as head girl, was busy both during school hours and afterwards helping to organise end-of-term activities. Dee, oddly enough, was ill too.

Only Richard was also at a loose end. Having taken his Oxbridge Entrance the previous autumn, his time was his own. His father had hoped that, until he went up, he might go into the factory and familiarise himself with the workings of what was to be, after his education had been suitably furthered, the source of his livelihood. 'He can stuff that,' Richard had said. He preferred to read Baudelaire and Rimbaud and attempt to emulate their accomplishments.

But for him the writing of poetry was not a purely private matter. Reaction was required. And Valerie, who was involved in the school play or the concert or the debate, never seemed to have a minute to spare. Besides, she was on the Science side. When he quoted Dorothy Parker at her: 'And I'll stay off Verlaine too; he was always chasing Rimbauds,' she hadn't the least idea what he was talking about.

So he took to visiting the ever-available Sophie. She and her mother lived in a studio-flat then. She remembered sunlight streaming through the skylight, illuminating his grave face as he recited his verses. She remembered his pale blue cashmere jersey – she was envious and begged it from him. (Usually in the holidays she'd get a job in Woolworth's or serving teas in the Marine Gardens Café, but this summer she was confined to barracks, so money was tight. She wasn't very good at doing without, so when she started going about with Graham Boyd who was thirty-five and drove a scarlet MG and had money to throw around, and he showed an inclination to throw some of it in her direction in return for her displays of affection, she never thought to refuse. He had more than enough and she had none; it was therefore redistribution of wealth and, as such, socially desirable.)

She remembered lying on a sofa with the sleeves of Richard's blue jersey knotted loosely around her shoulders while he read to her. She didn't remember much about the poems except that certain words seemed to crop up fairly regularly: 'sombre', 'fervid', 'yesternight', 'thirsting', 'immemorial'.

Sometimes he got her to read them to him. After all, she was the acknowledged queen of the verse-speakers, the one whose trophies – tarnishing for lack of polish – crowded the shelves of the bookcase. Occasionally, problems with scansion or rhyme made it difficult, but mostly she managed quite well. But it was boring. Even for one as in love with her own voice as Sophie. 'Best to leave them for a spell,' she'd say. 'Go back to them. See how they read then. Have some nut brittle,' she'd say. (Her mother was at that time being squired by a man who was in confectionery.) '*I* can't.'

She was supposed to rest and avoid stress and adhere to a diet of milk puddings and steamed fish. Don't, don't, don't, the doctor had said, but he never said don't indulge in sex because, as far as he knew, such a warning was unnecessary.

It started out with talking about Valerie. In telling her about Valerie's sexual coldness he worked himself up into a state of excitation. 'She makes me feel as though it's *abnormal* to want – you know.'

Sophie, who had lost her virginity some three years before to a judge of verse-speaking competitions on his car rug spread at a secluded spot at the far side of the pinewoods, and who had quite enjoyed the experience, did know. His excitement was contagious. Before long she'd unknotted the sleeves of his jumper and cast it off. Together with her cap-sleeved blouse, her pink checked gingham skirt, broderie-anglaise camisole top and petti-coat, Maidenform bra, stockings, suspender belt and Aertex school knickers.

His unsureness concerning the geography of female

private parts and the prematurity of his ejaculation made her suspect that he'd been a virgin. But he soon set out to remedy that state of affairs. Every afternoon he'd come up to the flat, read a little poetry, bewail Valerie's frigidity and then take off his clothes and climb on top of her.

Almost, but not quite, straight afterwards he'd dress and leave. Sometimes he'd arranged to meet Valerie near school. Sophie would take the rice pudding or the fish pie that her mother had dashed home at lunchtime to prepare out of the oven, eat it, put the dirty dishes into the sink and then get herself ready to meet Graham Boyd inside The Goat and Compasses, where she'd undo all the day's digestive good by drinking barley wine. Later, in bed in his flat, she'd pay for the drinks and the clothes and the perfume that he bought her.

It had been a weird summer: the sunlight in the afternoon as Richard entered her body; Graham's bedroom spinning around at night – the effect of the barley wine – as he did the same. It was the same act but performed so differently: her afternoon lover so importunate, her night-time seducer cool and controlled. (But neither of them took any precautions; she often wondered afterwards, when she knew better, just how she'd managed to escape getting pregnant. Perhaps, she thought, it was like money: the bad driving out the good. Or was it vice-versa?)

She never felt cheap, or used, or despoiled, or disloyal to Valerie; she never felt anything apart from mild curiosity and the requisite degree of sexual desire. It was a summer out of time, out of context. In October she left for LAMDA, at the same time as Richard for Cambridge. Graham Boyd she never saw again. And, Valerie, presumably, remained in ignorance for, three years later, when Mr and Mrs Philips were happy to invite her to the wedding of their daughter Valerie Ann to Richard Jonathon Lamb, he'd drawn her aside after he'd finished cutting the cake and said, 'I know I can rely on you, Sophie. To be discreet.' He'd looked so unfamiliar in his morning coat and sponge-bag trousers that she'd scarcely recognised him as the boy in the pale blue jumper and the permanent state of tumescence, and couldn't, for a second, figure out what he meant. When light dawned, she'd lit a Gitane and said in her most theatrical manner, 'Darling, discretion is my watchword.'

And continued to keep it that way.

Pixie's eyelids fluttered, her nose twitched and her eyes opened. She looked bewildered as she always did when she woke, and then she saw Sophie and she smiled. Sophie rose to her feet. 'Come on, my precious,' she said. 'Let's go back for our lunch.'

She hadn't really expected Valerie to be out of bed, and she wasn't. The breakfast dishes were still in the sink. She propped Pixie in a nest of cushions on the sofa and shouted up the stairs: 'Valerie, are you ever going to come down here again?'

She wanted to say: 'Valerie, it doesn't matter. Richard has slept with many women – including me – without it mattering. I doubt whether this Ba is the exception.'

Of course she couldn't say it, least of all the 'including me' part. Even as she thought of it, she thought also of Dominic coming in after some foray between another woman's legs, saying, 'I don't know what you're getting so het up about. It didn't mean a thing.'

It mattered to Valerie because Valerie had loved Richard. And Dominic's infidelity had mattered too. Was that also because *she* loved *him*? She'd always been what Constantine had called 'insanely jealous' and Hawley had described as 'pathologically paranoid'. This made it difficult for her to distinguish between love and mere ego-gratification. She closed her eyes while Pixie's beef and rice baby dinner warmed through on the gas and saw his face: young, handsome, cocky. He'd left her three months ago. Or she'd thrown him out. He'd been playing around, yet again. 'Well if I can't get it from you,' he'd shouted, 'what am I supposed to do?'

'I can't help the condition I'm in,' she'd shouted in reply.

'Your condition! Your condition! When are you ever not in a condition?' he'd yelled at her, cramming his clothes into a hold-all.

They'd been together, off and on, for nearly two years and, she had to admit, during that time the opportunities for normal sexual relations had been severely limited.

But if *he'd* loved *her* it wouldn't have mattered. People stayed faithful to paraplegics and accident victims in comas and persons who no longer knew what day it was and kept putting the shovel into the fridge.

Though perhaps they weren't people whose partners were fourteen years older than themselves.

When she was a child, standing in line with Dee at the barre in Madame Bertola's Academy of Dance, she'd been hired for two pounds ten a week to be part of the chorus in a pro-am production of *Maid of the Mountains*. She didn't remember much about it except for the refrain of one song: 'It's when he thinks that he is past love, it is then he meets his last love. And he loves her as he's never loved before.'

She had thought then, at the age of twelve, that those were the most tenderly optimistic sentiments she'd ever heard expressed. It had taken years for her to realise that it was not necessarily the case that the older one got, the better things became.

Anyway, the song referred to 'he' not 'she', as did all songs of that sort.

18

Dee

I rode the train back from London as urgently as if I had been carrying the good news from Ghent to Aix. In my head, I was repeating, over and over again, 'It will be all right now.' No need for drastic action, change of plan, promises made that I'd later regret.

Once before I'd been seriously stuck, almost physically incapable of forcing the pen to make marks on the paper. I'd been involved with a man then who wanted to marry me. There were bills outstanding and Tom needed shoes and I thought I might have to do it, but thank God there was a last-minute reprieve: I wrote one sentence and then another, and so on and they formed a chapter, and the man got fed up with my prevarications and married somebody else.

Of course that man wasn't Fred, wasn't a patch on Fred. So maybe the situation isn't comparable.

The euphoria soon evaporated. I tried all sorts of tricks to recreate it: I had my typewriter overhauled, bought a carton of the only sort of ball-point pens that I can work with, I even rang Fred and said, 'I'm not going to be able to see you quite so often for a while. I simply must get cracking on this new book.'

Despite this, all I seemed able to do was interrupt myself. I made cups of coffee one after the other, I mowed the lawn until it was bald. I hoovered carpets and cleaned windows and sorted out all my correspondence and emptied a wardrobe for Oxfam.

After a week of manic house-cleaning and drawer-clearing and caffeine-poisoning, I rang Fred again and said, 'Why don't you come round tonight? I need a break.' Fred, coolly – and understandably – said that he had a prior engagement, but being Fred: ever-optimistic in his interpretation of my signals, came round afterwards, bringing a bottle of wine with him.

'How's it going?' he said.

It would have been too cruel to tell him that I'd been eschewing his company merely for the sake of sorting through some moth-eaten jerseys and getting my bills in date-order, so I said, 'It's going. Let's leave it at that, shall we?' And he did, because being a bookseller he'd met authors and knew that you mustn't ask them about their current work in case its inspiration took fright and fled.

Besides, he wanted to talk about something else. A new approach to an old refrain. He was ever so subtle about it, but I gathered that something Sophie had told him while I was in London had convinced him that to succeed with me he must first devote himself to winning my trust. This apparently involved treating me the way they treat potentially violent patients in locked wards just until they've got their arms into the straitjackets: a kind of there, there – I understand all about it and know what's best for you – approach. It would have riled me at the best of times.

'It must have been a really cosy little chat that you had with Sophie,' I said. I hate people trying to tell me about me, particularly when they aren't in possession of sufficient of the facts to be qualified for the job.

That Fred was in possession of one particular fact was obvious from the pitying way he was looking at me. I cannot *bear* to be pitied. Damn and blast Sophie. Though she probably thought she wasn't telling him anything that couldn't be got quite easily from other sources. She probably thought she was helping: Sophie the match-maker. I remembered the matches she'd tried to make for me years ago: Andrew and Mario and Colin and Anthony. She'd always been well-intentioned. More's the pity.

'So what's she been saying to you? Did she tell you that I was a bastard, like my son after me and his daughter after him? Unto the third generation. Do you think that Pixie will get married and break the pattern?'

He sat nursing his glass and I knew that she'd told him more than that.

'It was my fault,' he said at length. 'I asked her.'

'Snooping,' I said.

'No, just trying to understand why you see me as some kind of threat.'

'You sound,' I said, 'like something I might write.'

He pushed his hair back from his forehead (a rather endearing gesture that he displays whenever he's embarrassed) and said, 'I think you tend to see everyone as a threat, not just me. But it's only me that I'm concerned about. Because I love you.'

There are times when that declaration is music to my ears, and times when it makes me squirm. I said, 'What do you mean: threat?'

'Your fear of closeness, the way there's always a part of you that you keep to yourself, as though it's so vulnerable that you daren't show it . . .'

'Christ,' I said, 'I go to bed with you, don't I? How much closer can I get?'

He said, 'Prostitutes sleep with their clients.' After a pause he said, 'That's sometimes how I feel: like a client.'

'And this disabling personality problem, this crippling character defect, stems from the fact that I was born a bastard, does it?'

He met my eyes. He wasn't a coward. He'd been in Aden, I believe, and Cyprus. All his jokes about never having heard a shot fired in anger were just that: jokes. But he dared not tell me what else he knew unless I opened the way for him to do so and I certainly wasn't going to do that.

'Why can't you just let things *be*?' I said. 'We're happy enough as we are, aren't we?'

'No,' he said. '*You're* happy, I'm not.'

'Well then, the solution to that problem lies in your own hands, doesn't it?'

'Is that what you really want?'

'I really want not to be blackmailed.'

'I'm not blackmailing you. You're blackmailing yourself. Dee,' he said, 'I don't think my demands are in any way extortionate, or odd, or untoward. I want to marry you. Because I love you and because I'm tired of being on my own. Because it would make sense: financially, practically. Because it's what people *do* . . .'

'I've never done what people do.'

'You don't have to make a religion of it,' he said.

It escalated into a row, of course, despite his intention to treat me with kid gloves. Voices were raised. I had the small satisfaction of being able to say, 'Listen! Now you've woken the baby.' He said, 'Are you planning on spending the rest of your life on your own?' 'Yes,' I said. 'Probably. I shall turn into one of those peculiar old women that you see.' 'I see you getting older and colder,' he said, 'and regretting it like hell. What's wrong with me? Is it because I'm a cripple?' I said, 'Don't be bloody silly. It's nothing to do with that. It's nothing to do with you . . .' 'Isn't it?' he said. 'Who are you waiting for then, Dee?'

I told him to go and he went, striding away from me as fast as he could – though his leg somewhat hampered what was meant to be a theatrical exit.

My head was pounding. One shouldn't combine good wine with a bad row. I took two aspirins and went to bed and tried to conjure up soothing images that might induce sleep but the only one that sprang to mind was that of Fred and Sophie earnestly swapping their bits of information about me, saying 'Ah yes' and formulating some logically-satisfactory equation: 'Dee grew up in a totally false situation, lived a lie from the very beginning, therefore it is not to be wondered at that the defences she built up to cope with the ambiguity are now quite impregnable.'

Of course Fred is right when he says that I am afraid of closeness. The bigger the skeleton and the darker the cupboard, the more careful one has to be to keep other people away from them. And for so long I lived in a terror of people finding out. They knew all along, of course; *they'd* been wondering all along if I did.

In fact, I can't remember a time of not knowing: I knew that I was being brought up by my Auntie B – that was the official version; that was one kind of truth. And I knew also that the other kind, the true truth, tacitly acknowledged, was that at the end of the war my so-called Auntie B, hitherto a quiet, reserved woman of immaculate reputation, had had a brief affair with a married Canadian airman who was stationed at St Wilfred's, during the time when it was requisitioned for troops and before it became a sanitorium. (There was just one photograph, hidden at the back of a drawer: an air-gunner, pencil moustache, nice eyes.) He went back home, she found herself pregnant. She went away too and became a mother. My mother. But when she came back it was as my aunt.

She had a story ready to explain me: that I was the child of distant relations who'd been killed in an accident, but it didn't fool anybody. Why then did she persist with it? Because, I suppose, the alternative was to expose herself to overt, rather than covert, pity and scorn and ostracism. Because she needed a construct to make her life liveable. Of course, this alternative truth depended – as I got older – upon my collusion. I realised that. Only once did I default from our unspoken understanding. It was when she found out that I was pregnant, when she was screaming at me and hitting me with a saucepan, a brush, anything that came to hand. I said, covering my face with

185

my hands: 'You hypocrite! It's only what happened to you, isn't it?'

She hit me really hard then. With the shovel. It was more than she could bear. I had made her ashamed of me. And that was a reversal of our normal relationship; it was I who was ashamed of her: because she was old and unfashionable, because she was poor and her livelihood depended on being nice to women like Valerie's mother, because she had involved me in her web of lies, spun so that she could delude herself into believing that she'd retained some self-respect.

'I'd rather you were dead,' she'd said to me that day, after she'd hit me with the shovel and I was mopping the blood from the cut above my eye and retching into the sink. All her careful nurturing, all the Virol and Scott's Emulsion and tap shoes and ballet lessons and tailored coats with velvet collars, all the treadling far into the night until her eyes went, so that I could go horse-riding and have a tennis racquet – brought to nought.

A double dose of shame would have been too much for her. That was why, when I had decided, in turn, that nothing would induce me to give Tom up for adoption, I didn't turn my footsteps in the direction of home, but sought instead anonymity. I kept in touch. And when she could, she'd send me a little money, though she'd started to be ill by then and wasn't able to work much. It was ten years before I returned and then only because she was almost totally incapacitated and there was nobody else to look after her. During those ten years: between '64 and '74, the world had changed a great deal, and a woman with a child and no husband was hardly likely to raise eyebrows, even in Ferryside Lane.

She was in a bad way. Her medication had to be increased all the time. It induced in her symptoms that resembled schizophrenia. Tom was disturbed by them, and her. Even the doctor suggested that a hospital might be the best place for her. But I knew my duty. She had kept me and raised me, and raised me well, according to her lights, when she could have given me away. I owed it to her at least to see that she could finish her days in the bosom of her family.

She shook like a leaf in the wind. Mostly she was demented. She scarcely recognised me. And ten years of fighting for myself and Tom to survive had made me hard – no doubt about it. But once, just before she died, she managed to say to me: 'I did it for the best,' and looked at me so beseechingly that I wanted to cry, to hold her and try to communicate to her poor befuddled brain that I understood why she'd lied, why – thinking that she was saving me from a worse fate ('Diana Wyatt's a bastard!') – she'd placed me in such an invidious position.

'Ontological insecurity,' Fred probably said to Sophie, referring to the effects of my upbringing. 'Existential anguish.' And Sophie, being fairly ill-educated due to lazy-mindedness, would have said, 'Who's dead?' or, 'Yes, we had one but the wheel came off.'

Well maybe it's true. But it's not also true that I am cold and incapable of loving. I resented my Auntie B, I was ashamed of her, I hated her for what she'd made of me, but I loved her too for loving me. I love Tom. I might even, given time and a following wind, get to love Pixie.

And I loved, oh how I loved – someone else.

Someone else, who left me at a railway station, saying that he'd be back.

He never did come back. But Fred was uncannily near the mark when he asked me who I was waiting for.

Because I am still waiting.

19

'Pixie's sort of – snuffling,' Dee said. '*Ought* you to take her out, do you think?'

'Fresh air's supposed to be good for colds, isn't it?' Sophie said.

'If you say so.'

She wasn't going to argue, not if it meant another hour or two to devote to her work – or, alternatively, to defrosting the fridge, or cleaning out the cupboard under the stairs.

'How's the Begum?' she asked. 'Attempted suttee yet?'

'Pretty much the same. And it's not a joking matter. I feel that she might just try it as soon as my back is turned.'

'Is that why you're staying on?'

Dee suspected that Sophie had absolutely no reason for going back: no BBC Television series, no Zeffirelli film, not even a voice-over.

'We're going to have to do something,' Sophie said.

'Such as?'

'I don't know. What *do* you do if someone looks as though they might be having a breakdown?'

Change their lives, Dee thought. Alter their circumstances. Failing that, call a doctor who will prescribe pills to block the take-up of certain chemicals circulating within the brain. The scenery remains the same but the colours of the lenses through which it is observed are substituted for those of a more cheerful hue.

'Could you come round later on?' Sophie said, dabbing at Pixie's runny nose with a tissue.

'Me? What can I do? I'm supposed to be in the dark, remember?'

'Not any more. I told her I'd told you. I thought it might produce *some* sort of reaction. She just shrugged her shoulders. Perhaps you can talk some sense into her. There's the estate agent on the phone by the minute. And somebody from the bank. I can't keep putting them off. I thought of getting in touch with the Twins, but I couldn't tell *them* the reason she's taken to her bed. Anyway there doesn't seem to be an address . . .'

'I know the feeling,' Dee said grimly.

'So you will?'

'I'm *trying* to get a book written,' Dee said, picking up a pen as she said it as if to emphasise the seriousness of her intentions. As she had been scrubbing the kitchen shelves when Sophie arrived, this demonstration was fairly unconvincing.

'Fair enough,' Sophie said. 'So if I take Pixie out now you'll have all afternoon free for it. So an hour or so later on isn't going to put you back too drastically, is it?'

There was really no answer to that. Sophie pushed the pram through the garden gate and Dee put the symbolic ball-point pen back on the mantelpiece and went to finish her shelves, scrubbing extra hard to assuage the guilt that she felt every time she picked up some implement that was not a tool of her trade.

The areas of guilt were limitless. Fred came by while she was up to her armpits in suds. It was half-day closing. He usually did the books on half-day closing. 'I've kicked them into touch,' he said. 'I'd rather see you. I'm not interrupting?'

It was rather difficult, in the circumstances, to claim that he was. Besides he looked so *nice*, standing there in

189

the doorway. He was nice. Hence her guilt. Far better to have truck with rotters, if one must have truck at all, then one would feel no compunction about treating them shabbily.

'Let's have a cuppa,' she said, and put the kettle on, gladly instead of grudgingly for a change.

'Fred,' she said as she waited for it to boil, 'hypothetical question: what would you do if you suspected that someone you knew was close to having a breakdown?'

'It would depend,' he said, 'on how well I knew them and how close they were.'

'Does one have the right to interfere?'

'Again, it would depend upon the seriousness of the situation. If it were you and me, well I'd do everything in my power to keep you safe.'

'Oh can't we keep it away from the personal?' she said.

'Everything's personal,' he replied. 'In the final analysis.'

After they'd drunk their tea he said he'd leave her in peace to get on. 'I'll see you on Thursday,' he said. He was driving down to a book fair in London early the next day. 'Miss me?' he'd say when he got back. And perhaps she would. But not as much as he'd have liked.

She finished her shelves and then she said to herself, 'I'll give it an hour. I'll sit at my desk and really give it a go. If it's a total dead loss then I'll go to Valerie's.'

An hour later she was backing the car out of the garage.

As she drove to Valerie's house, she was thinking wistfully about the vague assortment of ideas that she'd recited so glibly to her editor over lunch in Soho Square. She was thinking about whether Fred's niceness outweighed his irritating persistence. And she was thinking about Valerie: poor old Valerie, first up the creek financially and now being forced into an acknowledgement of Richard's infidelity. Anyone but Valerie, complacent Valerie, would have put a stop to it or left him years ago. Surely it wasn't possible that she really had been unaware? Wives were, traditionally, supposed to be the last to know, but she and Sophie had just somehow assumed that Valerie was content to turn a blind eye.

She was deep in thought and consequently not paying proper attention to the road. She had thought that the Pelican crossing was clear of pedestrians when, at the last moment, a woman dashed across it and she had to brake sharply to avoid a collision.

'You stupid cow!' she called after the woman – it was Sophie – who had disappeared into a throng of tourists at the entrance to the Pier.

What was Sophie doing on the Promenade? And where was Pixie? When she reached Valerie's and rang the bell and it was Sophie who answered the door, she stood for a moment or two dumbstruck.

Eventually she said, 'How did you get back so quickly?'

'Back so quickly from where?'

'From the Promenade. I nearly ran you over.'

'I haven't been anywhere near the Promenade.'

'I tell you, I nearly ran you over – '

Sophie looked at her closely. She said, 'I've been back here since about half-past three. Ask Valerie, if you don't believe me – if she's aware of my presence, that is. She must have heard Pixie though, she's been crying. You want your glasses changing. Or else take more water with it.'

'But she looked exactly like you, this woman.'

'Well they do say we all have a double.'

'Weird!' Dee said. 'Really weird!'

She kept saying it until it got on Sophie's nerves.

'For heaven's sake, shut up! Whoever it was most probably looked nothing like me; they never do, these supposed doubles. Somebody once told me I looked like that old bag Mary Murdoch. Just because she played my sister when I was Blanche in *Streetcar*. I wouldn't care, but she's about fifteen years older than me and as butch as they come . . .'

'Is Mary Murdoch the one who was Rosa Dartle in that

telly *David Copperfield* yonks ago?' Dee said. 'Actually she does look a bit like you.'

'She's got a *squint*, for Christ's sake!' Sophie shrieked. 'Anyway, shut up about Mary Murdoch. Just go upstairs and do something about the Sleeping Beauty.'

Valerie was neither sleeping nor beautiful. Valerie was staring at the wall. She had the greasy, unwholesome look of one who hasn't seen daylight for some time. She did however turn to look as Dee entered the room.

'Just thought I'd pop in to say hello,' Dee said, without any attempt to make it sound convincing.

Valerie did not return her greeting. She just said in a dull tone that matched her dull expression: 'Did *you* know?'

'Did I know what?' Dee said cautiously.

'You know. About Richard and that woman and the child. Were you one of the ones that knew?'

'No,' Dee said, truthfully.

'It's not knowing who knows and who doesn't,' Valerie said, 'that's the worst.'

'I don't suppose anybody else did know. Does it really matter, anyway? It was all a long time ago and you must stop dwelling on it, otherwise you're going to end up in the funny farm, never mind the workhouse.'

(Sophie, eavesdropping, cringed.)

'You can't lie here for ever,' Dee said.

'Why not?'

'You know very well why not. You've got to stop looking backward and start looking forward. Look to the future.'

'What future?' Valerie said mournfully.

The tears had started to flow again. They flowed effortlessly, dripped off her chin, drenched the front of her sordid nightdress and the quilt cover beneath. She said, as they fell, 'What future? A future on my own, with no money? A future of hardship? I can't even look back for comfort because the past was all a lie . . .'

192

But Dee had stopped listening halfway through this speech. 'Hardship!' Dee said. 'You don't know the meaning of the word.'

(Sophie, behind the door, thought: Cue for entrance, if ever I heard one, and entered.)

'. . . you've got a family,' Dee was saying, 'you've got friends. So you had a husband who was a bit too keen on nookie, and couldn't add up very well . . . It's hardly the end of the world, is it?'

Dee had once wept for love of Richard Lamb. Afterwards, after she'd gone away and grown up and returned home again, she'd been mortified by the memory of it. Grown up, he inspired in her only resentment: if it hadn't been for Richard Lamb's rejection of her (the fact that he'd been unaware of her passion for him was no excuse; he should have known, instinctively); if it hadn't been for that, then she'd never have been rescued from behind a sand dune, never transferred her affections, been abandoned . . . Her defence against the mortification and resentment aroused by those memories had always been to put him down.

'No big deal,' she said. 'No reason to act like a dying duck in a thunderstorm.'

A tear dripped from Valerie's chin. Tender gestures towards those of her own sex had never come easily to Sophie. Nevertheless, she took a corner of the sheet and gently wiped Valerie's face with it. 'Dee's right,' she said. 'Feeling sorry for yourself isn't going to make any difference. It's only preventing you from facing up to things.'

The tears fell as fast as they were wiped away. Valerie said, 'What am I going to do with the rest of my life?'

And Sophie, whose patience was wearing thin, due, in no small measure, to the fact that she was in a good deal of pain, said, 'At least you've *got* a rest of your life.'

They heard Pixie, from below, starting to cry. 'You go, Sophie,' said lazy Dee. 'You're better with her than I am.'

But this time even Sophie, who had discovered her

maternal instincts so late in life, had no success. Pixie cried from five o'clock until seven without respite. Nothing they did could appease her. She refused food, ignored cajolement or distraction, did not respond favourably to her back being rubbed or her nappy being changed. Sophie trod the carpet, to and fro, rocking her, singing anything that came into her head: Brahms' Lullaby, Frère Jacques, Oh Susannah and Polly-Wolly-Doodle and Camptown Races until Dee was prompted to enquire whether she'd ever had a part in a *Black and White Minstrel Show*. 'And it's "I bet my money on a bobtail nag, somebody won on the bay," not "I *put* my money on a bobtail nag, somebody *bet* on the bay."'

They argued about it for a while. Then Sophie confessed that for years she'd thought it was Kemp Town Races, as in Brighton.

Meanwhile Pixie cried.

Eventually Sophie went upstairs to find out whether there was a thermometer in the house. Valerie, head buried in the pillows, said no. There was, however, somewhere, one that the Twins had used to test the temperature of the water in the tank when they kept tropical fish.

'Pixie's not a guppy,' Sophie said, and came downstairs and told Dee that Valerie was further off her trolley than she'd originally supposed. 'Mind you,' she said, 'I can never get thermometers to *work*. And is a baby's temperature the same as an adult's, or what?'

Dee couldn't remember. It was all so long ago and she'd only ever been a part-time mother anyway. 'What do you think?' she asked Sophie as they surveyed Pixie. She seemed very flushed and there was a rattling noise in her chest every time she breathed.

'I think we should call the doctor,' Sophie said.

She got Valerie's book and dialled the number and was put through to a recorded message which told her to dial another one. 'I hope it's not that dumbo who came to see me,' she said.

It wasn't. It was a Dr Patel. He even looked like her own Dr Patel. He made her think of the letter from the Middlesex that still lay unopened at her bedside, and she thought, as he was examining Pixie, 'How ridiculous. It's only a letter. It can't *bite*. I'll go up and open it as soon as he's gone.'

She forgot though because Dr Patel, having sounded Pixie's little Vick-rubbed chest, and listened, and listened again, said, 'Can one of you take this child to the General? It will be quicker than waiting for the ambulance.'

'Ambulance?' Dee said, gormlessly.

'Yes. She needs hospital attention. She has a respiratory infection. I will write you a note to take with you,' he said.

At the door, while Dee went upstairs to find blankets and to alert Valerie to what was happening, Sophie said to him, 'Is she really ill?'

He didn't answer her question. Doctors so rarely did. And of course they were able to get away with it because their patients so rarely dared to put the direct question anyway. She wondered what her Dr Patel would have replied had she said, point-blank, 'Have I got cancer?'

This Dr Patel said, 'There is always a risk with such a small baby. It's best to be on the safe side.'

They wrapped Pixie in Valerie's best merino-wool blankets and Dee drove them through the fading daylight to the hospital. She was a good driver but she drove badly, crashing the gears, braking at the last minute for red lights and zebra crossings. Like most selfish people, her immediate reaction to being inconvenienced by somebody else's misfortune was deep resentment; concern would come later.

I should never have taken her out, Sophie was thinking, as she held Pixie close to her body-heat. A paroxysm of pain almost exquisite in its ferocity caught her unprepared. It almost doubled her up. She remembered that she'd left her tablets behind. Perhaps Valerie would find them and swallow them and put herself out of her misery. Well, so

195

be it. There was only so much precaution that one could reasonably take.

There were quite a few people in Casualty, but Pixie was given priority. A young doctor examined her. She was quiet now, except for the rasping noise that issued from her as her chest rose and fell. 'I don't like the sound of that,' the doctor said, not knowing which of them to address. The tall dark striking one didn't look like anyone's mother, but the one with the short curly hair looked somehow uninvolved, or as though she'd like to be. But he plumped for her anyway and said, 'Are you Mrs Wyatt?' One saw some fairly ancient parents what with people leaving it late these days because of having to put their careers first.

'*Ms* Wyatt, actually,' Dee said, unable, whatever the circumstances, to let the assumption pass unchallenged.

'Well, whatever,' he said. 'I want to admit this child to keep an eye on her.'

'What's wrong?' Sophie asked, having waited vainly for Dee to put the question.

'She has bronchitis.'

Bronchitis was disgusting old men with hacking coughs who spat on the pavement, who alternated drawing on their cigarettes with desperate inhalations of oxygen. Bronchitis was the result of living in dwellings so damp that the paper peeled off the walls and one's breath crystallised in the air during the winter months. Dee and Tom had lived in such places, but Tom had never had bronchitis.

'Sister will see to the admission,' the doctor said. He was turning away from them to deal with the next case when Dee plucked at his sleeve. 'Is it hereditary?' she asked.

He considered. 'Well,' he said, 'a predisposition to respiratory infections may be hereditary . . .'

'Do you mean all chest complaints, or just some of them?'

196

'We're talking about bronchitis, aren't we?' he said.

'So when you say hereditary, you just mean a predisposition towards *bronchitis*?'

'Look, what's worrying you?'

She moved agitatedly from foot to foot. She said, 'It couldn't be anything – more serious?'

'Such as?'

'Well . . .' she said.

He said, 'The child has a chest infection which is affecting her bronchial tubes. That can be serious enough in anyone very young or very old. Hopefully, if we can catch it quickly and treat it with antibiotics it won't develop into anything more serious. Does that answer your question?'

'Mother?' said the Sister, who was hovering. 'We're taking Baby up to Ward Nine.'

Ward Nine was filled with oxygen containers and ventilators and incubators, monitors and transfusion equipment – all the grim paraphernalia of resuscitation. There was a paper to sign. Beside 'Next of kin' Dee wrote 'Grandmother'. 'Oh,' the Sister said, 'I *thought* you looked . . .' but didn't finish the sentence and began another one instead. 'Will you be wanting to stay? Some of the parents prefer to stay, but with such a young baby . . .'

'I'll stay,' Dee said.

'I will too,' said Sophie, and gave the Sister such a Lady Bracknell stare that another sentence – which might have had to do with only relatives being allowed this privilege – also died on her lips.

'There's no need for *you* to stay,' Dee said, when she'd gone. Sophie said, 'Maybe not, but I'll stay all the same. Though I could do with my tablets.'

'Why? What's wrong now?' Dee said testily. Like most invincibly healthy people, she had little patience with life's invalids.

'I'll ring Valerie.'

But there was no reply, so she rang a taxi instead.

'Valerie!' she called when she got back. 'Valerie, can't you even answer the damn phone? You *know* the baby's ill . . .'

Valerie wasn't in her bedroom, or any other bedroom. A rapid search established that Valerie was no longer in the house at all.

She's finally gone over the edge, Sophie thought, racing out to the taxi with her pills. She's gone missing, making for the railway bridge, the canal . . . Police squads will have to be alerted, photographs circulated, lakes dragged . . .

It came as something of an anticlimax when she got back to Ward Nine and found Valerie sitting next to Dee, calmly drinking vending-machine coffee out of a polystyrene cup.

20

Sophie

I said, 'How on earth did you get here?' She looked up. 'I rang a taxi,' she said. 'What did you think?'

She appeared to have washed her face, so some good had come out of the situation. I said, 'How poisonous is that coffee?'

Valerie said, 'It's drinkable.' Dee said, 'It tastes like toxic waste.'

We sat in a little side room where there was a bed made up for the parents who preferred to stay. At intervals I went along to the day-room for a smoke and, on the third occasion, Valerie accompanied me, saying that she needed to stretch her legs. I wasn't surprised; I was only surprised that they hadn't atrophied completely after all those days in bed.

'You're feeling a bit better then?' I asked her. I was, thank God. One can only cope with bad pain for so long.

'No, not really,' she said. Her face was washed and her hair was combed but she still looked like someone who'd lost a shilling and found sixpence.

'Valerie,' I said, 'I'll have to go back to London soon, you know. And I'll feel dreadful leaving you in this state.'

Perhaps it wasn't the best time to broach the subject, but I needed to make it clear to her. I felt somehow responsible – which was ridiculous – as though my long-ago sexual relations with Richard might have had some

199

bearing on the course their marriage had taken, on his inability, or refusal, to find satisfaction within it.

'Oh yes,' she said. 'Everybody goes. Sooner or later.'

I wouldn't have minded so much but it was *I* who had come back to be nursed, not the other way round. I said, 'Valerie, you can only rely on the sympathy vote for so long.' And then regretted saying it when I saw the tears starting to brim again. So I apologised and changed the subject. 'What do *you* think about Pixie? Do you think they're making a lot of fuss about nothing, or what?'

She mopped her eyes with the disgusting piece of tissue that she seemed to have been clutching ever since she took to her bed. She said, 'I had a cousin who had bronchitis as an infant. It turned to pneumonia and she died.'

Well, with Valerie in her present mood, I'd have been over-optimistic in the extreme to anticipate any other sort of response.

When we got back to the ward we found that Dee had fallen asleep in her chair. She woke, rubbing her eyes and complaining like a small child and made no more than a token protest when we suggested that she might as well undress and get into bed and be comfortable. 'We'll go home,' I said, recognising how silly it was for all three of us to be hanging around simultaneously to no good effect. Shiftwork was the thing. 'Give us your keys,' I said. 'All these taxis are costing me a fortune.' She was half-asleep so she complied without demur.

It was half-past three by the time we reached home. 'I thought you'd been disqualified from driving,' Valerie had said, hesitating with her hand on the car door handle.

'Would you prefer to walk?' I said. 'Get *in* for God's sake.'

She put her alarm on for seven and so did I, but I slept through mine. She shook me awake. 'It's a lovely day,' she said, and even though she said it in a mournful sort of way I knew that she meant: 'Pixie's bound to be better. Nobody could get worse on such a lovely day.' But people

200

drop dead in heatwaves and expire slowly to the accompaniment of magnificent sunsets: Pixie wasn't better, not at all. When we got back to the hospital, Dee was being told by the paediatrician that it might be a good idea if the child's parents could be contacted.

Memory is selective. It has to be, I suppose, for the sake of one's sanity. They say that events that would be too painful to recall are generally forgotten. But I'll never forget that Wednesday in the hospital: the endless cups of polystyrene-impregnated coffee, a policewoman arriving and Dee giving her the sparse details that she possessed concerning Tom's and Sam's whereabouts, the awful deadly periods of nothing happening that were interspersed with flurries of activity, the glazed, inward-looking expression on Valerie's face being gradually transformed into one of normal anxiety, a glimpse of a tiny still form that they said was Pixie, attached to all sorts of tubes in a kind of glass chamber.

At some stage I said, 'Shall I ring Fred?' and Dee shook her head and said that he was in London. 'He's never here when he's wanted,' she said savagely and, I'm sure, most unfairly.

Pixie's chest infection wasn't responding to antibiotics and her condition had worsened. Bronchitis had developed into pneumonia. The doctor explained the process and a few phrases stuck: the substance of the lung becoming swollen and hard, the strain placed upon the heart. He could explain the process but couldn't supply prognosis: modern drugs could fight the infection, machines could take over one's breathing; the imponderable was always the patient's ability to resist.

I couldn't bear to think of her: having to engage in such a struggle. She was so little, so helpless. I concentrated instead on the way she smiled for me, the pure, unmixed motivation of the affection she showed me; her absolute trust in my goodwill towards her. And I closed my eyes and I prayed that if only God or whoever it was would allow her to live and recover, then God, or whoever it was, could have me instead.

And that meant, of course, acknowledging for the first time what was wrong with me; at long last taking my head out of the sand.

I'd had cervical cancer. When I told Valerie and Dee about needing to recover from a virus, I wasn't exactly lying, not if current medical opinion is to be believed: one used to pay for love with the traditional venereal diseases; now it's the virus that kills quickly rather than the bacterium that takes its time.

Well, they scraped me and froze me and burned me and pronounced me cured. I was lucky. Sometimes, I was told, a radical hysterectomy has to be performed. That involves removal not only of the womb, the cervix and the ovaries, but also of part of the vagina. In other words, you go in a woman and come out mutilated as well as neutered.

Cervical cancer, they say, if caught in time, is one hundred per cent treatable. Maybe mine wasn't, or I'm the exception that proves the rule. Or maybe different sorts of cancer aren't mutually exclusive.

They'd want me to go back into hospital in order to be butchered. They'd want to subject me to radiation and chemotherapy until my hair fell out, and expect me to be grateful for my life. My life as it stood was in a hell of a mess, but I didn't intend to settle for half of it. I'd rather be dead than dragging around as a kind of sexless half-being, arousing only pity or distaste or embarrassment. If that was to be my future, then if God or whoever it was would accept a trade-off: one used life in return for a new model, then that was fine by me.

During the endless reaches of the afternoon Dee remembered that she'd promised Fred to feed and exercise Sally, but obviously she couldn't leave her post. Valerie and I went instead. I had a bit of a nose – as one does in other people's houses – while Sally ate her Pal and crunched her biscuits. 'This is *nice*,' I said, surveying the exposed beams, the inglenook fireplace, the antique furniture, the pictures – and the books, books spilling forth everywhere, from shelves and tables and cupboards, stacked on the floor, as yet unpacked on the hall table. I remembered Dee at about age ten, saying how wonderful it must be to work in a bookshop, in the way that other children might have said, how wonderful to work in a sweetshop.

'We'd better get back,' Valerie said. But we lingered, looking out through the window (picturesquely leaded, sensibly double-glazed) across the marshes to where the sea shimmered beneath a fierce sun. In normal circumstances I'd have been wheeling Pixie down to the beach, telling her the story of my life, watching her face as she listened with rapt attention: her appropriate gravity, her encouraging little smiles.

'You're crying,' Valerie said.

'No I'm not. It's allergy.'

They said that if you could see Blackpool Tower the fine weather was due to change. I couldn't see it. Not even when I'd blinked away my tears.

Wednesday night became Thursday morning. The machine breathed for Pixie and the antibiotic waged war upon the bacterial infection. We watched the battle from the door, looking through the glass container that was Pixie's world. She hadn't even the contact of human flesh for reassurance, just the tubes that fed and drained and the pump that inflated and deflated her lungs.

There was a pile of ancient copies of *Woman's Weekly* on a shelf by the door. Dee read her way through every single one: every word of the stories, every knitting pattern and recipe and thought for the day. She responded to comments with curt monosyllables and it was obvious that she was holding herself together only by the most tremendous effort of will. I counted the tiles on the lower half of the wall of the corridor – there were two hundred and forty-eight (three of them cracked) – and watched a stripe of sunlight changing its position on the wall opposite, gradually moving closer to where Dee sat, tearing at her fingernails and reading about a new preparation for 'haemorrhoids, commonly known as "piles"'.

By four-thirty she was bathed in sunlight. And then the sun-stripe vanished as suddenly as if someone had turned off a light and we heard the rain pouring down and I thought: so much for Blackpool Tower and its visibility, and a moment later the paediatrician walked through the door and my heart began to bang and I said, 'Please God, please God, please God,' over and over again.

Dee's eyes were closed. I closed mine too. I heard Valerie saying, 'Is she any better?' And the doctor replied, 'Yes, she's bucked up quite a bit. At that age things can change as quickly as the weather. It's dark in here, isn't it?' And as I opened my eyes he was switching on the light.

They said that we should go home and get some rest. But we were reluctant to give up on the vigil, as though Pixie might be aware that we had abandoned her in her hour of need. 'I'll stay,' Valerie said (the old Valerie, the sensible, responsible Valerie). 'But it'll be all right. I'm sure it will.'

And for some reason we placed more faith in her optimistic prediction than we had done in the doctor's considered verdict.

It was still pouring when we reached Dee's car: lovely rain: cleansing, revivifying. 'Where to?' I said. 'Home?'

'Just drive,' she said.

'You know I haven't got a licence?'

'I don't care. Just drive.'

So I drove. With my foot down hard. Out into the country, along the by-pass, and turned off just before we hit the motorway and came back along the coast road. She wound down her window and the rain lashed in. 'You'll get drenched,' I said. But she stuck her head out into it, as though she too needed to be cleansed.

I parked beside the headland and reached over and wound up her window before we had another pneumonia case on our hands. It was a moment before I realised that her face was wet not only with rain but with tears.

She wept without restraint or decorum. Violently. It was as different from Valerie's slow dismal seepage as could be imagined. She soaked her handkerchief and then mine and most of a box of tissues that I found in the glove compartment. And then she began to talk. Because of the tears, most of what she said was, at first, incomprehensible, but eventually I made out the word 'punishment'. It seemed that she saw Pixie's illness as a judgement upon herself for resenting having to look after her, for failing to bring Tom up to respect the virtues of marriage and responsible parenthood, and for something else, something that had happened before Pixie existed, or even Tom.

The downpour stopped as suddenly as it had started. We got out of the car and walked along the embankment in the direction of the old sanatorium. The tide had just turned and the smell of decayed things was sharp in our nostrils. Dee said, 'I was afraid it might be hereditary — Pixie's chest trouble. I was always afraid of that. Even though they told me, over and over again, with Tom, that it wasn't.'

And I said, 'Why should her chest trouble be hereditary?' in the usual off-hand manner that I adopted when Dee seemed close to disclosure: a sort of 'tell me if you want, but it's all the same to me' tone of voice.

She never had told me. Perhaps Dee had always written the pain out of herself, but perhaps this time the emotion was so intense that it required verbal expression.

But it was also, I think, because she had realised as she got older that some secrets weren't all that important any more, that, in fact, it was the secrecy rather than the information it concealed that had become important.

We walked to within a few yards of the barbed wire — torn down in places — that enclosed the derelict building. During our fervid adolescence we had imagined ghosts: wounded soldiers, the coughings of consumptives. But there weren't any ghosts; it just looked decayed and sad and incongruous.

Tom's father had been one of the consumptives, Dee said. She told me about him, about her eighteenth summer when, as I entertained Richard in the afternoons and Valerie sat beside him at Bible study class in the evenings, she had cried in the sandhills because she cherished a passion and the object of that passion scarcely acknowledged her existence.

He'd literally stumbled over her, the consumptive. He'd been walking. They did a lot of walking; fresh air was important. He'd lent her his handkerchief and offered her a wine gum. His name was Tom Ransome and he was twenty-eight years old. He was tall and fair with laughter-lines around eyes as blue as the sea looked when the sun shone upon it: a true aquamarine, like Tom's, like Pixie's. 'You look a bit glum,' he'd said, but not in the accusing sort of way that other people said it, as though it was a crime not to have a smile permanently pasted across one's face.

'Cheer up,' he'd said. And, as the fog bell sounded down by Ferryside Lane and Auntie B started to worry, 'Worse things happen at sea.'

His name was Tom Ransome and he was a photographer. He came from London, and when he smiled it was as if the whole landscape changed, as though the beam of the lighthouse at the estuary's mouth had suddenly swivelled and bathed them in its radiance.

He could – within certain limits of acceptability – have been anybody. It wasn't exactly that she fell in love on the strength of a clean handkerchief and a wine gum, but by then, due to frustration and neglect, her susceptibility was at its peak: the longing she felt was unrequited; boys of our acquaintance were wary of her, put off by her prickliness, nervous of her scorn; Tom Ransome was old enough to be capable of interpreting her touch-me-not as come-and-get-me.

They met almost daily. Mostly they walked. Or drank tea and Camp coffee in the Wayside Café. Once she'd drunk from his cup by mistake and he'd snatched it from her. Tuberculosis was a highly contagious disease; sufferers had their own cups, their own cutlery, spat into their own personal sputum vessels.

So how odd it was that he who had been so anxious for her to avoid one sort of contact with him should have consented to, or pressed her to (she didn't elucidate, and I could hardly pry), indulge in another, surely far more risky, mutual activity.

Dee had had no experience whatsoever. I had succumbed to temptation years before, out of curiosity as much as anything; Valerie's hand went out automatically to remove Richard's from prohibited places on her body because decent girls saved themselves for a ring; but Dee, being unversed in sexual politics: the ambivalent signals, the come-on-but-come-no-furthers, the whole cynical business of barter, lay down with Tom Ransome in the lee of a sand dune for no other reason than desire.

He took a photograph of her and developed it in the dark-room at the sanatorium. She'd kept it all these years in her wallet (she showed it to me: it was a good photograph, made her look prettier than the girl I remembered), together with two strips of metal upon which she'd stamped their names.

She'd done that after he'd parted from her at the Church Street railway station, saying, 'I shall return,' or whatever his version of it happened to be. She knew his name, his age, his profession, that he liked wine gums and Jelly Roll Morton and the German Expressionist Cinema, that he played jazz piano sometimes and had an ambition to get into the film industry. She knew that he smoked Senior Service ('If I'm going to cough, then I might as well make it worthwhile'), that he could finish the crossword in the *Sunday Times* before she'd figured out the third clue, that he'd been expelled from school for gross and persistent insubordination, and that he had a way of kissing her and touching her that made her feel as though her flesh was likely to melt away to nothing.

She also had an address. He wrote it out for her: 'Flat 3, Robert Peel Mansions, Margaret Road, N19.' Years later, when she had her first novel accepted and was invited to sherry in Bedford Square, she made a detour and found what she already knew from consulting the *A to Z*: that Margaret Road did indeed exist. She had been prepared to discover that Robert Peel Mansions didn't, and she was right. But they had done once, before demolition. It seemed that the address had been genuine, even if her letters had been returned from it with 'Not known' written across them.

He went away and he never came back. Perhaps he'd died. (Although they were supposed to be curing his tuberculosis, shifting the shadow on his lung with penicillin, building up his resistance with rest and good food and sea air.) Perhaps he'd had a bump on the head that had resulted in amnesia. Perhaps he'd been a Russian spy and they'd recalled him.

'I never knew,' she said, shredding a handful of dune grass, looking fixedly at the building's blind windows as though expecting to see explanatory images appearing within them. 'And because I never knew, I could never stop waiting. In case. I don't mean I've spent twenty-five years thinking about him,' she said, 'because I haven't. In fact, if he hadn't made me pregnant I don't suppose he'd have mattered all that much. It was the combination: him just disappearing so abruptly like that and me having a child – if he'd known about it and said, "Bugger off", that would have been different. But he never knew. And neither did I – what became of him. Valerie thinks that not knowing who knows your secrets is the worst thing imaginable. But it's just not knowing that's the worst. Wondering. It destroys you. You can never write "Finish" under it and begin again. It's why I can't be very sympathetic towards Valerie. At least she hasn't been left wondering.'

'Wondering wasn't involved,' I said. 'She only found out by accident. In Valerie's case, ignorance was definitely bliss.'

Valerie and me, wanting not to know. Dee, never being able to let go of a memory because she never knew. Daft, isn't it?

21

The police located the personnel of Catastrophe Theory in Amsterdam the day after Pixie was declared out of danger. Fred drove Dee to the airport to meet Tom and Sam, and then stood astonished in the arrival lounge as Dee first screamed abuse at her son, then physically assaulted him, then burst into tears and hugged him and kissed him. Meanwhile Sam stood serenely apart, apparently quite unaffected by this display.

'I thought there was going to be bloodshed,' Fred said later, to Sophie. He was obviously used to rather more decorous behaviour between parents and their offspring.

'Oh, it's a very volatile relationship,' Sophie said. 'They're very alike, that's why. Though Dee can't see it.'

Dee, presumably, looked and saw shades of his father, whereas Tom resembled her in almost every discernible feature.

'They've always fought,' Sophie said.

Valerie had told her of epic battles. Valerie, with her two well-behaved little boys, always so distantly polite, was horrified by the evidence of violent emotions, unsuppressed: Dee, a bread knife in her hand, chasing Tom with his hair dyed blue, through the house and out into the garden. Valerie was also perhaps jealous: Dee and her son might shout and swear and sometimes hit one another, but violent emotions at least meant closeness and filial closeness was a precious thing.

'Not what you'd call a quiet life?' Fred said, pouring coffee into the Capricorn mug and handing it to Sophie. A camaraderie had sprung up between them. She felt that he regarded her as a confidante. It wasn't a role she'd ever played before, and she wasn't used to playing second fiddle to Dee or anyone else, but she had chucked in her twopennorth, for what it was worth: 'Fred's awfully fond of you,' she said. 'Why don't you put him out of his misery? Don't you get on together, or what?'

Dee had been busy making up the spare bed for Tom and Sam. She shook out a sheet. 'We get on well enough,' she said.

'Well then?'

'If I married him,' Dee said, 'he'd always be *there*.'

Sophie didn't tell Fred that. But she'd taken to dropping into the bookshop now that she had no Pixie to wheel through the town. She'd visited the hospital, of course, but Pixie's parents had priority. Obviously.

At least Fred always looked pleased to see her. He'd make her a mug of coffee and draw up a chair for her beside the fire. 'Do me a favour,' he'd say, 'check the catalogue for these orders,' and show her how to work the computer that told you whether a certain book was in print and/or in stock. 'Lucy!' he'd call. '*Did* you check those dates for me?' and Lucy would wander slowly to the doorway and say, pushing a swathe of hair out of her eyes, 'Oh, *sorry*, Mr Browning. It went completely out of my mind.'

Lucy wanted to be a model, not a shop-assistant. She had handed in her notice and spent most of the time gazing into the mirror in the lavatory while she worked it out.

'Why didn't you employ someone who was interested in books?' Sophie asked.

'Because there wasn't anybody who was interested in

books,' he replied. 'I don't suppose there will be this time either.'

He'd advertised in the Job Centre and the local newspapers. 'At least,' he said, 'this one wasn't bad at dusting.'

'Well I'm no good at dusting,' Sophie said, 'but I can do parcels, if you like.'

'That would be most awfully kind . . .'

It was quite pleasant – soothing – to sit beside the fire, listening to the ticking of the school-house clock, drinking coffee and wrapping up orders in stiff brown paper while Fred talked on the telephone or took a customer into the room at the back where the antiquarian stuff was kept, where they conversed in low serious voices as befitted connoisseurs and sneezed gently from time to time in reaction to the paper dust and mould spores that were liberated into the atmosphere whenever a page of an ancient volume was turned.

'He's been a good friend to me,' Dee had said.

He'd been a tower of strength, certainly. On his return from London, as soon as he heard about Pixie, he'd rushed to the hospital. He'd opened his arms to Dee and she'd walked towards him and been enfolded. Neither Valerie's presence nor Sophie's was required any longer. As they were leaving they heard her saying: 'I really do care about her, you know.' And he'd hugged her and said, 'I know. Poor, poor Dee,' he'd said, as he stroked her hair. 'You're not nearly as black as you'd like to paint yourself, are you?'

That was what Dee wanted – a friend. Sophie had never really had one, not a full-blooded male friend. It was a novel – and pleasant – experience. But a friend was not, ultimately, enough.

There was the smell of autumn in the air. Dee remarked upon it when she drove over to Valerie's to escape from Sam, who smiled vaguely and occasionally but was otherwise totally uncommunicative.

'She's like an alien being,' Dee said. 'Do you think she's

212

permanently stoned, or what? I mean, her baby almost dies and there's been absolutely no reaction. And she's never out of the bathroom.'

'Better than the other way,' Sophie said.

'I distrust bathroom fetishists.'

Sophie, on the strength of one brief meeting with Sam, had found her to be a quiet girl, but quite inoffensive. Perhaps she was shy; it didn't occur to Dee, whose self-image was arrested at age eleven, when she'd stood on a platform reciting 'They hunt, the tigers in the jungle,' and suddenly felt urine splashing down her leg, that anyone might find her daunting.

'Talking of fetishists,' Dee said. 'Where's Madame Ajax?'

'Giving the bedrooms what your Auntie B would have described as "A bottoming".'

She'd been forced from her bed by the Pixie crisis. They'd thought, once it was over, that she might return to it, but she had gone into overdrive instead: blitzing the house, scouring out every last dirt-harbouring crevice, thwacking away imaginary cobwebs with broom-heads bound in dusters.

'If it makes her happy . . .' Sophie said.

Although 'happy' wasn't exactly the word. Valerie rose from her bed and washed her face and cleaned the house and answered the phone. She even went to see the bank manager and mooted Sophie's suggestion that she convert the house into two flats. He had approved the plan and the workmen were due in three weeks. Until the place was once again habitable, she was to move in with Dee. Dee said, falsely optimistic in the face of the prospect of Valerie's gloom being contagious, 'Perhaps she'll have a job by then.'

They both knew how unlikely that was. And Dee was capable of conjuring up quite enough gloom on her own account. 'Won't it make it even more difficult for you to work?' Sophie asked. 'I'll work at Fred's,' Dee said. 'He's out all day.'

She knew that there was as much chance of that as of Valerie getting a job within the next three weeks; she'd simply read her way through all his books, but sufficient unto the day ... For a brief time all was right with Dee's world: Pixie was recovering and nobody blamed her grandmother for her illness, not even her grandmother; Fred was being extremely sympathetic and deliberately censoring the word 'marriage' from his conversation; darling Tom, whom she loved and hated with equal intensity, was home, in his proper place, even if he did have that sphinx-like consort of his in tow; and, perhaps most importantly, she had every excuse in the book for neglecting her work.

'September,' she said, sniffing up a great lungful of air. Everything smelt much sharper after you'd stopped smoking. There was just that hint of ripe fruit and early frost and woodsmoke in the air. But what autumn always meant to Dee was the smell of new gaberdine mackintoshes and leather satchels and the crisp cold feel that white school blouses have before the starch is washed out of them.

For Sophie, September meant a train ticket back to London. It meant a phone call to the Middlesex Hospital to book another appointment to replace the one she'd missed. It meant a plane touching down at Heathrow and disgorging its passengers, among them a young man with a suitcase covered in Canadian stickers.

He was twenty-eight years old. The same age as Dee's Tom Ransome who had been very much the older man, to Dee. But the age gap between Dee and her Tom Ransome had been in the acceptable direction; that between Sophie and Dominic-who-was-hers-no-longer was not, demanded a thick skin if you were not to be perpetually upset by the not-quite-out-of-earshot remarks: 'Toy-boy. Cradle-snatcher. Gigolo.' Gigolo was the most insulting – and the least accurate; she could scarcely support herself, let alone pay for sexual favours.

And even if she could have afforded them, she was in no condition to indulge. She had started to bleed again on the night they admitted Pixie to hospital and now, ten days later, she was bleeding still.

'You've not come on again?' he'd say, the young man who wasn't her gigolo. Or, 'Christ, isn't it finished yet?' as though she bled deliberately to thwart his amorous intentions. He was impatient and unsympathetic and juvenile in so many ways – and yet . . . She remembered their first meeting, at a read-through in a draughty rehearsal room in Acton. They were doing a television play for Channel 4. She was a high-class ex-prostitute who'd married a peer of the realm and he was her lover who was actually selling state secrets to the highest bidder. She remembered seeing his picture in *Spotlight* in the casting-director's office: dark, handsome and with the sort of expression that indicates an awareness of it, and thinking, 'I bet he's insufferable.'

He was lazy, she remembered, about lines, was still clutching a script when everyone else was word-perfect. She remembered him sitting with one leg slung over the arm of another chair, remembered a challenging look. On the third day they did their big love scene. She felt embarrassed and knew before he touched her that she was falling for him; embarrassment was always the sign.

Weeks later, they did the take on a closed set. They had to simulate sex in the sleeping compartment of a train. He said afterwards, 'That wasn't entirely simulated – as I'm sure you could tell. How about you?'

She was padded with towels and wadded with Tampax; she had a bad sore throat too and had been numbing it all day with sprays and lozenges, but despite all that his excitement was contagious. That night he went home with her. (It had to be that way round: he had a girlfriend in residence at his own flat.) He sulked a bit when she told

215

him she was out of bounds (her six post-operative weeks were not yet up), but then he brightened up. 'I suppose a blow-job's out of the question too?' he said, as she sucked on another honey and glycerine pastille. 'Come on! I'm only joking. Let's just sit here and exchange life-stories. Well, as your throat's sore, you'll just have to listen to mine . . .'

She was remembering this, and all the subsequent loving and fighting when Dee said, 'September' and sniffed the air. 'I must ring up the railway station about the train times,' she said. She kept saying it and then not doing it.

'Sophie,' Dee said, with a typical Dee oh-so-subtle sideways glance, 'Sophie, what did you mean the other day when you said that at least Valerie had the rest of her life?'

Sophie, who had forgotten completely that she'd said any such thing, merely looked vacant. 'I can't imagine,' she said, at length.

'It seemed such a peculiar remark to make.'

'It does, doesn't it?' said Sophie, who had, by now, remembered the circumstances and the remark.

'Are you ill?' Dee asked, as Valerie had done earlier, but Valerie was too polite to be challengingly direct; Dee had no such qualms. Dee said, 'Is it to do with all this bleeding business?'

'What bleeding business?' Sophie said, deliberately altering the stress on the word and thus the sense of the sentence.

'Oh come on, Sophie, don't make a joke of everything. You know something? I think the only time you're not acting is when you're on the stage.'

'Thanks for the compliment.'

'You're welcome,' Dee said. 'It's no skin off my nose. You just shouldn't go about making melodramatic statements, should you, if you expect to be taken seriously.'

'I don't,' Sophie said, 'I don't expect to be taken

seriously. I can't imagine anything more dreary than being taken seriously.'

Dee, miffed, walked to the door. She said, 'I only came to invite you both round on Friday night. It's Sam's birthday, apparently, and Fred says I owe you some hospitality – he's doing the cooking, so fair enough – and he thought you'd like to see Pixie when she comes out of hospital and before they take her back to London. They're going next week. They've got a recording contract and a proper flat, for once, in Kentish Town. You'll still be here, Friday?'

Sophie nodded and Dee drove back home. Screw you, Sophie, she thought. There had probably been no substance to the remark anyway. Sophie had always been prone to the outrageous pronouncement: pubic lice, abortions, going to bed with three different men in the space of one day, sitting next to a member of parliament in the Endell Street clap clinic . . . always the attention-seeker. No wonder, Dee thought, no husband or lover had been able to put up with her for very long. She braked as a woman began to push a pram across the zebra, and then did a quick double-take. Christ! she thought, I'm going mad. But when she looked again she saw that *this* woman looked nothing like Sophie.

Could I have told Dee? Sophie wondered, going slowly up the stairs in search of Valerie, following the sound of the vacuum-cleaner. A jingle from the early days of television advertising came into her head: 'Hoover beats as it sweeps as it cleans.' She thought of articles she'd read about the body's defence mechanisms against invaders: sweepers, there were, and clumpers, messengers and killers. She'd thought of an army of little vacuum-cleaners gobbling up all the alien dust in their path. But cancer was different, cancer was when the normal defences were made useless, the power was cut off and the messages got scrambled and nobody knew any more who was fighting whom.

Sophie's first job, traditionally, was as an ASM in rep. She learned the ropes from another one, an extremely thin, pale girl who seemed to grow gaunter by the minute. The girl would stand, shivering, with three cardigans pulled tight around her, issuing instructions in a powerful voice that belied the frailty of her appearance: 'Stand by tabs. House lights to a half. House lights out. Tabs going up.' One day they said Sophie was to take over. The girl had been rushed into hospital. 'The big C,' another girl had said. 'Poor old cow,' that girl had said, but perfunctorily. She was young and pretty and full of sexual vigour and the big C was like pregnancy: something that only happened to other people.

'Valerie,' called Sophie, who had not cared at all that that girl was in hospital, but had rather been glad of the chance to call, in her place, 'Stand by tabs,' and 'House lights to a half.'

Valerie was in one of the back bedrooms polishing a chest of drawers. Sophie had said earlier, 'Valerie, does it make sense to clean when in three weeks the builders will be here, covering everything in brick dust?' Valerie had paused, cloth in one hand, packet of Flash in the other, and given the question her serious consideration. Eventually she'd said, 'Probably not,' but continued to do so all the same.

'Dee's just been round to invite us to dinner on Friday.'

Valerie looked up and said, 'Must we?'

'Yes, we must. You need some company. And so do I. I told you weeks ago I was beginning to feel as though I was in the middle of a very long run of *Ladies of the Corridor* or *The Children's Hour*, or something equally female and enclosed.'

'What's wrong with female company?' Valerie said.

'Nothing. In moderation.'

'*The Children's Hour* wasn't exclusively female,' said Valerie. 'There was a man in it. That's what all the trouble was about.'

Sophie went back downstairs and rang British Rail. She could have rung the Middlesex too, but she didn't. She wasn't sure whether ringing the Middlesex meant fulfilling her part of that bargain she'd made during those desperate hours outside the door of the Special Care unit, whether placing herself at the mercy of medicine was likely to prolong her life or rush it to its close.

At various times Sophie had made bargains with fate which, for the sake of focus, she chose to personify as the Almighty. 'Dear God,' she had prayed, 'if you let me get that part, I'll stop messing about with Elvira's husband. Dear God, if you let me not be pregnant, I'll never be unfaithful again. Dear God, if you let me be pregnant . . .'

Usually, fate didn't keep its part of the bargain, but the few times that it did, she usually reneged on hers. By the time she heard that she'd been chosen for Rosalind, or Tess, or her agent had got her the voice-over for the chocolate bar, or the test had come back either positive or negative, she would have forgotten her promise. But this was different. Never before had she put her life on the line. Never before had she been unsure whether it was a feasible proposition, a going concern, that could be *put* on the line.

22

Valerie

I didn't want to go anywhere, least of all to Dee's dinner-party. I said to Sophie: 'If I don't go, at least the numbers won't be quite so uneven.' She said, 'Uneven?' 'Yes,' I said, 'two men to four women.'

'Good God!' she said. 'The life you've led!'

I can't help the life I've led. It may have been bourgeois and bound by what she sees as meaningless rules, like balancing the number of male and female guests at dinner-parties, but there it is. Anyway, those rules are very meaningful, if you think about them; they say a lot about the arrangement of social structures. One may not agree with them, but that doesn't mean that they are without significance: however at ease Sophie may be at Dee's dinner-table, I shall feel like a spare part.

I suppose it's a feeling that I shall have to get used to – given that I have to carry on living. (I think Sophie was afraid that I'd slash my wrists. One afternoon while she was out doing her surrogate mother bit I did actually draw the edge of a razor blade across that big blue vein that's so prominent there. It was one from a packet that I'd bought for Richard during my weekly trip to the super-market on the day before he died. For such a half-hearted, superficial attempt it bled an awful lot. And it hurt too, out of all proportion to the damage I'd done.

I didn't have the courage to try again. It's a terrible

thing to have to accept: that you're going to carry on living only because you haven't the guts to stop.)

Neither Sophie nor Dee seem able to understand just quite how terrible I feel. I know the facts that I have to come to terms with: that Richard betrayed me, that my married life was a counterfeit article, that Barbara Hilliard's unspoken inference: that she was merely one of many, might actually be true, but they're so hard to accept. I want to go back to the days of not knowing or, perhaps, of preferring not to know. Richard was an attractive man and, sexually, I was a total dead loss: perhaps, subconsciously, I preferred not to know because if he was sleeping with other women then he might not want to sleep with me. Maybe there are former sexual partners of his at every turn; maybe the only women that I can be sure of not having slept with him are Sophie and Dee.

I simply don't know what to believe any more, how to behave. There are no rules, no guidelines. I went to the cemetery and I said, 'What am I to do?' but answer came there none. There was just the tearing sound that the offshore wind makes as it hurls itself across the beach and flattens the dune grass and rips through the poplars that are planted at the far side of the graveyard. That and the rain dripping on to the limestone chippings from the petals of the tattered carnations that I brought the last time I came.

I know that the longer I isolate myself, the harder it will be to face the world, but I feel that I need more time. At any rate, I know what I don't need, which is to have to be sociable at Dee's dinner-table, but once her mind is made up, Sophie is not to be thwarted. I let her alternately cajole and bully me into washing my hair and putting on a frock and calling a cab. She stopped it at the off-licence while she went to buy a couple of bottles of wine, although I told her that if Fred was doing the catering he'd be doing the drink too, and it'll be considerably superior to anything that can be purchased locally. She said, 'Oh you can never have enough. We'll drink it later on when our palates won't know the difference.' They seem to run on drink, these people. I wish I could; it might cheer me up.

While she was gone, the taxi-driver wound down his window and glanced out and said, 'Looks like we're in for a storm.'

The sky was violet with a greenish haze and we could hear distantly-rolling thunder.

Then lightning flashed directly overhead just as Sophie came out of the shop carrying her brown paper parcel. 'Strewth!' she said, as she got into the taxi. 'Fasten your seat-belts. It's going to be a bumpy night.'

It began pleasantly enough: there was Pixie tucked up warm in the back room (we were led in by Dee, a finger to her lips, to gaze upon her); Sophie looked wistful. (I'd never seen her look wistful except when she was once cast as Margaret in *Dear Brutus* and had evidently decided that wistful all the way through was the only way to play it.) There was Fred in a butcher's apron coming in from the kitchen to welcome us with sherry before going back to his basting; there was Sam: spectrally-white-faced with chopped hair dyed matt-black and wearing those badly-fitting Charlie Chaplin sort of clothes that those in fashion's vanguard seem to favour these days, receiving congratulations on her twenty-second birthday with a distant smile; and there was her male counterpart: Tom. Sophie says they look like the Bisto Kids, but actually he's more like his mother. They are so alike that it makes you wonder whether the mysterious father ever existed, whether instead you're witnessing an authentic case of human parthenogenesis.

He has a readier smile though, a less prickly outer skin at any rate. He looked up and said, 'Hi, Sophie,' and, 'Hello, Mrs Lamb.'

I am Mrs Lamb, I suppose, because you can't call the mother of your contemporaries by her first name. At least I hope there isn't a more sinister reason for the distinction.

When he was younger he looked angelic. This made it

difficult to think ill of him even when presented with incontrovertible evidence of his mischief. He's a grown man now, of course, but you can still see traces of the naughty little boy beneath the designer stubble.

'Hello, Mrs Lamb,' he said, and offered me some cashew nuts. He said, 'How are the Terrible Twins?'

'Very well, thank you. They're in America at the moment.'

He lit a roll-up. 'I expect they're pretty high-powered by now, aren't they?' he said. 'Red braces and Porsches, that sort of thing?'

'Well, actually, they've only just finished university. They're going on to do scientific research.'

There'd always been a mutual aversion. They'd recognised him as being dangerous; he'd despised them for their conformity.

'Still,' he said, 'I expect they're getting there. It's what my mother wanted me to do, you know: Get somewhere. Isn't that right, Mater?'

'Don't call me that,' Dee said.

'All right: Grandmater, then.'

She shuddered and looked away from him. Though, generally, wherever he was in a room, her eyes followed him. I'd noticed it before.

'Yes,' said Tom, refreshing our glasses from Fred's sherry bottle, 'my mum wanted me to be a bank manager. Isn't that right, Grandmater?'

Sam sipped orange juice and smiled that remote little smile of hers that doesn't fit at all with the vividly-exaggerated make-up on her clown's face.

'If I became as famous as the Beatles and made money till I stank of it,' Tom said, glugging down his sherry, 'my mum would still be bemoaning the fact that I hadn't become a bank manager.'

It was obvious that we had walked into an atmosphere. Dee, who was drinking her sherry in a very regal way,

223

said, in a dangerously even tone, 'What's wrong with that? Valerie's father was a bank manager.'

'So what's the word then, Tom?' Sophie said quickly. She knew Tom less well than any of us but got on with him best.

'The word is,' he said, bestowing upon her the full radiance of a smile that he'd inherited from Dee – although with Dee it was rarely displayed, 'that you may not realise it, but you could be looking at a star.'

It was such transparent, childish boastfulness that it was rendered quite inoffensive. And how coincidental, I thought, that one whose star was ascending should be talking about it to another whose star, these days, seemed to be in permanent decline.

'The word is,' said Tom, 'that we've only been signed up by RCA, that's all. This is it, the biggie.'

I seemed to remember this being it a couple of years before when they'd been signed by some small independent label, and a couple of years before that when he'd been on tour, backing that big female singer with the cropped hair and shoulders like Garth who sounds as though she has a cleft palate.

'You were Heavy Metal when I heard you last,' Sophie said. 'I believe you've changed your style.'

She'd actually been to one of their gigs in London and reported that their songs were mostly to do with blood and Satan and nightmares.

'Yes,' he said. 'It was a bit juvenile really, all that stuff.'

'New Age Music?' Sophie said. 'Is that the sort that they play in supermarkets?'

'Now, now, Sophie,' he said. 'You're showing *your* age.'

'It's the sort that sounds like white noise,' Dee said, 'the sort that they use to torture political prisoners with when they subject them to sensory deprivation.'

They both ignored her. Sophie said, 'Are you still with the same line-up?'

He'd introduced her to them at the gig. I'd seen them

when he brought them back to Dee's. They were temporarily homeless and needed somewhere to practise. I
remember thinking that it was as well that Auntie B's
cottage was fairly remote from its neighbours as the surly-
looking youths with their ragged jeans and yards of frizzy
hair bashed the living daylights out of their massively-
amplified instruments.

'Oh no,' Tom said, 'we split last year. Different musical
directions, see.'

'Don't tell me: your new personnel are called Tristram
and Marcus and – Benedict.'

'Close,' he said, 'Tim and Robin, actually.'

Sam smiled. Dee, who was perched on the edge of the
sofa, studiously not taking part in this conversation, said,
'And do Tim and Robin keep in touch with *their* families?
Or do they too consider it unnecessary?'

He shot her a look from beneath his lowered eyelids.
'Leave it out, Ma,' he said. 'We're not in the kindergarten
now.'

Dee crunched a handful of cashew nuts. She said, 'Oh,
aren't we? Funny, that's the impression I've had all these
past weeks. As though I've been running one, anyway.'

Fred made a timely entrance with a couple of bottles of
wine and a napkin over his arm. 'If you would care to be
seated,' he said, 'ladies and gents – sorry, ladies and *gent*
. . . *Now*, please, if you wouldn't mind, before my soufflé
goes all – what's the word?'

'Deflated,' I said.

'Detumescent,' said Sophie.

'Flat,' said Dee.

We sat. Sophie reckons that Dee ought to marry Fred
for reasons of financial security. But – if she has to adopt
such unromantic criteria – she could equally well marry
him for his culinary prowess: his soufflé was brilliant, and
the poussins that followed it. Delicate cooking, surprising
from such a big man – but then Fred seems full of
contradictions: a military man with a love of literature; an

outwardly conservative sort of man who likes doing things properly and yet loves Dee who eats jam straight out of the jar and despises the rules and has only just about got out of the habit of only washing her neck if she's due to get her hair cut.

Even I, who have had no appetite of late, and Sophie who never had one, were stimulated into eating. 'Mm!' Sophie said. 'Little mushrooms! These didn't come out of a tin, did they, Fred, or off the supermarket shelf?'

'No,' he said, 'I rose at dawn and took my basket and tip-toed through the dew-spangled fields . . .'

I must have looked up at him enquiringly – I'm never absolutely certain when people are making jokes – because he said gently, 'No, Valerie, not really,' and went on to tell Sophie about the specialist stall in the market which can occasionally supply such delicacies.

They talked about food for a while. Sophie doesn't much care for eating but she enjoys talking about food just as much as Dee obviously enjoys writing about it. Tom and Sam ate as though they hadn't had a square meal in weeks, which – by the look of them – might well have been the case. Although Tom has always been thin and anyone, even someone quite robust, wearing the enormously baggy clothes that Sam wears would look slender by comparison.

Tom said, with his mouth full, 'Why don't you teach my mama to cook like this?'

Dee, who'd been inspecting her fork very closely like a health-inspector in a suspect restaurant, said, 'Why don't *you* teach yourself?'

'I do cook, don't I, Sam? I do pretty much all the cooking.'

Sam chewed and swallowed and sipped her wine and then actually spoke. 'Yes,' she said. 'He's very good.'

'*Some* sorts of cooking,' Tom said modestly. 'I'm not much on roasts and stuff but my vegetable curries are pretty good.'

'If you says it as shouldn't,' Dee said, but not in a particularly amiable tone.

'Fred, tell me how you did these potatoes,' Sophie said. 'They are *delicious*. Do you boil them first and then fry them? But they'd be greasy then and these aren't . . .'

'They have to be just *dipped*,' Fred said, 'and *very* briefly. You get your oil really hot . . .'

'I remember *something* similar at Mijanou . . .'

'For God's sake!' Dee said. 'What is this: the Oxford Bleedin' Food Symposium? God, I hate foodies. They are only slightly less repellent than wine-bores, or people who go on about what their houses cost. Or people who have initial letter abbreviations for everything – all that Dinky and Nimby crap . . .'

'Not much you do like, is there, Ma?' Tom observed in a deceptively equable tone.

Dee directed her animosity towards a softer target – me. 'Valerie,' she said. 'You're in another orbit again, aren't you? Beam yourself down, for heaven's sake.'

I'd been thinking about the Twins, who were probably preparing to fly home from America, and Ba and Melissa who were probably preparing to fly towards it en route back to Australia. Perhaps they'd pass each other in the customs hall; perhaps their aircrafts' flight paths would cross. Life is full of such little ironies.

Fred was smiling at me to make up for Dee's rudeness. I remembered that Fred had a daughter in Australia, not only Australia but Queensland. Perhaps even Bundaberg. Perhaps she lived next door to the Hilliards, or whatever constitutes next door in Australian terms . . .

'Can we talk about music?' Sophie asked Dee. 'Is that allowed, or does it come within your list of prohibited subjects?'

'Feel free,' Dee said, and speared a carrot savagely.

So Tom and Sophie talked about music: about trends and gigs and deals and packages and rip-off managers. They talked in the argot common to the subject. Dee's lip curled. At one point, when Tom said something about having taken a pause after Dead Reckoning had broken up in order to 'get his shit together', it was curled so exaggeratedly that it almost disappeared up her left nostril.

Fred kept trying to issue warning glances but their respective positions made it difficult: he was seated at one end of the table opposite Tom and she was between Tom and me and therefore out of his direct line of vision.

We were just finishing the chicken when we heard the sound of crying from the back room. I saw Sophie almost start to her feet before remembering that she had ceded that privilege. Tom looked at Sam and said, 'Your turn,' and then he said, 'But seeing as it's your birthday, you may be excused.'

Sam, who had scraped back her chair, pulled it forward again and went on eating, quite placidly.

'Just wanted a nappy change,' Tom said when he came back. 'She's gone off again, as good as gold. Well,' he said, looking at Sophie mainly, 'what do you think of her? Isn't she quite the most brilliant baby that you ever saw?'

That Sophie did think so – Sophie who used to blench if anyone under the age of twelve came within shouting distance – had become obvious to all of us. But she just said, 'I think you've done her a terrible disservice with that name. Whatever possessed you?'

'Blame Sam,' Tom said. 'It was her idea. Why, what's wrong with it?'

'It sounds so Thirties' cocktail party. You know: all those Pixies and Trixies and Bunnies and Binkies and so forth . . .'

'She looks like a Pixie,' Sam said. She reached out her fork and stole the last carrot from Tom's plate. He attempted to prevent her from doing so and for a moment or two they tussled good-humouredly.

'Well, yes,' Sophie said. 'It may be appropriate now, but she's not going to look like a pixie when she's forty, is she? You must admit that the name lacks a certain

228

gravitas. You could have given her another one, for when she gets older.'

'She can choose her own then,' Sam said, fairly indistinctly. She had won the carrot and was now eating her prize.

Tom said, 'And what's a name with gravitas, exactly?'

Sophie considered and then said, 'You could have called her after her grandmother – Diana, that's *very* dignified.'

Dee, normally a quick eater, had bolted her food even more rapidly than usual. She sat tapping the tines of her fork against the edge of her plate. She said, looking straight ahead of her, 'Grandmothers do not warrant the courtesy of having their grandchildren named after them; grandmothers are just useful for acting as nursemaids. When required.'

Fred winced and, apparently, decided to tackle her head on. 'How's the book coming along?' he asked.

'Don't ask,' Dee said, sticking out her chin so far that she looked like Popeye.

'From what I gather,' Sophie said quickly (her interjections were so obviously intended to defuse developing situations that their effect was quite diminished), 'from what I read in the papers,' Sophie said, 'writing novels these days must be a pretty hairy business.'

'Always was,' Dee said.

'Yes, but they seem to have dichotomised totally, don't they? It seems to me that I have a choice between two inches of formulaic garbage and slim volumes that tend to disappear up their own intellectual arses . . .'

Dee, who might normally have been disposed to agree with this point of view, said, 'You exaggerate, as usual, Sophie.'

Sophie appealed to Fred. Fred said, 'A great deal of what satisfies public taste is meretricious, but that's always been the case. I suppose it's the sophistication of modern sales techniques that makes the divide more obvious. But good books are still being published.'

'Are they?' Sophie said. 'All I seem to get hold of these days are perverted, padded-out, sexual fantasies, or else those frightfully well-written books that go on and on being fearfully symbolic and sensitive and are actually about nothing at all ... Oh, and then there are those earnest sort of feminist tracts in which all the male characters are consecutively dispensed with as the book proceeds ...'

Fred smiled and said, 'It's just that the conventions have changed. It used to be that certain sorts of novels ended with a woman meeting a man, now they end with a woman discovering that she can do without men ... Is drama the same, Sophie? Do you find that the fashions change in the same way and at the same rate?'

I thought for one terrible moment that Dee might say, 'When did you last read a script, Sophie?', but she didn't.

Sophie said, 'Fashions change all right. Everything seems to be old people at the moment. Death-bed reminiscences. There was a play on the telly the other night about some great social reformer – a woman – who was about to croak. The theme was how she'd always put her public life before her private concerns. She'd never married or had children, even though masses of men had asked her to marry them. Have you noticed,' Sophie said, 'how, whenever anyone is asked in old age why they didn't marry, they always say, "It wasn't for lack of offers." Nobody ever admits to never having been asked.'

I'm sure she didn't intend to be provocative. Fred took a very long drink from his glass. Dee went dark red and then said, 'To have to wait to be asked! How degrading!'

Every topic was a minefield. Even the pudding that Fred carried in: a bavarois of summer fruits which, after tasting, we were all moved to remark upon in the most glowing terms. Fred said that he'd made it using a recipe that his wife used to follow. I thought, for another terrible moment, that Dee was going to say, 'Fred's wife was a

230

marvellous cook,' and she did, in quite the snidest way imaginable.

And all the time the thunder rumbled distantly and the lightning flashed.

Tom had three helpings of the pudding and then he stood up and said, 'Would you please charge your glasses and raise them to Major Frederick Browning, DFC, DSO and Bar – what decorations have you actually got, Fred?'

'Not those, that's for sure,' Fred said.

'Well anyway, Major Browning, late of the Queen's Own Something-or-others, bookseller *extraordinaire* and chef even *extraordinair*-er, for providing this magnificent repast.'

We raised our glasses. Tom and Fred got on fine, Dee said, mainly because as they had so little in common, there were very few grounds for misunderstanding between them.

'To Fred!' we said. And Fred said, 'Actually, it's to Sam, isn't it? Happy birthday.' And Tom clapped a hand to his forehead histrionically and said, 'Oh Christ, I almost forgot!' and rushed out of the room and into the kitchen and came back carrying a cake. It had rosebuds on the top and a single candle and when Tom lit it Sam became animated for the very first time since she'd arrived and clapped her hands together and then shut her eyes tight and blew it out.

If a video camera had been trained upon us at that precise moment the image captured would have been one of family and friends enjoying a happy occasion; fifteen minutes later and it would have recorded the very different and more accurate picture that was the truth.

Over the cheese and biscuits Sophie had asked Fred whether he'd had any suitable applicants for the departed Lucy's job. Fred said he hadn't, just the usual crop of young persons who held their pens awkwardly and breathed very hard through their noses when writing their names, young persons who would be off just as soon as something better came up. 'I need someone who sees the job as being permanent,' Fred said. 'The ability to read and write would be an added bonus, of course.'

Sophie put down her knife so suddenly that it clattered off the side of her plate. 'Are we all quite mad?' she asked rhetorically.

'Only some of us,' Dee said. She had eaten hardly any of Fred's wife's bavarois and accepted only a sliver of Sam's birthday cake.

Sophie ignored her. She said, 'Good grief, what idiots we are! Fred, Valerie can read and write like nobody's business. Valerie has a university degree, for heaven's sake. Why didn't we *think*?'

Me, because I didn't know that Fred was looking for an assistant; Fred, because it probably didn't occur to him that I might fit the bill.

'Well then,' Sophie said, 'problem solved, isn't it?'

Fred looked at me and then at her and made a sort of calming gesture. 'Easy does it, Sophie,' he said. 'The job might not suit Valerie at all. I can't afford to pay much, for a start . . .'

'Not much is better than nothing,' Sophie said.

'Sophie!'

Both Fred and I said it at the same time. Then he said, 'This isn't really the time or the place. Valerie, if you're remotely interested, perhaps you could call into the shop next week?'

I nodded. There was nothing to lose by simply calling into the shop. Dee said, 'Well now! Philanthropy is alive and well and living in Ferryside Lane.' And Fred said sharply, 'Philanthropy isn't involved. I've a job going. Did *you* want to apply?'

'Nice one, Fred,' Tom said. 'That would really suit the Mater down to the ground: a job in a bookshop. She'd read all the latest offerings and be in a state of permanent despondency. It's bad enough on a Sunday when she gets hold of the reviews. We have sour grapes then, if you like, and wailing and the gnashing of teeth – '

'How would you know?' Dee said. 'You're never here on a Sunday. Nor any other day either, for that matter.'

'I do have to earn a crust,' he said mildly. 'I can't do it here, can I?'

'No,' she said. 'And you can't even pick up a phone either. I could be laid dead here for all you know – or care. You never spare a thought for me, unless it's to send you money or look after your offspring . . .'

Tom gave her a look that said, 'Pas devant les autres,' or would have done had Tom put in regular attendance at his French lessons at the Comprehensive.

But the vessel of her resentment had been too long on the boil not to spill over. She said, 'I'm just sick of the way that you use me and don't give a toss about me otherwise. I might as well not have a son. I might as well be on my own . . .'

Tom said – once again quite mildly – 'I've got my own life to live. You know that. And it's not as if you're on your own.'

That was quite the wrong-est thing to say. In vain did Sophie interject and Fred sketch peace-making gestures in the air. Dee said frostily, 'Oh yes. Very good. Excuse your neglect by handing over your responsibility to someone else.'

'My *responsibility*?' said Tom.

'Yes,' she repeated. 'I get the picture: it's get married, isn't it, and then you can stop bothering about me altogether? When I think . . .'

'. . . of all your sacrifices,' Tom said.

'Yes,' she said. 'As a matter of fact. And you give nothing in return, not a thing . . .'

'They wouldn't *be* sacrifices, would they,' Tom said, 'if you got something in return?'

But she wouldn't stop to listen. She was saying, 'Well you're not on. You're not just unloading me like a bloody parcel. I'm not getting married to please you or anybody else.'

Fred looked appalled. As well he might. Even Sophie appeared to be at a loss for words. 'I don't suppose you'd have deigned to come home if the police hadn't come after you,' Dee was saying. 'I suppose I'd have had to look after your child indefinitely . . .'

'She *is* your grandchild,' Tom said.

'Yes, and you're my child. But you might as well not be. You're just thoughtless and careless and clueless. You just drift through life without pausing to consider the consequences of your actions . . .'

Tom's supply of patience had been exhausted. He snarled at her. 'Get off my back, will you? What in hell's name's the matter with you, anyway? Is it the menopause, or what?'

'How *dare* you!' said Dee.

Sam slid off her seat and left the room. So did I. I stayed in the lavatory until the shouting had diminished. As I passed the back bedroom I saw that Sam was sitting on the edge of the bed with Pixie in her arms. She was rocking the child, crooning to her. I looked in and I said, 'You mustn't pay any attention to Dee. She's been going through a bad time lately, that's all. They're very fond of each other, she and Tom, really. They'll be hugging one another by morning.'

Her big eyes stared from the little white triangular face. She said, 'Yes, I know. But she's right. He doesn't think. He arranged that European tour without thinking. I didn't want to leave Pixie, but I couldn't let him down, could I?'

I could see in that face, those eyes, what she really meant: that Tom was an elusive character, that to be sure of keeping him, she dared not let him too far out of her sight. It made me feel profoundly sad. I had thought that this new generation were free to do things differently.

Downstairs, Dee sat at one side of the room and Tom at the other. They were not speaking. Fred was carrying the dirty dishes from the table to the kitchen. He looked very tight-lipped. I said, 'Can I help?' He shook his head. 'Sophie's in the hall,' he said, 'ringing a taxi. I'd run you home but I'm probably over the limit. I think maybe we're all a bit over the limit.'

The eye of the storm was coming closer. I peered fearfully out of the taxi window. I'm a coward when it comes to thunder. Sophie watched it unconcernedly. '*Götterdämmerung*. How appropriate,' she said. She's used to rows and shouting, of course. Presumably they don't make her stomach churn as they do mine.

'Poor Tom,' I said. 'He really got it in the neck.'

'It isn't really about Tom,' Sophie said. 'Or worry about Pixie. Or even writer's block. What it's about is whether or not she wants to be married.'

'Do you think she does?'

'Oh yes,' Sophie said. 'But I think she's scared witless that she won't be able to cut it. She's been on her own too long, has Dee. There'd be one hell of a lot of adjustment required.'

I thought that maybe she was too long in the tooth for those sort of radical changes. Can we re-make ourselves, I wondered, beyond a certain age?

While Sophie paid the driver, I ran through the rain to unlock the front door. I'd forgotten to leave a light on in the porch so I didn't see that it was occupied until I opened the door and almost fell over the figure that was squatted down on the floor inside. I screamed, though I should have recognised its identity, having seen it once before, unexpectedly, in the dark. I recognised the voice immediately. 'I've been here ages,' it said, in a most aggrieved tone. 'I was just about to bugger off. You're Sophie's friend, aren't you? Well, Sophie's friend, we simply must stop meeting like this.'

23

'What happened to the tour?' Sophie asked, while Valerie grilled rashers of bacon and tomatoes and fried eggs, one after the other, and delivered them on to Dominic's plate.

He ate ravenously. All his appetites were voracious. He heaped a slice of toast with marmalade. 'Don't you read the papers?' he said. 'They do *have* papers up here in Ecky-Thump land?'

'There is one beside your plate,' Sophie said. 'Why, what should I have read?'

'Pym died,' Dominic said. 'Literally dropped dead. Heart attack. Just came off at the end of Act Two of the Scottish Play and gave up the ghost. Well, we could hardly continue, could we? Iona was out of action and everyone else was filled with superstitious dread – so it was so long Montreal and not hello Calgary and Vancouver. You'd have expected Pym to have had better timing, wouldn't you; taken his final curtain on stage rather than off?'

Pym was the actor-manager whose Shakespearian tour Sophie had been tentatively invited to join, on the strength of old acquaintance – there had been a brief affair between them years before. Iona was his wife. A woman with a long memory. She had put the kibosh on the offer as soon as she got to know about it.

'Poor Pym,' Sophie said. He'd been a large, boisterous man, a womaniser who, privately, was eaten up with sexual insecurities. She'd slept with him out of sympathy as much as for career advancement.

Dominic was not much given to sentiment. 'Yes well,' he said, crunching toast, 'he'd had a good innings. So anyway,' he said, licking marmalade off each finger in turn with cat-like delicacy, 'here I am.'

'So here you are,' Sophie said.

It was the first chance they'd had to talk. The night before she'd started to interrogate him, but Valerie had said scoldingly, 'Sophie, give him a chance to get out of his wet clothes, at least,' and ushered him forthwith up to one of the bedrooms where she'd made up a bed and switched on the electric blanket. It was only time, presumably, that had prevented her from sorting out suitable bedside reading matter. 'Tomorrow,' Valerie had said, handing him warm towels and a bathrobe of Richard's.

They couldn't talk properly now with Valerie hovering between table and stove, a fish-slice in her hand. She had put Dominic's clothes into the washing-machine overnight and, after she'd washed up the breakfast things, set about ironing them.

'You are most awfully kind.'

Dominic treated her to his undying gratitude look.

'Have you got any other clothes?' Sophie asked him. 'If so, put them on and we can go out.'

'But it's pissing down,' he said.

'It's always pissing down. And we have to talk.'

He pulled a face. It was the exact same face that she pulled if anyone required her to be deadly serious. He said, 'Are you going to smack my legs?'

'I'm going to ask you how the hell you found out about this address. Valerie didn't give it to you, did she?'

Valerie, turning jeans inside out so that they could be ironed thoroughly, pursed her lips and shook her head. Dominic said with remarkable dignity for one clad only in a bathrobe: 'Valerie very kindly gave me her telephone number.'

237

'A telephone number,' Sophie said, 'is not an address.'

'It can be, if you chat up the operator nicely.'

'You bastard.'

She always had to curb the impulse to call him a little bastard. Little implied young. Dee called Tom a little bastard sometimes when they were having a barney. It struck Sophie that Dominic wasn't that much older than Tom. Dom and Tom, she thought, Tom and Dom, rhymed it to herself as she dialled Dee's number. Tom and Dom, Dee and me.

'Not likely,' Dee said in answer to her request to borrow the car. 'Not unless you've suddenly got your licence back.'

'I only want it for the morning,' Sophie said. 'I need it. I can't walk in this weather.'

'I've told you, no. You haven't got a licence.'

'No, but Dom has.'

'Who's Dom?'

It was very difficult to think of a way to describe him when he was sitting not five yards away from her. At length she said, 'What I thought of as being my past which suddenly seems to have become my present.'

'Oh yes?' Dee said.

'Just a few hours, that's all . . .'

'Oh well then all right. But if you're stopped, you took it without my consent. And I want petrol money . . .'

It was most definitely the morning after the night before at the cottage, which, in the case of Dee and Tom, meant calm after the storm. They were beginning to be friends again: he had made tea and carried a cup up to her bedroom; she had responded by asking him if he was all right for money. It was just the normal pattern of their relationship: she heard nothing from him for months, then he got in touch and she was delirious with relief, then she felt obliged to voice a catalogue of complaints which escalated into a row on the grandest of scales and then there was sweet reconciliation; nothing much changed.

238

'You must drive this carefully,' Sophie warned Dominic.

'Like a baby-carriage,' he said, cheerfully grinding the gears and kangaroo-hopping away from the kerb.

Quite unprompted, he drove to the sea wall and parked close to where she and Dee had sat and wept when Pixie was in hospital. Now, as then, rain streamed down the windscreen. He sorted through Dee's tapes, said, apropos them, in his Lancashire, flat-cap, comic's voice, 'It's being so cheerful that keeps me going,' and settled for Satie as being – presumably – the least gloomy of a very gloomy bunch.

For a time they sat quietly, smoking, listening to the Gnossiennes and watching the tide edging across the sand, stealing a few more inches with each encroachment. Then she had a pain and couldn't stop herself from wincing and he noticed and asked her what the matter was.

'My guts,' she said. 'It's nothing.'

'You should get them sorted.'

'You don't get guts sorted, you live with them. It's nothing. I had a bit too much to drink last night, that's all.'

Fred had kept filling their glasses as the battle raged around them, assuming, wrongly, that alcohol might be a calming influence rather than an inflamer of the passions.

'You drink too much,' Dominic said.

The last notes of the music died away. Sophie looked straight ahead of her and recited: 'I often wonder what the vintners buy one half so precious as the goods they sell. So do you,' she said.

'I can handle it better. I'm younger than you.'

'Now is that a fact?'

The tape clicked off. They watched the rain. He said, 'This fucking climate!' and then started to tell her about Canada, about the tour – what there'd been of it before Pym's death: who had had it, who couldn't cut it any longer, who was knocking off whom. It all seemed so

239

distant, as though she was listening to a child at the end of term, recounting obscure school customs.

'Everyone was asking about you,' he said. 'Seb and Adrienne Mercer and old Maisie. Oh, and in the Prince of Wales before I left, I ran into Terry . . .'

'And what did you tell them?'

'Told them what you told me: that you were recuperating. That's crap though, isn't it?'

She drew deeply on her cigarette, felt another spurt of acid being released into her stomach to wash over the surface of her ulcer. She said, 'I'm one of the ones who can't cut it, aren't I? You know, I kept believing that everything was all right long after it must have been obvious to everyone else that it wasn't. I kept on believing that I was just going through a bad patch and that things would right themselves. But once you start slipping, once you get beyond a certain point, you can't halt the slide.'

'I'll bear it in mind,' he said.

'You don't need to. It won't happen to you. You'd get by on your natural attributes. Even if you weren't as hungry as you are.'

That was it, she supposed, the lack in her: hunger. It was what motivated you to fight, to hustle, to hang on in. A different appetite from that which had first nudged her towards acting; that had been a need to compensate for an insufficient sense of identity. Acting had been her chance not just to be somebody else, but to be somebody, to make herself up as she went along.

'So there's not much kudos attached to consorting with the likes of me,' she said, looking at him through the driving mirror.

'You talk balls,' he said.

She found his face difficult to read, principally because it was expressionless. When neither of them was acting they were at a loss. She knew though that she, at any rate, must try. It was the worst role of her life and demanded her best performance. That in itself would have been bad

240

enough, but she had also – in this instance – to write her own script.

'Let's get out,' Dominic said.

'It's still raining.'

'So?'

'We'll catch our deaths, as Valerie would say.'

Actually the rain was stopping, had stopped completely by the time they reached the headland. He walked with long strides; she had to trot to keep up with him. Whenever he stopped, he thrust his hands deep into his pockets. Dominic was the sort who always thrust his hands deep into his pockets, no matter how tight his jeans. This stance was usually accompanied by a hunched-shouldered, beetle-browed stare, as in Olivier playing Richard III. It was the attitude he adopted for interrogation. Therefore she had anticipated the question by the time it came: 'Why did you do a runner?' She said, 'Why did you come after me?'

Each awaited the other's response, as though one was dependent upon the other. Which may have been the case. She spoke first. She knew that theirs was an unequal relationship and that she would always have to speak first. She said, 'To get away from all sorts of things I don't want to face.'

'Which are?'

'Which are, among other things, you, and my career being in a shambles.'

'Well you've brought that about yourself,' he said sharply. 'You're your own worst enemy.'

That was another cliché she'd never fully understood, despite being accused of it before today. 'Why?' she said.

'You find excuses. Either you're on the juice or the part's beneath you or you're having an emotional crisis or you're ill – '

'I *am* ill,' she said. To screw oneself up to spill the terrible beans and then be derided was too much.

' – oh I know all about your gynaecologicals,' he said,

picking up a piece of driftwood and hurling it towards the rapacious tide, 'but there's a danger that you're going to turn it into a way of life.'

She watched him picking up pieces of wood and hurling them seawards, watched his face. Success in the theatre was to do with either having a face that was totally anonymous, a face designed to be fitted with masks, or else one that obliged you to look at it and keep on looking. Dominic's was the latter sort. She'd admonished him on many an occasion when he'd assumed that the look was sufficient. 'Hey,' she'd say, 'you're doing your Richard Burton again.' But she could understand the temptation.

'It's not you, Sophie,' he was saying, 'the Elizabeth Barrett Browning bit. Not you at all . . .'

'What is me?' she said. 'Tell me. Because I don't know.'

Suddenly she felt very tired, and tired of attitudes struck and verbal games played. She didn't want to be walking with a self-regarding young man in the rain on a wind-swept beach; she wanted to take off her make-up and be tucked up tight into a warm bed by – someone kind, someone who cared, the sort of mother perhaps who hadn't been obliged to go out to business and have boyfriends. 'Why did you come?' she asked abruptly. And he threw up a stick and kicked it skywards and said, 'Because I love you. I think that's what it must be.'

She'd heard it so many times before: from Constantine when he was doing his Paul Henried, from Hawley as Joe Lampton (or was it Jimmy Porter?), from Dominic himself as Rupert Brooke and Byron and – many times and soulfully – when they cast him as Harry in *Fanny by Gaslight*. But nevertheless it was, usually, good to hear.

It was good to hear it from him. But love, for him, meant, first and foremost, sex. And as far as sex was concerned she was – as he'd have put it – 'out of the game'. She said, 'I've got cancer.' She said it so easily, she surprised herself.

She said, 'I had one operation. Now they want me to go

for further investigation. You know what that means. I didn't want to know. That's why I did a runner.'

He seemed to move in slow motion: raising his arm above his head and throwing the stick towards the sea, watching its arc of trajectory. She said, 'I'm forty-two, I'm sterile and I've got cancer. These are conditions that would not look too good on an application for Computer-Date. So if I were you I'd bugger off back to London and one of your little girls.'

She watched his arm falling back to his side. He said, 'You're not me, thank Christ. How do you know about computer-dating?'

'I once filled one up for a laugh.'

'That's what we're short of,' he said, 'a laugh. Let's go and have a drink.'

He put his arm around her shoulders. Until he did so she hadn't realised how much she'd missed that kind of physical contact, how starved she'd been. 'You've just told me I drink too much,' she said.

'Well if you've got the big C, what's one drink too many in the great scheme of things?'

Flippant. She didn't want flippancy. In the Crown and Anchor she sat apart from him, refusing to drink from her glass. He downed a pint of Guinness and ordered another. 'You'll end up like me,' she said coldly.

'What? With cancer?'

'With no driving licence,' she said. She said, 'You may want to make a joke of it, but it happens to be true. I probably stand to lose half my insides when I get back to London.'

'No shit?'

'No shit,' she said. 'So there's nothing to be gained by hanging around.'

'Can I finish my drink?' he said, and when she raised her hand to hit him, grabbed it and held on fast to it. 'Can I stay?' he said.

'I've nothing to offer.'

A girl at the other side of the bar nudged her companion. She'd probably recognised him from the Sunday afternoon serial on the Beeb: 'St Ives': all galloping hooves and knee-breeches.

'We always fell out before because I was so often off-limits for sex. It'll only get worse.'

'Possibly.'

'So what's the point?'

'I'll take bromide,' he said. He had noticed the girls noticing him and was preening. She said, 'If I might crave your attention for a moment . . .'

'Yes, yes, it's all yours.'

'You keep saying you love me – '

'I do. I think.'

' – what is it that you love? I'm a failure, as an actress, as a woman, even as a properly-functioning human being . . .'

He turned the hand that he was grasping and began to kiss its palm. The watching girls spluttered into their Malibu and Lemonades. He said, 'If I tell you that I wasn't attracted to you in the first place because of your yellow hair, you'll only get vexed.'

'Why will I get vexed?'

'Because you're vain.'

'Well,' she said, 'so are you vain.'

'I know. All actors are vain.'

'No they're not.' And she reeled off a list of non-vain actors of their mutual acquaintance. He said, 'You could start a fight in an empty house.'

'Only with you. All the more reason why we should leave each other alone. You're too young for me, anyway.'

'If that's supposed to be cruel,' he said, 'it misses the mark by a mile. The cruel one is "You're too old for me." '

She snatched her hand away. 'I'm too ill,' she said, 'too ill for all this nonsense. What I need is peace and quiet and looking after . . .'

He started to laugh. He said, 'You sound exactly like

244

Sonia Lieberman as Mrs Alving in *Ghosts*; you remember, at the Aldwych? Christ!'

She laughed too. As the audience at the Aldwych had laughed at poor old Sonia Lieberman's silent-film method of expressing strong emotion.

He said, 'That's more like it. More like Sophie. I'll look after you, you know.'

'You?' she said. 'You couldn't look after a pot-plant.'

'I'll look after you,' he said, unoffended, '*if* you need looking after. Now, if you can dispense with the histrionics and tell it like it is . . .'

She told him: about the lack of work and her precarious financial situation ('Get back and get on to David and get him to move his arse. He's a lazy cow unless pushed, as you know,' he said. David was her agent, and his); about her haemorrhages and Dr Patel and his speculum and the letter from the Middlesex. ('Christ!' he said, 'You've constructed this whole doom and gloom scenario on the basis of a letter calling you in for an appointment? It might be for nothing more than – ' He sought for some minor gynaecological complaint but was too young to be acquainted with most of what can go wrong with the female organs of reproduction.)

She told him how she'd hoped that by returning she could make some sense out of what seemed a botched existence, try to get a perspective on things . . .

He took up her hand again and held it firmly within his own. He said, 'You can only talk about making sense and getting a perspective when something's finished, and you're not finished, Sophie, not by a long chalk.'

She said, 'Getting old is bad enough. Getting old and becoming a medical *case* – the idea is unendurable.'

'Better though than not getting old at all?'

'Is it?' she said.

'I think so. Come on back to London and go to the hospital and find out.'

Big tears splashed on to the back of the hand that held hers. 'I don't want to fucking *know*,' she said.

The girls who watched were embarrassed. They looked away. He kissed the tears from her eyelids. He said, 'Yes, you do. I do as well. Come on, Sophie, we'll beat it. Won't we?'

She wiped her eyes. She knew that he believed he was being sincere. But the words sounded faintly familiar. She was tempted to ask him what script they came from, knew herself the danger that faced all actors, the occupational hazard of confusing seeming with being. But it was such a good moment they were having that it seemed a pity to spoil it.

After that first night Dominic's bed was not slept in again. On Sunday morning Valerie heeded the evidence and stripped it of its sheets, thought it was lucky that she'd put Sophie into the room that had the double bed in it, and tried to remember how it felt to lie beside a man all night but found it difficult, even after so short an interval.

I am an unnatural woman, she said to herself as she carried the sheets down to the wash: a woman who never enjoyed cleaving to the man she loved and now, so soon, has come to enjoy the freedom of an unshared bed. And then she wondered if she really was all that unnatural, and whether there weren't hundreds of thousands of women who felt exactly the same way but were too scared of seeming aberrant to admit to it.

She washed and ironed and packed bed-linen and clothes, some into tea-chests ready for the removal men, others into the suitcases that she would take with her to Dee's. Dee, on the phone, had said, not 'I'm glad you're coming to stay' – that would have been expecting too much, but, 'I always feel so terrible when Tom leaves. As though I'll never see him again,' the implication being that company would not be unwelcome, initially at least.

Tom and Sam were leaving on Monday morning on the

246

same train as Sophie and Dominic. The tedious journey made merry, Valerie supposed, by much anecdote, theatrical and musical, and many trips to the bar. 'Who *is* this Dominic, when he's at home?' Dee had asked when she rang up. 'He seems very nice,' Valerie had said. But Dee was too taken up with her son's impending departure to evince much interest.

Dominic did seem nice. He was good to look at and dispensed a practised charm. Valerie liked him as well as any middle-aged woman likes a polite and attentive young man. She certainly didn't blame him for the fact that Sophie was undoubtedly making a fool of herself over him; she blamed Sophie for that.

And then felt guilty when Sophie went out early on Monday morning and came back with her arms full of flowers: great frilly carnations and freesias with an inebriatingly-heady scent and those sort of dark red, tightly furled rosebuds that cost a fortune, and pressed them upon her to the accompaniment of a quite untheatrical kiss and said, 'Thanks for putting up with me and mopping up after me and – oh you know.'

Typical, Valerie thought, after they'd gone, as she was unpacking carefully-packed vases from tea-chests – even so she didn't have enough and had to resort to a bucket; typical of Sophie to buy up half the flower-shop when something more practical would have been appreciated: a packet of tea-bags, say, or a couple of pairs of tights.

Stifling such uncharitable and parsimonious sentiments, she waved them goodbye from the front doorstep and then went back upstairs to transform herself into the embodiment of an efficient woman for her forthcoming interview with Fred: the dark blue suit, the court shoes, the crisp white blouse. When she'd finished, the image of Barbara Hilliard stared back at her from the glass. She closed her eyes. She felt that when she opened them it would be a different bedroom that she saw reflected: a hotel bedroom containing a king-sized bed, and Richard lying upon it, his tie loosened, his arms opened to receive her, her or Barbara Hilliard, or any other woman who matched the description.

But when she finally dared to blink it was the same familiar setting that confronted her and herself, alone, within it.

There was a letter with an American postmark on the mat. She read it as she waited for the bus that would take her to County Road and Browning's Bookshop and discovered that her sons would be returning to the family home for the weekend prior to the builders arriving to transform it into something entirely other.

She felt a little surge of joy as the number eight bus, at long last, arrived. She knew, beforehand, that the visit would not, could not, live up to her impossibly high expectations, but as Sophie's mother used to say in that huskily-attractive accent that attracted so many men who either could not, or would not, marry her: 'Hope springs eternal.'

24

Dee

It doesn't get any easier: saying goodbye to Tom. Although he never stays long any more, and invariably travels very light indeed, after he's gone it always seems as though his visit lasted ages and I can't get used to the place not being littered with broken guitar strings and hair gel and discarded copies of *Blitz*.

I always weep, sitting there in the lounge that seems empty, listening for a baby crying or a drum solo or a blast of electronic noise – all the racket to which I objected so strongly when it was actually occurring.

It's then when I need Fred, to cry into his nice white hankies, to hear him say: 'He'll be back again before you know it.' But this time he's not here. Not simply because he has a shop to run and a Valerie to interview; he isn't here because my behaviour on Friday evening appalled him. He hasn't said so, but his face said appalled from the crown of his head to the heel of his left foot which, since the accident, doesn't quite touch the ground.

People are always conspicuous by their absence when most needed. I wiped my eyes and put some Verdi on the record-player. Verdi's usually guaranteed to cheer me up: the Choruses especially; you can't listen to the Choruses and still believe that life consists only of partings and betrayals and twilight's last gleamings and all the rest of it. At some point you start to believe in luck and unexpected cheques in the post and the way that you feel when you wake up in the morning and remember, when first you fall in love.

But this time it didn't work. And neither did Rossini, nor even Strauss, Senior or Junior. I just moped the day away, re-running the morning's departure scenes in my head. Even a change of location: a drive to the cemetery, couldn't dislodge them. (Cemeteries usually induce composure and a certain serenity within me: 'Not long to go,' they say, and, 'Nothing new under the sun,' and, like my Auntie B: 'Worse things happen at sea.')

Her grave is a disgrace. Perhaps I could ask Valerie to have a go at it after she's tended Richard's, which she does on an admirably regular basis.

That'll wear off. She thinks now that the rest of her life will be spent in deepest mourning, doubly sub-fusc in her case on account of not only his death but also his faithlessness, but Valerie's not the type to remain forever rooted in the past.

Not like me. From the graveyard you can just about glimpse the headland and the shape of the building that occupies it: the building out of which came first my father and then my lover. I wish they'd pull it down. I don't want to be a cemetery person, roots so firmly tangled up in memories that I can't break free. (Memories so insubstantial, so unreliable, so downright *fallacious* – how can they exert such a hold?)

Although pulling down the sanatorium alone wouldn't do; I'd have to: never look upon Tom's countenance again – or Pixie's, probably. Or Sophie's, come to that – now that she knows.

We were strained with one another when she came to say goodbye: it was the embarrassment consequent upon the telling of a secret and the sharing of it. She was flippant and so was I. The young man stood by, chatting to Tom. Every so often he glanced at his reflection in the mirror above the fireplace. I daresay I might be tempted if I was that goodlooking.

'He's come to drag me back, kicking and screaming, to civilisation,' she said.

I supposed that he'd run short of money or perhaps needed an introduction that she could supply. His ears had certainly pricked up when she told him that I was a writer. 'Writer' is such a hugely umbrella-type term: it can embrace anything from unpublished poet to West End playwright with lovely juicy parts for up-and-coming actors.

The only time that Sophie ceased to be flippant was when she was saying goodbye to Pixie. She lifted her from her cot and – although Pixie was very wet – held her tightly against her posh frock and said in a very imperious manner, addressing both Sam and Tom: 'Now you really will give this child the very best possible care and attention, won't you? And for God's sake give her another name while you're about it.' And then, quite humbly, she asked if she might go round to their place in Kentish Town occasionally to take Pixie for a walk or whatever.

'Sure!' Tom said. I think – if it was up to him – Sophie might find herself acting as permanent foster-mother, if not quite wet-nurse. Sam smiled her smile. She's polite and she's inoffensive but I can't get through to her at all; Tom might as well have taken up with a Chinese. ('Married', I nearly said, but that's a little premature or, more probably, a complete category mistake. Tom says that he knows of no one in his social circle – which is extensive – who's married. People may live together and have children, but marriage is seen as being irrelevant. Despite myself – for there's a part of me that hankers after engagement parties and wedding-present lists: all the paraphernalia of conformity – I'm as pleased as punch. Auntie B should have lived to see it: the time of nobody batting an eyelid. Except she'd probaby have disapproved.)

There wasn't room in my car for everybody so Sophie

251

and Dominic took a cab to the station. We exchanged a quick word at the platform barrier. She said, 'Well, get your finger out.' And I said, 'You too.' 'Oh yes,' she said, 'Dom was telling me that Owen Griffiths is touring a new play after Christmas.' I said, 'Once I was a tour-de-force; now I'm forced to tour,' and she laughed. She looks better since Young Lochinvar came on the scene: less – wasted. But then she's an actress and part of being an actress is the ability to look anything from Olympic-fit to two-breaths-away-from-the-death-rattle.

Tom handed Pixie over to Sam. I gave them both a quick kiss. That directed towards Pixie being the more enthusiastic of the two. She was almost entirely obscured beneath baby-gro and bonnet and blankets but I found a scrap of cheek upon which to leave the imprint of my lips. I had come to be fond of her. I'd get fonder still, I knew, as she got older. If I had the chance to know her as she got older, that is.

'Mama!' Tom said, and drew me towards him in the general direction of his shoulder. Like me, he is not demonstrative and therefore all public displays of affection have to be clothed in the same kind of flippancy that Sophie and I now seem to have adopted.

He said, 'Take care of yourself and take it easy. No, don't take it easy. Get going, I mean. It's only a question of time, isn't it?'

He's still young enough to have an answer for everything. He's not yet afraid.

Is Sophie afraid? She sweeps through the barrier like royalty with an entourage and you can tell that the ticket-collector is thinking: Haven't I seen her somewhere? I don't think she's a particularly good actress but she's good enough to conceal successfully what she doesn't want you to see.

They stood waving for a moment before they boarded the train. Just as he did: Tom Ransome. Stood in a shaft of sunlight beneath the vaulted roof, blazed within it so that I had to close my eyes, and when I looked again he was gone and so was the train, and all I had to commemorate our summer were the two silly bits of tin saying Thomas Ransome and Diana Mary Wyatt that I went and stamped from the machine.

I suppose that's the reason why, every time I say goodbye to Tom, I feel that *he* won't come back again either, why I need Fred to hold me tightly against the solidity of his large frame and to say, 'With respect, Tom is like the proverbial bad penny.'

It was nine o'clock that evening before Fred rang me. And then it was only, ostensibly, to say that he and Valerie had decided upon a trial period of employment, during which they could see how well they were suited.

'Very nice,' I said. 'I hope it works out for you both.'

I was sure that it would. Valerie was on the Science side but she's polite and helpful and a wizard with lists.

There was a long pause during which we could hear faint snatches of another conversation on a crossed line. Then he said, 'Have you been able to do some work?'

'No,' I said. 'I've been walking in the graveyard all afternoon.'

'Is that a source of inspiration?'

'No. It's just that when I'm gloomy, I feel I might as well go the whole hog.'

'I had noticed,' he said.

Then there was another pause until I ended it by saying, 'Aren't you coming round then?'

'Why?'

Why had never before entered into it. Not even when there wasn't a specific reason for his visit: a fence to be mended, a ball-cock to be adjusted, an escort-service to be provided. So I couldn't think of an answer. It didn't occur to me that a simple: 'Because I'd like to see you' might have sufficed. Eventually I said, 'I could do with some company. I haven't got used to being on my own again yet.'

He said, 'Why don't you go round to see Valerie?'

'Because we'll start talking about offspring, and the last thing I need to know is how Stephen and Simon have got their careers mapped out from now until the age of sixty-five. I thought,' I said, 'that you might bring a bottle round and we could drown our sorrows.'

'Which sorrows, Dee?' he asked.

I said, 'Oh – you know.'

'Yes,' he said, 'I ought to by now. By heart. But I've sorrows of my own and they don't seem to be drownable.'

'What's up?' I said. 'Look I'm sorry about Friday night, if I said anything to upset you, but whatever it was, I don't think it justifies acting like a mardy child . . .'

'You expect me to behave as if everything's just fine and dandy after saying what you did?'

'Saying what I did? I can't remember saying anything so very terrible.'

'No? Your memory, I think, is subject to convenient lapses.'

'I have a phenomenal memory,' I said coldly.

It's true. It's my curse.

'You, Dee,' he said, 'have a phenomenal capacity for self-deception. That I do know.'

'If there's something bothering you,' I said, 'then let's have it.'

He said, 'I can just about cope with the fact that you turn me down with monotonous regularity. I realise that's the risk you run when you love someone more than they love you. But to have it announced to the world in general that one's attentions are nothing more than a source of irritation . . .'

He was about to tell me what a terrible person I am. There was nothing he could say that I wouldn't be prepared, privately, to confirm, but I'm no good at taking criticism, either personally or professionally. I let him get as far as 'incorrigibly self-centred' and then I put the phone down. I didn't see why I should have to listen. I don't criticise other people – apart from when it's justified.

I drank my own, somewhat inferior, wine and when that ran out I drank some terrible stuff that Tom had left behind – stuff that I expect the citizens of Bordeaux use to soak their feet in after a hard week treading the premier cru. So it was no wonder that I slept badly and dreamed the anxiety dream. At dawn a bird started to sing. The one that sings 'Frederico' over and over again. I wondered if it was a permanent resident of my garden or was this in the nature of a swansong before it took flight for more welcoming climes.

The tide was up and the sea was roaring. It frightens me sometimes. I suppose it's because I never learned to swim. I could never trust anyone enough to allow them to teach me. Fred offered once. Maybe I'll take him up on it. One of these days.

25

If Fred mentioned Sophie and Valerie to Dee, he called them – naturally enough – 'your friends'. And it was how they described themselves to others: 'my friend Valerie', 'my friend Dee'. But Dee sometimes wondered if they weren't perhaps over-stating the case: friendship implied certain obligations, among them a propensity to be well-disposed towards one another and a willingness to keep in touch. After a month of having Valerie as a house-guest, such kindly feelings as Dee might have cherished towards her were evaporating fast, principally because of Valerie's determination to repay her for her hospitality. Dee would lock herself in the bathroom while she tried to suppress the murderous impulses that came over her every time Valerie insisted upon cleaning the oven or ironing non-iron sheets or dividing the household expenses down to the last halfpenny or creeping about the cottage in case she disturbed what she supposed to be Dee's newly-descended muse, whereas Dee was probably only filling in the crossword or reading her way through *The Oxford Dictionary of Quotations*.

Having Valerie to stay made her realise just how difficult it would be to adjust herself and her domestic routine to include another person on any sort of permanent basis.

As for keeping in touch – Sophie simply didn't, didn't even deign to reply to the two letters that Valerie sent, failed to respond to a message left on John Wainwright's answering machine. It was obvious, Valerie realised, eventually and resignedly, that Sophie had resurrected their relationship only because she needed a bolt-hole. Now she was back with Dominic, old acquaintance could safely be forgot.

Had it not been for Tom they would have been unaware of Sophie's whereabouts after John Wainwright reclaimed his flat. Tom said that she and Dominic had moved to Islington. He knew because she came to Kentish Town now and then to see Pixie. She was doing some radio work, she told Tom, and Dominic had a film.

But since Dee only heard from Tom whenever there was an R in the month, any information relayed was not only second-hand but also extremely belated. For instance, they didn't get to hear about her hospitalisation until some three months after the event, and by that time Valerie was in the throes of flat-decoration and Dee was in the midst of coming to terms with the fact that, for herself and Fred, the time of ultimatums had come and gone. He'd begun to withdraw himself from her, little by little: two evenings apart, three days; a broken fence that once he would have mended now left for a tradesman's attention; her lawn long and lush with spring growth and never the offer of his Flymo, let alone his services at its helm.

'Sophie had to go into hospital for some tests,' Tom told Dee. Something to do with her insides. Oh well, they'd thought, *that* was nothing unusual; Sophie had had trouble with her insides since she was seventeen. 'What was the outcome?' Dee had asked. But Tom hadn't seen her since then.

They hadn't given it another thought. Valerie had continued to decorate her flat, vigorously stripping from the walls the papers that she and Richard had once chosen together; after that she'd gone down to London for two weeks to help the Twins settle into their new flat. Dee, who hated holidays, decided that if she *pretended* to like things that normal people liked she might actually, despite herself, get to like them without any pretence being involved (normal people liked companionship, proximity, the prospect of permanent coupledom); and a holiday might help to unblock her block, so she booked a last-minute bargain break and spent a thoroughly-disgruntled fortnight fending off fellow-tourists in Dubrovnik. When she got back the phone was ringing. 'Are you never *in*?' Tom said when she picked up the receiver.

She listened to what he had to tell her in complete silence. 'Hello,' he kept saying, because the silence continued after he'd finished telling her. She simply couldn't take it in. Tom had started to speak again but she cut him short. 'Ring me back later,' she said. She said it so commandingly that, for the first time in his life when thus requested, he did.

But had to try several times before he got through because her line was engaged for the best part of an hour.

She'd rung Valerie and then found herself physically incapable of communicating Tom's incredible news. She hummed and hawed for such a long time that Valerie – that most patient of souls – said eventually, 'Was there anything in particular? I was just getting ready to go to the cinema. It starts at eight.'

'Sophie died last night,' Dee said, as baldly as that. If she'd been passing on the information by letter she'd have led up to that brutal climax by gradual degrees: 'Sophie had to go into hospital for tests. The tests showed something malignant. She was given a life expectancy of nought to six months, which turned out, actually, to be four weeks.'

Valerie couldn't take it in either. Eventually she would ring a cab and go round to Auntie B's cottage and they'd sit talking and remembering all the night through, talking about Sophie with her toes turned out reciting 'I come from haunts of coot and tern,' on some platform or other; Sophie drinking barley wine in The Goat and Compasses with some older man or other; Sophie ringing up to say, 'I'm getting married. Isn't it a hoot?'; Sophie being late, for exams and auditions and appointments with film producers, talking about Sophie alive, because they had made no provision, none whatsoever, for Sophie *not* alive – any more than they had for themselves.

26

Sophie Stephenson *was* late for her own funeral. Apparently the hearse got stuck in the traffic. Dee and Tom and Valerie waited with those assembled at the church (quite a crowd – Dominic must have twisted a few arms. Or perhaps arm-twisting had not been necessary; since the new film version of *Hangover Square* had picked up a handful of awards, Dominic was very hot property indeed and worth cultivating).

Dee was more interested in Harvey Hawley. (She'd forgotten that that was not, actually, his name.) She kept peering along the pews and nudging Valerie and saying, 'Is *that* him? The one in the blue overcoat?' Or, 'Isn't that him? That one who looks as though he's had an unsuccessful nose-job?' Valerie kept saying, 'No,' and, 'Hush!' She remembered what Hawley looked like and was pretty certain that he wasn't present.

Tom, superficially so laid-back, was celebrity-spotting. *He* kept nudging Dee and asking whether that wasn't such and such or so and so. Eventually Dee told him to stop behaving like a gawping provincial. 'That's our role,' she said, 'mine and Valerie's. Only we aren't impressed.'

Valerie was, rather. Dee rubbed shoulders with soap-opera stars in the canteens of television studios, but Valerie was still something of an autograph-hunter at heart. And anyway celebrity-spotting might just take her mind off what was happening, why they were gathered together, might just help to staunch the flow of her tears.

What a difference a year makes, Dee thought, para-phrasing. She was terrified that *her* tears would begin to flow. Valerie spent the greater part of her time sniffling, but Dee hadn't cried – publicly – since about 1965.

The waiting seemed endless. 'You see what I meant about not bringing Pixie?' Dee said. Tom had been all for it, seeing that Sophie had been so fond of her. 'You can't take an eighteen-month-old child to a funeral,' Dee had said, watching as the child pushed a horse on wheels around the carpet, carefully picking her way through the untidiness of Tom's living-room. 'Funerals are not for children,' Dee said, putting out a guarding hand in case Pixie should venture too close to the fire. She'd personally had a fire-guard sent down from the North and a gate for the stairs, since the child's parents didn't seem to have a clue and let her wander unchaperoned in the vicinity of plugs and pans and sharp corners.

Not that she'd come to any harm as yet. Dee had to remind herself that the only time that Pixie had come to harm was when under her supervision.

'Who *are* funerals for?' Tom had said, putting on a black jacket. His wardrobe, being all in black, like Sam's, was custom-made for such occasions.

'God only knows. Bury me under the apple tree.'

'Gran'ma,' Pixie said and handed over a piece of orange peel that she'd found on the carpet with the air of one bestowing a precious gift. '*Thank* you, my darling,' Dee said, accepting it with due reverence. A year had made a lot of difference to Pixie. She'd filled out, become bonny, stood upright, toddled, walked, uttered sounds that became words. These were quite normal stages of devel-opment, but Dee found them uniquely fascinating and was of the private opinion that Pixie was remarkably precocious.

'God, I hate funerals,' Dee had said, lifting her grand-child on to her knee. 'I wish we didn't have to go.'

'*Mother*,' Tom said. He was genuinely shocked. There were signs of a sneaking regard for convention emerging in his personality.

They left Sam with her hand on the vacuum-cleaner (it so often seemed to be there, yet the flat never looked any less dusty or debris-strewn) and went to meet Valerie at the Tube whence she had been escorted by one of her sons. He lingered for just as long as politeness demanded – which wasn't very, Simon (or was it Stephen?), nodded to Tom who enquired where they were living now, he and his brother. 'Stoke Newington,' Stephen said (or was it Simon?). 'We've just bought a maisonette there.'

'Oh, Stokie,' Tom said, fiddling with his earring. (Dee had thought that he looked quite conventional in his dark jacket and trousers – even his Doc Martens had proper laces in them that matched – until she saw him side by side with Stephen/Simon.) 'I've got some mates over in Stokie. D'you ever drink in the Prince of Wales?'

Valerie's son shook his head. No doubt he lived in an entirely different Stoke Newington from that with which Tom was acquainted.

Valerie fretted all the way to the church. It was all wrong, she said. Funerals were not, traditionally, con-ducted in this way. *Traditionally*, the hearse left from the home of the deceased with the cortège travelling behind it. Mourners did not just meet up at the church as though they were – going to the theatre, waiting for curtain up. Eventually Dee said, 'Put a sock in it, will you, Valerie?' and she subsided into tears until they reached the church, whereupon she wiped her eyes and said, 'I remember getting lost round here that time I stayed at Sophie's friend's flat. I was quite frightened.'

Her tone of faint self-mockery suggested that she would no longer be frightened by such a harmless experience. Her foray into the big wide world – even if it was only as

262

far as Browning's Bookshop in County Road – had instilled into her a measure of confidence. She could smile now at that pathetic creature of a year ago who had been thrown into a panic at the thought of venturing alone out of familiar territory.

Not that she ventured alone much now. If and when there was any venturing done, it was in company. The occupant of the other flat converted from Valerie's house was one Blanche Heywood, an unmarried woman of boundless energy and healthy self-esteem, who was used to making her own way in the world. Blanche Heywood filled every waking hour with activity. If she wasn't improving her mind with Workers' Educational courses, she was golfing or rambling or brass-rubbing or visiting Tuscan churches. Thus far, Valerie had been persuaded to accompany her on a hike up Kinder Scout and to an antiques weekend at York. And they were tentatively planning a coach trip to the Tyrol for the following summer. Dee called Blanche Heywood 'your lesbian lodger' or 'your dykey friend', which was most unfair because, although it had occurred to Valerie since the time of Richard's death that perhaps, fundamentally, she might be female- rather than male-oriented in terms of her sexual preference, she'd come to the conclusion that she really wasn't any way oriented. Blanche was simply a friend – the best sort: a friend whose strengths complemented one's own weaknesses, a friend neither scathing like Dee nor unpredictable like Sophie. A friend – living as she did in such close proximity – who could offer the same companionship as a husband without making any of the unwelcome advances.

'Tom, you can't smoke in here!' Dee hissed as she saw him taking a packet of Benson and Hedges out of his pocket. 'Are you mad?'

'Well *I* don't know,' Tom said, putting it back again. 'I don't know about churches. I've never been in one. If you were a proper mother,' Tom said, mischievously, 'you'd have made sure I knew the score.'

'Don't be ridiculous,' Dee said. 'Of course you've been in a church. You were in a Nativity Play once. You were Mary.'

Tom said, 'Why the f – , why was I *Mary*, for God's sake?'

'Because the child who was supposed to be playing the part was ill, and you knew the lines, and you were prettier than the other little girls,' Dee said proudly.

'How could you *do* such a thing? How could you endanger my sexual identity like that? Why didn't you go the whole hog and dress me in skirts like whoever it was did to her kid – that poet woman who was always being ill – Christina Rossetti?'

'Elizabeth Barrett Browning,' Dee said, and fell silent.

Valerie looked at her and wondered how she would guard against breaking down. On the train, she'd been as callous-seeming as ever, but she'd kept disappearing into the lavatory and returning red-eyed before saying, 'Oh God, are you *still* skriking? Give it a rest, can't you? Tears won't bring her back. Not your tears, anyway. You cry at nothing.'

Valerie knew that it was true. She knew that when she saw the coffin strewn with wreaths, when the organist stopped playing those indeterminate background chords and launched into Abide With Me, she'd weep until she could weep no more. But those would only be the sort of tears that she was liable to shed when they played God Save The Queen at the Olympics or Land of Hope and Glory on the last night of the Proms; those tears would have nothing to do with Sophie. The tears for Sophie were of a different sort: they came up from deep, they hurt, they did not assuage.

'Where have they *got* to?' Dee said, fidgeting with her order of service. She wanted it over and done. The whole thing was a farce, a charade, a *performance*: most of the people present probably hadn't given two shits for Sophie or, possibly, even known her.

She fixed her gaze upon her surroundings, hoping for distraction, hoping to quell the involuntary quivering of her upper lip. Dominic had certainly staged things on a grander scale than they had anticipated: organ and choir-boys and incense; the first surprise had been that the ceremony was to take place in a Roman Catholic church.

'Well, yes of course,' Valerie had said. 'If you remember, Sophie always used to be excused prayers at school . . .'

'But she never *practised*,' Dee said scornfully.

'Perhaps she took it up again,' Valerie said, 'her religion. When – you know – when she knew she was ill.'

A minor female film star entered the church. She wore a tightly-fitting black suit and a scrap of veiling atop her tousled corn-coloured hair and she held a handkerchief to her eyes. There was every chance that she hadn't ever met Sophie, but the photographers were outside. Tom drew in breath sharply and then made lip-smacking noises. 'Wicked!' he said, watching her undulating progress along the aisle. Dee jabbed him with her elbow and said that she hadn't brought him up to be *that* sort of man. He said that judging by her predilection for dressing him in girls' clothes she hadn't intended to bring him up as any sort of man. Valerie had to tell them to be quiet because the organ music was beginning to change from burbling J. S. Bach into something in the nature of overture.

Dominic walked behind the coffin. Every eye was upon him. 'The bereaved,' Dee said to herself, and accompanied this silent observation with a sarcastic sniff. Dominic slipped into the front pew, the priest moved into the chancel and the congregation, depending upon whether they were performers or non-performers, knelt and made ostentatious praying gestures or else reluctantly went through the motions.

Just a performance, Dee thought again: Dominic's impeccably-cut dark suit, the priest's theatrical gestures, the sham solemnity of the choirboys' demeanour; it had nothing at all to do with Sophie Stephenson who had stepped on to verse-speaking platforms and clasped her hands behind her back and said, with enviable articulation: 'Is there anybody there? said the traveller, Knocking on the moonlit door;', whose mother had received not-very-expensive presents from men with moustaches who carried suitcases full of samples, who had believed in the sincerity of those whose constitutional insincerity was apparent to everybody else at ten paces.

Valerie will really start to cry – as opposed to her constant snivelling – when they sing Ave Maria, Dee thought. But actually Valerie held out until one of the choirboys who had a deeply unintelligent expression and the usual heart-breakingly beautiful voice stepped forward to sing Panis Angelicus.

All the stops were being pulled out, with a vengeance; it was a deliberate assault on the more superficial and easily-aroused of the emotions. Dee's face was wet. 'I must be pre-menstrual,' she thought. She'd been pre-menstrual for longer than usual on account of her last period not having arrived. She was worried at first until she remembered that it is not normally possible to become pregnant without an act of sexual intercourse having previously occurred.

It was her age, she supposed. The hiccups were starting. As they had started for Sophie, earlier still. But that was all they had been: hiccups; her cervical inflammation had been cured by laser treatment; her haemorrhages had been due to a combination of hormonal imbalance and fibroid growths; all her shilly-shallying vis-à-vis the hospital summons had made no difference in the end. It was her guts that killed her: the long-standing, lived-with condition had altered, turned nasty, become cancerous. And when the bad pain came, it was too late. She'd not taken it seriously enough anyway; she'd co-existed with that sort of pain, intermittently, for too long. She hadn't realised that it doesn't do to concentrate wholly on new problems at the expense of the old.

Dee saw that Tom, too, was screwing up his face as though attempting to stifle a sneeze in the way that people do when they are trying to disguise the fact that they're holding back tears. Tom had visited Sophie in hospital just before she died. She was full of drugs but had managed to smile and joke a little. 'How's the New Age Music?' she'd asked. 'Or is it pretty old-hat by now?' Well, yes, he'd said. They were no longer New Age Music, they were Acid House. One had to keep up with the changing trends. 'We're playing a warehouse party Saturday,' he'd said. 'How about I get you a ticket?'

She'd smiled and moistened her lips and said, 'If I'm still here.' And he'd told her not to be so morbid, she'd be around to see a good many trend-changes yet. And then her eyes had closed and she'd mumbled something about having to pay your dues and then she'd gone to sleep – he'd assumed it was sleep.

'What did she mean?' he'd asked Dee when she arrived for the funeral. Dee said she didn't know, but Sophie was right: dues always had to be paid, one way or the other.

There was the usual trek from the church to the burial plot which, like all new burial plots, was at the very edge of the consecrated ground. Dominic would have done better – and cheaper – to have arranged a cremation, but that, Dee realised, would not have given him the same dramatic scope: he would not have been able to dash a tear from his eye as the priest intoned above the grave, to take the small silver shovel from the undertaker and scatter a little soil on the surface of the coffin and then follow it with a single red rose. There was a singular vulgarity about the gesture that made the hairs rise on the back of Dee's neck; it seemed to go with pink champagne on yachts berthed in the port at Marbella and large faceted diamonds flashing on fingers that ended in regularly manicured red talons. Sophie herself would have laughed it to scorn.

Dee nudged Valerie and said, 'Oh how I suffer! See me suffer.'

Valerie mopped her face and said that perhaps Dee was misjudging him. 'He didn't have to stick by her, did he?' she said. 'There was nothing in it for him as far as I can see.'

'Only the chance to act like Heathcliff, that's all.'

'Oh don't be so cynical. Not everybody has an ulterior motive.'

He exchanged a few words with them as the mourners dispersed. There was a buffet laid on at the Tennyson Hotel but Dee and Valerie had excused themselves from attendance. He did look fairly wretched, but it was his job to be able to look wretched when called upon to do so.

'She was most awfully brave, you know,' he said.

'She shouldn't have kept it to herself,' Dee said.

'She didn't. Not at the end.'

'Well she told *you*.'

The implication being that while she and Valerie were friends of long-standing who had every right to be taken into her confidence, he was merely, and accidentally, the last in a line of lightweight lovers, unfitted for the sharing of such a terrible secret.

'You're sure you won't come back?' Dominic said.

'Absolutely.'

Although she felt such a deadly sensation of anti-climax. She kept expecting Sophie to appear among them and start to pass comments about the company: 'She's a nympho. He sleeps with goats.' There should have been something of Sophie here and there wasn't, not the ghost of an echo.

'Excuse me,' Dominic said. He chatted to Valerie a little longer. Of course Valerie couldn't see through him.

'You're not coming then?' Tom said. 'To this do?'

She shook her head. 'You go,' she said.

He wanted to go, naturally. There was the chance of

making influential contacts – and he needed some influential contacts since the deal with the record company hadn't turned out to be quite as watertight as he'd been led to believe – as well as to admire at close quarters the attributes of Femma Fatale, or whatever the hell her name was: the sex-bomb who had forgotten to be grief-stricken and was sharing a joke with the man who might or might not be the surgeon in *On Call*.

'I shan't see you again before you go.'

She had a meeting with her agent and then she was leaving for home. He gave her the usual despite-himself hug and said, 'Give my regards to the Galloping Major.' Then he said, 'Isn't it time that you two stopped farting about and moved in together?'

She didn't tell him. She just said, 'He'll be up here himself in a couple of weeks. It's the book fair in Bloomsbury.'

And it's Valerie, not I, who will be accompanying him, she might have added, but didn't because Tom would have been bound to make the obvious sort of suggestive comments and – whatever else – Dee was pretty certain that there wouldn't be any hanky-panky of that sort between them.

She stood looking down into the grave for a few moments longer. If you did nothing else, Sophie, she thought, you were instrumental in bringing Fred and Valerie together and therefore founding one of the great partnerships of history: Rolls and Royce, Gilbert and Sullivan, Laurel and Hardy. Valerie was meticulous, conscientious and eager to please and, being eager to please, learned quickly: how to keep the catalogue up to date, chase up orders, interpret customers' clumsily-expressed requests and guide them in the right direction. Fred was often away at house auctions and trade fairs. His previous assistants had sometimes taken advantage of his absence to turn up late, but Valerie always had the door open at nine o'clock prompt. Fred's speciality was military history so Valerie, who wouldn't have known an automatic pistol from an arquebus, read up on the subject. She was also a dab hand at dusting.

'Fred's awfully upset,' Valerie had said accusingly. Though he had not taken her into his confidence, it was plain to see.

'I am not responsible for Fred's upsetness,' Dee had replied. 'Nobody is responsible for the way anybody else feels.'

That seemed to be the fashionable feminist opinion. It meant that women were not responsible for men being unhappy, not the other way round. And it was pure garbage, of course.

'Well I don't think it's very fair of you to ignore it,' Valerie had said. It was she who now offered to do his ironing and saw to it that he rested his leg when that frown of pain appeared between his eyebrows. He was nine years older than she was but you'd have thought the gap was twice as big and in the opposite direction.

At the end of August Fred had put his cottage up for sale. He was looking for a place at the other side of town, over Parklands way, perhaps (convenient for Valerie: he could give her a lift into work). Then he wouldn't be so upset, having to pass Auntie B's cottage every day, being reminded constantly of his rejection.

There'd never be a better man. Dee tried not to think of that fact. She lingered still, looking down into the grave where, beneath the scattered soil and the furled rosebud, she could just glimpse the glint of the plaque that told of Sophie's relatively short existence. ('I thought we might call Pixie after Sophie,' Tom had said the night before. 'Kind of remembrance, isn't it? And she was always going on about Pixie being unsuitable.' 'Sophia,' Dee had said. 'It was actually Sophia.')

'Sophia Magdalena Stephenson' it said on the plaque. Dee read it and wondered why Sophie had kept the truth from them (Was it because she thought they wouldn't have been able to cope with knowing? *Would* they have coped?), remembering suddenly that misidentification she'd made last summer: the woman on the zebra crossing whom she'd taken for Sophie. A doppelgänger, perhaps? Were these things preordained? *Do* people die when they're due to, Dee wondered, or is the timing of death as random as the ordering of the life that precedes it? Maybe the timing was right for Sophie: to go out believing that she was loved, to have the curtain rung down on a triumphant West End opening rather than the last night of a run to an empty house in the provinces.

Dominic was chatting to the film star. Perhaps he had only pretended to love Sophie, but did that matter if the pretence was convincing enough?

'Are you coming?' Valerie said, plucking at her sleeve. She wanted to get back to Stoke Newington. She was staying the night with her sons. They would work hard at trying to cheer her up, take her out for a meal, buy her a box of chocolates. Her delight in their courtliness and pride in their achievements would temporarily over-ride the wistfulness that came over her whenever she contemplated the impenetrability of their exclusiveness.

Tom was exclusive in a different way: always retaining some part of himself, keeping it back, requiring a secret place. On the previous day they'd walked from his flat in Kentish Town past the demolished mansion block that had once been his father's address. She'd looked around her, as she always did when making this pilgrimage, for a face, unseen for twenty-odd years but kept familiar via Tom's face and now Pixie's. It wasn't there. It never would be. Phantoms had existence only in fevered imaginations. Fred was real. And it might not be too late. 'I just want to be *normal*,' Dee cried within herself. 'I always did.'

She got off the Tube at Tottenham Court Road and walked through to Bedford Square. It looked rather beautiful and somehow sad in the late afternoon sunlight. I shall miss Sophie, she thought; even though months, *years*,

271

could pass without any contact between us, I shall miss her like hell. Somehow, so much of what I've done has been done with Sophie in mind: to upstage her, to say 'So there!'; to share with her a secret 'Up yours!' at all the Valeries of this world – at least before we discovered that Valerie wasn't one of them after all.

No one understood her like Sophie. Not even Fred. Fred believed that she could be changed. She knew it was unlikely, if not impossible. I'll miss Fred too, she thought. Sophie gone, and Fred; my life will be a desert – or a dessert, as Sophie used to spell it.

After a fairly dispiriting talk with her agent and a good cry in the Superloo at Euston, she went into John Menzies to furnish herself with reading matter for the homeward journey. On the train she tried hard to concentrate but the words just ran into each other, became blurred, absorbed the odd tear that still insisted upon falling despite the rigidity of her upper lip. But just after Bletchley and into her first lager she had a bit of an idea. She laid aside the *New Statesman* and TS Eliot's *Letters* and picked up her pen and began to write on the blank endpapers of *A View of the Harbour*. It would have been overstating the case to say that she was happy; the most that could be safely assumed was that she was no longer quite so sad.